BLUE NESTIRA

a novel

ALIETE GUERRERO

AUXmedia
Detroit, Michigan

Editor: Lisa Allen

Cover art: Aquarius Press

ISBN 978-1-7322091-9-0

AUXmedia LLC

www.AUXmedia.studio

Printed in the United States of America

*This book is dedicated to my husband and sons—Gabe, Willie and Chris—
for the great support while I was writing it.*

Chapter 1

Someday, I will be one with the Blue Nestira butterfly. She is the most extraordinary of the Morpho species. Her sapphire hue dazzles the onlooker. She is rare, mythical, and elusive. My metamorphosis will be so mesmerizing that the old Sofia will become but a memory—a memory that only I will have.

It is Ash Wednesday, and before the day is over, I will catch a plane to Los Angeles. The black carry-on isn't large enough for all my things, but Didier tells me that he will provide me with everything I need to succeed in my endeavors. I'll do anything to sing on a stage again, but right now, I'm wondering which is farther away: America or my dream?

I dash down the hallway lined with photographs of me onstage and leave the apartment. The elevator descends quickly, and in no time, I'm buckled into my seat in the cab. "The tall building across from the Blind Institute, please. Thank you, Ronaldo. I'm glad you were available." I tell the thin, black man I rely on to get to places fast. When I'm not in a hurry, I take the bus or drive, both of which I dislike.

Ronaldo takes off and dashes down the avenue. The traffic is light. Carnival madness is over. There are floats left abandoned after the big parade. Costumes were tossed off into municipal trashcans. Rio de Janeiro is littered to the core after Carnival. It's the beginning of Lent; citizens kneel down to do their Stations of the Cross.

I unfold *O Jornal do Brazil* and read the news story once more:

NEW EVIDENCE IN THE DEATH OF TENOR ELI LEVATTER POINTS TO CAPTAIN RICARDO ALMEIDA AS THE KILLER

Federal Judge Daniel Levien has convened a Grand Jury seeking to indict the officer from the Special Police Operations

Battalion, BOPE, who allegedly committed the murder and orchestrated a cover-up to avoid justice. The long investigation has revealed that the captain is a member of a well-known neo-Nazi group. The officer is known by his nickname: Totenkopf, a reference to Hitler's 3rd SS Panzer Division, also known as the "Death's Head Division."

I am not a violent person, but when it comes to him, I feel that I could kill in cold blood. When I remember what he did to the person I loved the most, I think I could pull the trigger in the flick of a second and never look back.

A bolt of thunder shakes the whole city. A string of red traffic lights ahead makes me nervous. The traffic begins to inch slowly and then comes to a halt as one by one the cars are inspected. A huge swarm of military police on motorcycles escort a military bus filled with agents of Rio's Police Special Battalion. As soon as they stop, the cops begin to build a barricade. The BOPE agents leap out of the bus. They are in their black uniforms and wear huge, shielded helmets. They have M16s with bayonets on them and are heading in the direction of the favela, the slums, with a license to kill.

I feel cold even though the temperature is above normal. The air is oppressive. Our turn to stop is coming, and I'm terrified when I see that the officer in charge of the blitz is no other than Captain Almeida, Totenkopf himself. He sticks his head in. "Oh, look who we have here, the daughter of my commander." His eyes are fixed on me. His gun is drawn. He opens the back door and gets in.

He grabs the newspaper. "If I get indicted by this grand jury, I'll have you killed, Sofia."

His brutality reminds me that there are hundreds of us who are raped and battered and at risk when we confront our oppressors. Many try to escape their circumstances, while others are stuck and remain victims. He also reminds me of the madness that surrounds me at the clinic. The women tell me about all kinds of violence committed against them by the men in their lives.

He leans closer and outlines my lips with the barrel of his gun. "Do you understand, sweetie? And by the way, someday I'll be the commander of the BOPE, and you'll be mine." He lets us go.

I take several deep breaths to calm myself down.

Copacabana is a restless world of broad streets, dense traffic, and a crowd that does not know where to go. The air is charged. Dark clouds swirl faster and faster. The swirling Portuguese mosaic of the sidewalk echoes the frantic clouds. Heavy rain begins to fall. People rush down Avenida Atlântica looking for shelter. Will this storm be the final one, destroying Rio's broken paradise?

Finally, the taxi starts to pick up speed. Efficiency is not the norm. Inefficiency abounds in my city, thanks to bureaucracy and other obstacles, like rainstorms. The traffic is sheer madness, but like millions of us, I take it in stride.

"Sofia, there is a cruiser following us," Ricardo says. He shows dread in his voice.

"Can you get rid of him? I'm sure it's Officer Almeida."

"Here's right behind us."

"Do something, please. Get in front of that bus right there, go." I clutch the bracelet my late grandmother gave me. It's decorated with intricate filigree and has a solid black jaguar with amber eyes. The natives of her Indian nation have blessed it, and it's supposed to ward off the evil eye. She was the daughter of the Aruaques, and so am I.

He accelerates and moves ahead of the bus and then swerves right to get in between the bus and another car. He continues to drive above the speed limit but I know that there are no guarantees that we won't be followed.

"Get off the main road as soon as possible and take a side street."

"Okay, Sofia, give me a bit more time." He changes lanes again and accelerates while I look on the map for alternative ways to get to Dr. Lev's office.

I give him directions as he drives fast through the dangerous streets of Rio. The good news is, by driving erratically, he is acting like any other driver in my city. Everyone speeds, everyone cuts in front of other motorists, and everyone honks their horns as soon as a light turns green. Driving in Rio is sheer madness. I'm sure we are behaving normally except that I have a great reason to act like a mad woman. I'm running away from the man who can kill me in the blink of an eye, just like he did Eli.

The cab stops across from the Braille Institute. I pay my fare and then rush inside Dr. Lev's building. In the elevator, lights flicker as if a blackout might take place. I get out of the elevator, walk down the silent hallway, and ring his bell.

Lev opens the door and I walk in. He takes my carry-on, puts it down. "I'm glad to see you, Sofia." He shuts the door and leads me through a narrow hallway that connects to a smaller room. I sit down on the couch, and he sits next to me. "Is everything okay? You seem unsettled." Even though he towers over me, he has a calm demeanor.

"Officer Almeida threatened to kill me when my taxi stopped at a blitz by the Rocinha favela. The gun he pointed at me was the same type of weapon that he used to kill Eli." I'm trembling. "I'm so enraged that I could kill him with my bare hands and put the body in a freezer somewhere. All I know is, I'm more determined than ever to testify at the trial and get justice for Eli, even if death is the price I pay." I open my handbag and pull out my Glock 17. "I should have used it on him, but I froze with fear."

Dr. Lev looks stunned. "Where did you get this pistol? Civilians are not allowed to have guns."

"My father gave it to me when I turned eighteen. Would you keep it for me? Didier says I can't take it to America."

"Have you ever used it?" He puts it down on the desk.

"No, but a month ago, when my parents were in Argentina, I came home to find Officer Almeida there. He had the key to my house, somehow. He said he was going to kill me if I went ahead with the motion to reopen Eli's case, so I walked straight to my room, picked up my gun, aimed at him, and told him to get out. I guess he got even today."

"Why didn't you tell me about me about his breaking in and threatening you, Sofia? I wish you had. I would have had him arrested." His gaze is on me. "You have my word that he will be convicted for his crimes." He looks resolute.

I dread it that Lev's father is taking on my father's right-hand man. The judge is putting himself and his son at risk.

"Please be careful, Dr. Lev. If you defy my father, he might throw you in jail—or worse." My eyes well up with tears. "I'll die if anything bad happens to you."

"Don't worry about those things, Sofia. I promise you that powerful people have my back."

"They'd better be good." I lean toward him. "Thank you for always listening to my tales of woe. Most people won't. They say they're always walking on eggshells around me. I get down on myself a lot, and I leap down their throats when they call me a dramatic diva. I guess I'm complicated."

"Complex. And you are the bravest. I'm in your corner." He looks straight at me. "I need to check on an important email. Will you be okay while I'm gone? It will take just a few moments."

"Don't worry, Dr. Lev. I'll be fine."

He walks away. He's a rare person. Even though hard science is his vocation, he is far-sighted, and his ethics are flawless.

I survey the room. It's decorated with Brazilian ceramics, and paintings hang on the white walls. There is an upright black piano, a white leather couch, a mahogany desk, and a tall display cabinet next to a bookcase. The painting next to the bookcase is acrylic and varnish on jute with geometric shapes: a turquoise square and a red rectangle with a yellow Star of David in the center, along with the words: We Will Always Remember.

I walk across the room and look outside the window. The rain has lessened, and a group of revelers is gathered in front of the Blind Institute. I spot a BOPE cruiser parked down below. My blood pressure takes a plunge, and I take a step back. I'm sure Officer Almeida has sent someone to spy on me. I walk away from the window and stand in front of a shelf by Dr. Lev's desk.

He comes back in and stands by my side. "Are you ready to leave for the airport?" he asks.

"Yes, but I'm afraid. There's a BOPE cruiser down below."

"We'll leave through the back. I'll get you to the airport safely."

"Thank you." I grasp my handbag and follow him out of the room. He picks up my carry-on, and I follow him into the dim hallway.

The fast elevator stops at the parking level in no time. He leads me to his car. I hear the rain pounding the city. Soon, there will be flash floods, mudslides, and red lights that never turn green.

He drives out of the parking structure and makes a right. Crossing a double yellow line, he makes an illegal U turn. I'm astonished. As far as I knew, he was one of the few Brazilians who obeyed all laws.

Torrential rains fall, reducing our visibility to almost zero. Maybe we'll crash, and I'll die having never realized my dream. My passion for opera has driven me to the edge and disrupted my own sense of security, but I welcome the shakeup. I crave the deep passion that only my art can offer.

I reach inside my purse and take out an envelope. "Here is the key for the guesthouse at Capella—the building where I stay when I'm on the ranch. Thank you for offering to check on my horse from time to time. Vento will miss me very much. Please show him one of my videos on YouTube. He loves to hear me sing."

When he stops at a red light, he presses Number 1 on his CD player.

I hear my own voice singing "Un bel di Vedremo" from the opera *Madam Butterfly*. I sound so dazzling that I wonder how I ever had the courage to abandon my art. The aria is haunting.

"Where did you find this?"

He reaches across me, draws a CD case from the glove compartment, and hands it to me.

There is a photograph of me on the case in which I wear a kimono dyed with tones of reds, purples, and indigo-blue hues.

"You sure look the part."

"Well, I am petite and have black hair and am a brown woman, but that's about it, Dr. Lev. Cio-Cio San was only fourteen when she sang this, and I'll be twenty-seven in four months. Besides, my hair is full and if I sleep with it wet, it's a bird's nest in the morning. Not so *Madam Butterfly*-ish." I laugh. "And whenever I ride my horse, my hair is a total disaster. It's just as wild as my Vento."

"Still. It's an astonishing voice I hear when you sing this aria. The tempo is just perfect, and so is the pitch. I'm sure you'll win the Met competition." He signals and moves into the airport exit lane. "As soon as I get to Capella, I'll take photos of Vento and post them on your Facebook timeline."

"Thank you. He's my baby."

Night falls. He parks at the garage structure across from Terminal 4.

I can't believe I'm saying goodbye to him. We've been working on this case for a few months and have become inseparable. At the end of the day, after seeing my own clients at the clinic, I have found it healing to discuss the trauma I've been through. He helped me shift my perspective and inspired me to make the most of my life after it had been shattered.

He supported me when my father's own anti-Semitism allowed an evil person to murder the love of my life. My father was blind to Officer's Almeida's hatred of Eli's heritage. I couldn't be more grateful for Judge Daniel's efforts to take a dangerous man off the street. I hold a grudge against my father for allowing a cold-blooded killer to have accesses to me even after he killed Eli. I'll never forgive him for taking Totenkopf's side. So much for the man who sheltered me all my life and watched every step I took.

We stop at the entrance of Gate 3.

Our eyes meet. It is not the first time I notice how blue his are, like sapphires, especially against the black hair that frames his intelligent face. I see a certain vulnerability about him that I never saw before. Maybe all the goodness in his heart makes him a target of hateful people, or maybe being the grandson of a Holocaust survivor has left its marks.

"I wish I could stay. I'll miss Rio, my ranch, my horse—and you—so, so much."

"My father can put you in the Witness Protection Program, Sofia. You don't have to go. I promise you'll be safe."

"Brazil isn't good for opera. Most divas leave to make a name for themselves elsewhere. But it is my biggest dream to be recognized as Brazil's number-one prima donna one day and sing at the Amazon Opera House Festival."

"I'll be your accompanist if you need one."

"I will, and you're a great pianist. We have a deal." I reach out, put my arms around his waist, and lean against his chest. "Goodbye, Dr. Lev. Thank you for everything."

"Goodbye, darling. Keep me posted."

I turn and walk down the terminal as my tears fall. I can't believe I'm leaving everything I love behind. Yet, like Madam Butterfly, who gave up her own life to save her family's honor, I'll give up anything to have my opera back. I'll do anything to sing at the Met, including tethering myself to a man I hardly know—a man who will take over my career and life. I'll give up my own freedom to soar on the stage again. I'm as sure of that as I am about catching a plane to America before Ash Wednesday is over.

Chapter 2

Didier drives up a hill, across a busy boulevard and down a road called Avoka Avenue. It amazes me that, fourteen hours ago, I was still bound to Brazil, and now I'm a free woman, away from the watchful eyes of my father and the grip of Totenkopf.

Didier has done all the talking, all the questioning, and he has set all the rules. All I've done so far is to think of Brazil and yearn for Rio and my ranch. I'm afraid to forget where I came from, but he has promised to reboot my career, and now that I've met him in person, I believe him entirely. He came into my life like any other fan, writing letters, asking for autographs and other things groupies ask for, but later he revealed himself as an impressive businessman who has the connections to turn my career and life around. It is clear that he is a powerful man. He is a chef and owner of a well-known restaurant. He is nice looking, blond.

He drives up to where the street forks and continues to the very top. He stops in front of a deep-blue house. It is perched on top of a hill, standing alone. It seems a bit eerie, but the tall black ash trees are astounding.

"We're home." He presses a button on a remote control and the garage door opens. He parks his SUV and turns the motor off. "Why are you so reserved, Sophie? Are you unhappy, or are you just tired? You barely said a word on the trip home."

"Crossing three different time zones must have worn me out." I tighten my grip around the irises he gave me at the airport.

The shelves in his garage are stocked with cans of car wax, motor oil, and antifreeze. Steel trowels hang down from a perforated board. The red outline of a missing hand pruner stands out.

"Why do you outline your tools on the board?" I ask as I get out of the car.

"By outlining their shapes, I can immediately see what's missing." He gets out of his black SUV.

"I've never found anything I've lost, Didier. I don't even remember what I've lost, except for a book on etiology my friend Isabella gave me for Christmas." I lean against him. "I always lose things."

He has his hand flat against my back as he leads me inside. "I'll have to discipline you, Sophie. I've heard how disorganized Brazilians tend to be." He opens the kitchen door. "From now on, you'll always recover what you've lost. Better yet, you won't lose anything."

"That's the plan." I certainly came to America to stop losing things, or maybe to stop losing altogether.

Wooden cabinets hang from the walls in the kitchen. All his appliances are silver and black. Several deep-blue Mason jars are arranged on the counter. His knives are arranged in gradation from the smallest to the largest on a wooden block. There are at least twenty of them. The clock on the oven marks 4:58 PM. Rio is melting in February, but L.A. is cold, just as it is cold in August in Rio, especially at Capella. The world is upside-down and quiet. There is a draft coming from a vent. Night begins to fall.

He turns the lights on and hands me a purple vase with water. "For your irises." The yellow blossoms look fragile against his black trench coat. He is so different from most Brazilians I know, although my own mother is blonde like him, and just as steadfast.

I put the flowers in the container and set it on the glass table. "Whose dog do I hear?" I ask, as he leads me out of the kitchen.

"That's Phantom, my Doberman Pinscher, named after *Phantom of the Opera*, my favorite musical." He lets out a loud whistle.

Phantom barks.

He guides me toward the living room and turns on the central heat.

It's a blue world—a Prussian-blue carpet, a cobalt-blue couch, and marine-blue shelves. A chandelier hangs down very low. So far, I've not seen anything green except for the fichus tree by the window. I haven't seen anything brown, either, except for the skeleton-leaf bowl sitting on the glass coffee table.

I look out the window. A star shines on top of some distant hills. I think of my Capella from where I would be able to see millions of stars, and I am comforted for a moment. That ranch was my refuge from the chaotic life in the city. I miss my marigolds the most. I loved looking at the abundance, so many in bloom. But in my last year there, they all wilted and died.

There is a gradient color wheel hanging on the wall above the mantel.

"It's beautiful, isn't it?" I hear Didier's voice from behind me.

"There is no yellow in it," I say, thinking of the sunflowers I also left behind at Capella.

"It's a blue wheel of color. We'll get a primary wheel one so that you can have your yellow." He turns me around with a soft touch. "Anything for my diva. Let's go see your studio up in the attic."

He guides me out of the living room, up the stairs to the second floor, and then up another short flight of stairs. I see a thick wooden door. Didier opens it and turns on the overhead lights. The large room is padded with heavy marine-blue material. There is a baby grand piano, a music stand, and a tall shelf with dozens of books. A huge TV hangs on the wall across from a red couch by the window. There is a large poster of me on the wall above the piano. I'm dressed in my *Madam Butterfly* kimono with red maple leaves and white cherry blossoms motif. My hair is even longer than it is now. I forgot about making that poster.

Even more uncanny is another poster hanging next to mine of Didier's mother dressed in her own *Madam Butterfly* garb. We look like clones of each other, except that her eyes are blue. She wears a black kimono and has long, dark hair. The look on her face comes from a dark, lonely place. She must have been in her forties when she sang the aria and probably knew how to capture Butterfly's pain even more intensely. It was my first major role, and I was only seventeen. I was very much in love with Eli then, and thrilled that I was going to have his child. Maybe I would have the same look as Didier's mother had I sung it after the abortion.

"This is breathtaking." I turn to face him.

"It used to be my mother's singing room whenever she stayed in America. Shortly before her death, she and my father decided to go back to France, and I kept this room exactly as she had left it. You'll find the scores and librettos of all the arias she used to sing. She left many outfits behind that are at your disposal when you begin to perform at Maison Sakura, my restaurant. It has a small stage, and it will serve as your training ground. You'll shine, Sophie. I promise. You'll live your dream as my mother lived hers." His gaze is spellbinding. He steps closer and holds me tight.

His embrace takes me aback, but I'm so overwhelmed by what I see and hear that I remain quiet. Have I come to America to live my dream? Is this country a dream-maker? Or is it a heart-breaker for a woman like me, who is one with her land, her horse, and her flowers?

He guides me to the sofa. "Have a seat, Sophie." He sits next to me and picks up a menu on the coffee table in front of us. "From now on, I'll be taking care of your meals. Your Brazilian foods require significant quantities of dendê oil to prepare. They are loaded with saturated fat. I'll be cooking most of your food, and you'll love it, though it will be nearly all-vegetarian. We'll cut down on your sugar intake, as well as coffee." He continues to talk about the special menu, but I tune out.

All I know is that I already miss the smell of acarajé, vatapá, and moqueca de peixe. All my favorite dishes require a lot of dendê and coconut oil. Still, I am willing to give up any food I love to accomplish my goal.

I must make sacrifices to be able to win the contest at the Met. I quiver just thinking that I am going back to what burns and blazes inside me. If something were to happen to my voice, I'd never recover. Maybe it is an impossible dream, even though Didier says that everything is possible in America.

Didier speaks louder. "As soon as you master the English language, you'll be ready to give interviews and make a few appearances. The publicist will make sure people notice you. You haven't been on stage for five years, and you have a lot of catching up to do." His Portuguese is pitiful, but I still love it.

"This is a projected schedule for you so that you don't feel so lost in your new country. But you must know that, later on, your life will be scheduled years in advance. As a diva, you'll always be going somewhere in the world to show your art."

I look at the long list of instructions, and then at the clock on the wall, and realize that I'm at least seven hours behind schedule. I'm dreading this regimen, but I know I need someone as decisive as Didier to guide me through the intricate world of opera singing. Like any diva, I'm well aware of my curse.

"As specified in the contract, pregnancy is not acceptable, and I have provided you with these contraceptives just in case you need them." He hands me a package with a box of pills.

"I'm sorry, Didier, I don't take pills. I'm allergic to them."

"American pills are different."

"If you say so."

"I say so." The look of inevitability in his eyes is a bit alarming to me.

"I don't think I'm the right person for this, Didier. Your standards are very high. Maybe this is all a mistake."

"Nonsense. You're the very thing I've been waiting for all my life. And you're not signing the contract until your first performance in my restaurant. Besides, there is a target on your back in Rio, Sophie, and your own father is backing that criminal. You're safer here. I'll protect you."

"I suppose you're right. I guess I'm just a little tired."

"Of course, darling. Let's take care of you. Your bedroom has a private bath." He stands up and helps me up. He lets my hair down. "I love your tresses. Tomorrow, I'll take you to Alondra Libertad. She'll be your hairdresser and makeup artist. She'll prepare you for the stage."

I feel that he wants more from me, and I don't know how to respond. When we get down to business, maybe he will realize that I only came here for my opera. He leads me out of the opera studio and straight to my bedroom. As soon as I enter, I hear the sounds of *Madam Butterfly*. The television mounted on the wall across from the bed is as large as the one in my studio. Even though the heater is on, it feels cold for a Brazilian from tropical Rio. The bedroom is large and spacious. The walls are a rich blue in all its gradations. The indigo shutters hide a glass door that leads to the balcony. It feels as though I fell inside a gloomy world that dulls my senses. There are no sounds of buses cutting through busy streets, no stormy weather, no smell of coffee brewing in the percolator, no lagoon reflecting the silver light of the moon.

"This is your YouTube channel, called 'Sophie Morpho.' There are clips of you as well as of other divas. This is my mother Genevieve singing Madam Butterfly's aria." He puts my carry-on down by the desk.

Genevieve Guisan wears the same outfit as the one in the poster hanging in the studio. *Madam Butterfly* indeed touches the soul: a story about a rush of love that sets the universe ablaze with great intensity. It is complete bliss. But things don't end well for the young geisha. It's a sad and poignant tale. Hopefully, I'll sing it again. Genevieve's voice is rich and full of pathos. I think we have a lot in common as artists. Too bad I'll never meet her.

"My room is down the hallway. Don't hesitate to call me if you need anything. We'll have dinner at six p.m. Please be on time."

"Thank you, Didier. I'll shower and rest a bit."

"Okay, darling. Welcome again." He leans closer, kisses me on the cheek, and leaves the room.

I walk to the desk and sit down in the purple swivel chair. A skinny black vase holds a single iris. I unfold the note he has left. It's written on creamy stationery with the name Sophie Blue Morpho on the top margin. The bottom of the letterhead displays jagged silhouetted orchids with a Blue Morpho sitting on a flower on the left side.

> Petite Butterfly,
> Welcome to your new life. I've been planning your arrival for months and will provide you with anything you need. I'll ask much of you, but I will give you your dream in return. You'll become the most important diva of the twenty-first century if you put your life and career in my hands. Brazil will finally make you their number-one prima donna, and you will sing at the Amazon Opera House Festival. It's a promise.
> Yours,
> Didier Guisan

I open my carry-on, take out a picture of my family, and put it on the desk.

Papa, my sister Madalena, and I stand behind a piano at Rio's Conservatory. Mama is sitting on the bench. Her blonde hair is waist length, and so is my sister's. Mine was bobbed at the time since it was too hard to manage when I spent hours on end practicing and then performing. Mama has played the piano for as long as I can remember. I used to lie under the instrument and listen to her playing the classics until I fell asleep. I was fifteen when I sang the aria from *La Sonnambula*. In the portrait, Papa is beaming with pride. He did everything in his power to make me into an opera singer, but before that, I was his baby and he braided my hair every night so that it wouldn't be a bird's nest the next morning.

I hold a photograph of my grandmother Iracema. I look exactly like her. She worshiped me, and I revered her. She was the daughter of the Aruaques, but encroachment made the city her tribe. She longed for her forest of staggering trees and mesmerizing iguanas. I promised her I'd never forget the stories she told me as a child—they are pressed onto my skin and into my blood and bones. I can still hear the songs, the drums of my ancestors, and their voices in shades of green.

I grab my iPad from inside my handbag and call Dr. Lev.

"Sofia," he answers. "How are you doing? Did you arrive safely?"

"Yes. Tudo bem? Any news?"

"I'm fine. Your father came to my office, looking for you. I told him that my father put you in the Witness Protection Program after Officer Almeida threatened you."

A chill goes down my spine. "You shouldn't have. Officer Almeida will hurt you when he finds out, Dr. Lev. He's an evil man."

"He won't. I told your father that you're safe, Sofia, and that Officer Almeida will have his day in court, and so will your father. I'm afraid he's testifying for the defense if there is an indictment. I'm sorry."

"That's my father. I told you; he's unforgiving. He'll do anything in his power to help Totenkopf win this case."

"But they will lose. Brazil may be slow to deliver justice, but it always does in the end. We just have to keep at it. Totenkopf will be convicted."

"I hope so." My eyes well up with tears. "Do you want to come here, too, so that I can protect you?"

"No need, querida. I have my own protection. I just want you to be safe, Sofia. One day you'll be free and happy again. It all shall pass, I promise. I've got to run. Be well. Beijos."

"Beijos. Adeus. Bye."

There is so much more I want to say to him. I miss him and Brazil so much already. I'm dying of saudade, a Tupi-Guarani word that means loss of soul; a longing, a yearning for what has never been. It can also mean the presence of an absence, like a lover who is gone yet ever-present. I then remember the word desatar, to undo, to untie, to burst out laughing or burst into tears.

Chapter 3

The Hive is a spacious salon. The ash-grey walls make the atmosphere a bit somber, but the cobalt-blue furniture lends the place more hope. A painting of an amethyst on the wall reminds me of Brazil's abundance of natural resources in contrast to its astonishing amount of poverty and hunger. White smoke rises from an oil burner sitting on a blue table. I smell plumeria, a tropical flower that grows everywhere at Capella. I worry about my ranch, but the thought of Dr. Lev visiting there to comfort Vento and keep an eye on my plants calms me down.

A curvy woman with brown eyes and wavy hair approaches me. She is a bit taller than I am and has a full figure. "I'm Alondra Libertad, Sofia. Nice to meet you." She is wearing an earth-toned dress and cardigan, which reminds me of the brown people of my country, people like me.

"Nice to meet you." I smile. "Good place, good perfume, good lights. Everything is very good." I try to get my English right.

"Thank you. What a beautiful smile you have."

She turns to Didier. "Do you want me to do an assessment today or just go ahead with the hair plan?" Alondra asks.

"Let's do a full consultation and then the hair." He continues to talk while looking around.

It feels strange to be dealing with looks and beauty again. All this preparation before finally getting onto the stage has made me weary, but I have no choice. I'll have to be transformed into a glamorous diva again. I'll have to get used to it as I did in the past.

"Let's go to the back, then. Please follow me." Alondra guides us into a large room painted a sea-glass green. It has a massage table, a shelf with all kinds of products, a sink, a sound system, and a black room divider. "Please have a seat." She pulls out two chairs for us and sits down in one. "Let's begin." She opens a beauty salon program on her laptop.

She maneuvers the mouse, creating a face on the Lenovo. She gives it eyes, a nose, a mouth, ears, hair, a tan, and a warm skin tone. "This is you, Sophie. You have an oval face, the most harmonious of all shapes. You have large green eyes, seductive lips, and a killer smile. Your nose is slightly skewed, but elegant." She continues to talk about every aspect of my face, emphasizing that Brazilians like me have the most exotic look.

While they talk, I think of Capella. Unlike millions of Rio's citizens, I love to be lost in the woods, away from the gentrified and crazy life of the city, but like millions of Cariocas, I'm my happiest sitting on the beach in a bathing suit, admiring the sea, and then taking a dive instead of tweeting on my iPhone from an expensive club or eating at a fancy restaurant. It's going to drive me crazy to be indoors day in and day out, but Didier has been an opera manager since the days when his mother was alive, and he'll get me to where I want to be.

"I'm identifying your season," Alondra says in Spanish. "I truly believe you are a Winter woman. I'll give you a new hairstyle, show you new makeup techniques, including colors that go well with your complexion." She points at my double on the screen. "We'll decide what to keep, fix, and get rid of in your closet, as well as how to put outfits together. And, of course, we'll go over how to conceal body flaws and accessorize, and we'll talk about wardrobe shopping."

"Thank you," I say, thinking that the Sofia I know will be gone in no time. She will be just a memory, a memory that only I will have. I remember my days at Capella riding Vento and picking fruit from the trees. All of a sudden, I want to return to my land and everything I love.

Didier turns to me. "I have to go back to work, darling. I'll be back in two hours. You're in very good hands. Bye." He turns to Alondra. "Don't cut her hair too much. And I also want you to give her a keratin treatment. Make the hair as flat and straight as you can. She'll be my geisha."

He's obsessed with my hair and wants it long. I was hoping she would cut at least five inches, but I guess he wants me to be just like Cio-Cio San, even though I won't be playing that part anytime soon. He listens to the opera constantly. I love the score, but the story is troubling to me; it's so wrenching, maybe because of Butterfly's city of origin. Like Hiroshima, Nagasaki was also destroyed by the A-Bomb.

"Ready to wash it? Lavar?"

"Yes, thank you. You are very good." I walk to the sink. It's a good thing The Hive is within walking distance of Didier's house, and I'm glad Alondra is a Chicano girl. She might understand me better than an American woman would.

I tilt my head back. Alondra turns the faucet on. I love the warmth of the water on my scalp. It's soothing. The smell of coconut shampoo is tropical. It reminds me of the sunscreen I used to wear when I sat at Copacabana Beach under the tropical sun. I dread the world I'm about to dive into. Didier says I'll be in the studio many hours a day practicing for the Met competition.

"Ready?" She guides me to the chair. She smiles. "You're cute, Sofia." It's nice that she calls me by my given name, rather than Sophie. She begins to trim my hair. Her hands are steady. She's focused on what she's doing.

Afterwards, she pours a small drop of golden liquid on her hand and rubs it. She massages the silky liquid into my scalp and hair. I can't help but think of my father braiding my hair every night so that it would not look like a bird's nest in the morning. I miss that father, but not the one who still supports the man who killed my lover.

"I'll put you under the heat for fifteen minutes. Acalentar, okay?" She guides me to another chair across the room, and I sit down. She turns on the hair drier and walks away, adjusting a timer.

She gives me a folder, a guide on how to dress to impress—distinguished and stylish. There are photos of outfits for every season, but she has marked five evening gowns for New York so that I can steal the show. There is a guide on braids and the bare necessities for hair removal. There are also dozens of tips on makeup, including an ad for extra-dark mascara that lasts without smudging.

A tall black woman comes in. She has dreadlocks. She's dressed in tribal attire, but more refined, a tie-dyed dress with a lot of oranges, reds, and greens to it. She also wears large, golden hoop earrings. She has a huge smile. She greets Alondra. I can't hear what they're saying because the blow dryer is too loud. She waves and smiles at me. She shows me her key chain, which has a Brazilian flag medallion. I smile and wave back, hoping that it's not just the key chain that's Brazilian.

Alondra guides her to the back. She comes back about ten minutes later, followed by the woman, and turns the dryer off. "I want you to meet Valéria Vasconcelo. She's Brazilian."

"Oi, Sofia, eu sou da Bahia." She smiles.

Like millions in the state of Bahia, she is black and beautiful. I smile back. "Nice to meet you."

She continues to speak in Portuguese, which feels as good as the treatment on my hair. "I work here in the evenings on Mondays, Wednesdays, and Fridays. I also read Tarot. Do you have any interest in it?"

"De verdade? I love it. Can you read for me, today?"

"I'm free for the next half hour."

Alondra smiles. "Please use the room in the back. I'll finish with the hair later."

Valéria guides me to the adjacent room, and we sit at a small table facing each other. She opens her canvas bag, takes out a wooden box, and shows it to me.

"Que bom. Que felicidade. My angels are helping me."

"They are, querida. There are angels all around you. Let's get started. Let me pour you some orange-lime-infused water. Water is good." She opens the refrigerator, picks up a glass, and fills it up with the golden liquid. She hands me the glass.

"Do you have Guaraná?" I hope it's not my imagination, but I see a stack of the Brazilian soda in her fridge.

"Yes. I have a stash of Brazilian things that I can't live without. The berries from our forest make the drink potent and healthy." She hands me a can.

I look at the sugar content, which says 24 grams. "Sorry, my manager wants to limit my sugar content to 15 grams a day. He has his reasons, and I don't want to go against his advice."

"Drink it, amiga. Listen, girlfriend, don't let no white man tell you how much sugar you get to have." She opens the can for me. "I never give in to the white man."

"Thank you, but I'll pass. I have to be able to fit into a bunch of outfits that were made especially for me. He is my sponsor, and I have to follow his instructions."

"Be careful, honey, don't let him walk all over you." She picks up a stack of cards. "Pick two of them, please." She unfolds a white napkin to display seven small cowry shells. "Tell me what you want to know."

"Did I do the right thing following this man? Should I let him manage my career?"

She flips a card. "I see the Moon and the House of God. "It's a part of your karma to be with him again." She throws the cowry shells. "He has wronged you in the past and has come into this world to rectify that and help you grow spiritually."

"Is he going to give me my opera back?"

She flips another card and throws the cowry shells again. "He will. He'll work hard to make you a great opera singer, but he'll ask much of you. He is in love with you, even obsessed, and will take you very far. He'll help you achieve your dream. But I see a shadow looming. Is there anything putting your life in danger?"

"There is an officer in my father's battalion, the BOPE, who promised to kill me if I testify against him in his upcoming trial. He killed my fiancé, and my testimony is very important. That's one of the reasons I entered into the contract with Didier."

"Your father is the commander of the BOPE?"

"Yes."

"I'd never have guessed, Sofia. How could he be the father of a girl like you?"

"The father I know isn't the commander. The father I know became the head of the BOPE so that he could finance my opera career."

Alondra comes in and hands me a gold box with a black bow. "Didier wants you to wear it after I do your hair."

I open the gift and see a brilliant and translucent hair ornament that shimmers in the light. It's shaped like a Nestira, and it looks so real that I hesitate to touch it. I read the note attached.

> Petit Sophie,
>
> This is a real Blue Nestira. It was prepared with a special type of varnish so that it will last forever. There are tiny diamond studs around the edges to make it even more exceptional. It was conceived and made especially for you, my Butterfly.
>
> From your greatest admirer,
> Didier

My heart sinks. I turn my head away, wondering how anyone could freeze and kill one of the most astounding creatures in nature. All of a sudden, I feel like dropping everything and running back to my ranch. I feel like I've been snatched from nature in the most harrowing way. I panic, thinking that Didier's world of ostentation and intricacy will drive a wedge between me and my beloved natural world.

"I can't possibly wear this today, Alondra. Would you please tell Didier to save it for a different occasion?" I give the package back to her. "Please make something up."

"Okay, Sofia. I'll let him know that this is to be worn with a kimono."

"Gracias."

Valéria touches my shoulder. "Would you like to do a brief guided imagery? Let's get rid of those dark thoughts. I'm sure this gift affected your mood. You look rattled."

"Yes, please. I feel a bit unstable."

"I'll help you get rid of this negative stuff. Breathe in and out."

I shut my eyes and take a few deep breaths as I hear Valéria's voice leading me into solace.

In my mind's eye, I see the Amazon forest. I enter the woods and follow a trail guided by my grandmother, Iracema. Along the serpentine path, there are ceremonial vestiges of tribes that live nearby. The afternoon birds sing their joyful calls. The trees are so staggering that I feel a bit dizzy. The dark-green foliage guides us farther down the path. Iguanas roam free, their emerald-green gleaming in the sunlight that breaks through the gaps in the canopy. The magenta laelia orchids grow by the thousands on thick tree trunks. It's magical to be in this world with my grandmother. She was my own goddess of love and beauty, the person I've loved most in the world.

"At the count of five, open your eyes, Sofia," Valéria says. "One, two, three, four, five."

Opening my eyes, I take a few deep breaths and focus on the painting of the amethyst.

"How do you feel, now?"

"Peaceful."

"Good."

Alondra comes in. "Are you girls done? Sofia's hair will take a long time to dry."

"We're done." She puts the cards back in the wooden box. "Next time, we'll do a Reiki massage. Just remember that nothing is lacking. All you need is within you—now! I'm simply here to remind you."

"Thank you so much. I'll be back for the massage." I get up, kiss her goodbye, and follow Alondra back into the salon. I sit on the chair, and she washes my hair again. I wonder how long I'll be able to endure this life of glamour without having my Capella to fall back on. But Didier says that if

I don't let go of some of my old ways, I'll never make it onto the biggest stage in the world. He says that, in America, what matters is talent and way you look.

Alondra dries my hair and leads me to another chair. She picks up the blow dryer and begins to work on it after applying keratin and detangling cream.

I'm glad she didn't insist on putting the hair ornament on me today. Later, I will try to explain to Didier that I can't wear something so loathsome. I hope he will understand that there is a limit to what to what I'm willing to do for this transformation.

"Done." Alondra turns off the hair dryer. "Gorgeous. Shiny, smooth, healthy. You have such beautiful hair, thick but fine, and heavy, too."

"Thank you for everything. No wonder Didier said that I'd like you a lot."

I study myself in the mirror. He'd asked her to make my hair look very flat and straight. I'm small, but even so, I don't think he can make me look like a fourteen-year-old Japanese geisha. I'll do my best, but I don't think I can pull this off.

She shows me the back of my head with a mirror. "We're going to be girlfriends. You can stop by anytime if you have questions.

"It is so wonderful to be around a loving and spiritual woman. I'm so happy." I get up. "Is Didier coming, now?"

"Soon. Do you have any questions, Sofia?"

"Do you use any animal-tested makeup?"

"No, darling, don't worry. I'll be right back." She walks away.

I focus on a series of photographs on the wall above the large mirror. The pictures are portraits on heavy textured surfaces in the gray scale. The colors are missing, except for the deep-red lips of a woman who seems to be in mourning. She is dressed in an ornate and expensive kimono. Not a strand of hair is out of place even though the winter scene seems to include a faint wind blowing at the few leaves left on a flowerless myrtle tree.

Alondra returns with a black satin bag in her hands. "These are some of the products I used on your hair today. Please follow the instructions. Didier is waiting in the car."

"Thank you for everything." I grab my purse.

She hands me a chart showing me a variety of tattooed eyebrow designs. She tells me Didier wants me to have mine done in this fashion. I gasp. I'm not ready for that. A tattoo is something permanent, and I don't yet know how permanent my life in America will be. I kiss her goodbye and leave the salon.

Chapter 4

It has been a month since I arrived in Los Angeles. I've given up a lot of things to be able to realize one of my greatest desires, but it is all worth it. There is nothing more important than singing Madam Butterfly at the Met and winning the contest. Didier demands that I spend hours warming up my voice and working on different arias with Noah, the pianist from Maison Sakura. There is a lot of work ahead, but I won't give up.

The red-and-gold butterfly art nails took two hours to get done, at least an hour of which was spent on gluing on the rhinestones. Alondra has become a friend, and so has Valéria.

I sit down on the swivel chair and turn on my laptop. I navigate to a webcam streaming a view of Copacabana Beach. South Atlantic waters stare back at me. I have never seen anything so blue aside from the Nestira's wings. I can see the spot where I used to hang out. I used to lean over the edge of the tallest rock, mesmerized by the whirlpool below. There are dark clouds rushing in, and soon the rain will come, bringing flash-floods, landslides, and strong winds.

A new view shows a billboard announcing the new Coke Zero. America is colonizing Brazil as swiftly as the Portuguese did six hundred years ago. I wonder if future generations will have "Made in America" imprinted on their products rather than my generation's "Made in Portugal."

I log onto Facebook. Isabella posted a picture album of Dr. Lev's party at the clinic. My best friend and colleague still works there and keeps me posted. She is so concerned about the well-being of others that my admiration for her knows no bounds.

There is a picture of Dr. Lev and Dr. Cristina, his fiancée. She is standing next to him, facing the camera, with her arms looped around his neck. His arms are around her waist. She is gorgeous, but she looks a bit uptight with her blonde hair pulled back in a low bun. She gazes straight at the camera, but he seems distracted by something to the side of them. He's an atypical man—most of the men I know use their power and position to boss people around, especially women. Dr. Cristina is lucky to be engaged to someone who will never put her down or act like he owns her.

Didier's YouTube channel plays an aria from Madam Butterfly, the moment in which she gives her child away to Lieutenant Pinkerton and his American wife. Her husband has betrayed her and is leaving her behind to return to his country. She gives up one thing after another for her dream. I've been doing the same. Will there be a limit for me, or will death be the final price tag?

I change into the new kimono Didier bought for the special night he has in store for me. It's a fabulous thing with motifs of mint leaves, chrysanthemums, and plum blossoms. The background is blue, and it's made of silk. The sash clasp resembles a camellia carved from pink coral and jade and set in ivory. My hair has been styled in a bohemian braid. The Blue Nestira hairpin seems too expensive to be worn at a private celebration, but he wouldn't have it any other way. The hardest thing to get used to are the geta, the clogs that geishas wear, but he says I'll have to wear them when I sing on the Met stage, and I might as well start practicing.

I put on the sapphire choker necklace that Didier gave me and then put on a drop of Sakura eau de toilette. I walk to my desk, sit down, and finally open the FedEx package Dr. Lev sent me. Since I'm not allowed to use electronics during working hours, we've been communicating through letters, as well. I open one dated March 20, 2015.

> Cara Sofia,
>
> As you read this, Officer Almeida is being arraigned for his crime. The Grand Jury indicted him on first-degree murder with a depraved heart. My father is taking him off the streets, as promised. He will set the bail very high in hopes of keeping him locked up until the trial takes place. I'm not sure when it will happen, but my father will expedite this case. Sadly, racism and anti-Semitism are on the rise in Brazil. My father also ordered the removal of an article online that compared Moses to Hitler and Judaism to Nazism, written by a lawyer called Marco de Souza Pereira who happens to be associated with Officer Almeida. He also ordered the Centauro Editorial to stop selling Mein Kampf and other books of anti-Semitic content. This is

just the beginning. In most cases, federal prosecutors refrain from getting involved in cases involving abuse by state police, but my father is not relenting and promises justice for you and Eli.

I hope all this makes you happy. As I said earlier, my father can still put you in the Witness Protection Program, and there will be nothing to fear if you decide to return to your homeland. However, I must be clear that even though Officer Almeida is in prison, there are no bars for a criminal of his stature, especially when your father still believes him, and if you choose to return, I'd need a few weeks to figure out a plan. I know he means it when he says he would have you killed. But rest assured, I will never let it happen. Plans will be made for your safety when you come to testify.

Um carinho, Lev

I fold his letter, stunned by the news, wishing I were there to see it all with my own eyes, but I guess it wasn't meant to be. The most important thing is that Eli's death will be vindicated.

The stereotype in Brazil is that America has the greatest material advantages but lacks warmth in human contact. It's too soon to judge, even as a therapist who knows a great deal about interpersonal relationships, yet it has always been clear to me that, while Brazil is a third-world country, relationships are more important than material possessions. Being Brazilian means I'll never put business affairs in front of human affairs.

***

I walk down the hallway in my geta, taking tiny steps toward Didier's bedroom. Holding his camera, he stands at the end of the hall in front of his room. He wears a black tuxedo and looks imposing.

I'm nervous and trying to keep my balance as I walk. This idea of turning me into a geisha is a pain, but he insists, and I hate to disagree with him. After what seems like an eternity, I reach his bedroom and he gestures for me to enter before him.

A round table has been set with black dishes graced with white sakura flower motifs. There are wine glasses, champagne flutes, black wooden placemats, and black chopsticks. There are two tall, silver name holders. He wrote our names in the new font he's perfecting for the new menu at Maison Sakura. It's inspired by Kanji characters and looks very elegant. There are two tall candelabras with blue candles and an ikebana flower arrangement at the center of the table. It consists of concentric rings of flowers. There are red roses, white saxifrage, and blue grape hyacinths. The display of elegantly placed blooms in a shallow black container is stunning.

The aria "Ah! Non credea mirarti" comes out of the speakers. The Cavatina from *La Sonnambula* by Bellini reminds me that, like Amina, I have been sleepwalking through my days since Eli died. I think of my shattered dreams. No matter what they say, I'll never find the closure I want. Will I ever wake up from my somnambulism? Will I ever love again with the same passion? Didier seems to want me in a romantic way, but I have made it clear that our relationship is strictly business, even though I do find him attractive and persuasive. Still, I just want to concentrate on my opera. Love hasn't really worked for me.

"This is such luxury, Didier. You shouldn't have."

"It's a special occasion. We're having hirame sushi, which is made of halibut, salmon, and a kabashira roll, which is made of scallop. I have a bottle of Vinho Verde to go with it since you told me you love Portuguese wine. Plus, a delicate sashimi made of puffer fish, called fugu. It will be served with Moet & Chandon, darling, just for you."

"When I was fifteen, I ate fugu, but it had traces of tetrodotoxin, and I fell into a weird sleep that lasted twelve hours. I suppose that sushi chef in Rio didn't do a good job."

"That would never happen here. I'm a certified fugu chef, trained in Japan. I spent a year there learning about Japanese food to incorporate a few items into my restaurant's menu. I extracted all the poison myself." He shows me the tray with the sashimi.

His food is sheer elegance. His life, sophistication. I wonder if there are any flaws in this universe.

"Do you speak Japanese, too? I heard it's very difficult to learn."

"Yes, and six other languages. Do you speak any other languages?"

"I speak Latin."

"Why Latin? It's a dead language."

"Not for me. It's alive in my heart. I wanted to read from the *Carmina Burana Codex* on its own terms. It's very special to me."

"Well, that's excellent, since I've included "In Trutina" in your repertoire, as well. I guess you won't need a language teacher for that."

Maria Callas sings "Ah! Non Credea mirarti" perfectly. She holds the F note for so long. I tremble at the thought that, one day, I, too, may be singing at the Met. Pretty soon, I'll be practicing seven hours a day to get my voice up to speed.

All of a sudden, I realize that I don't really know how things will work out. All of a sudden, I realize that talent is just part of the story; hard work is what truly shapes the voice. Discipline without end is required, and I'm terrified to begin the journey toward singing with perfect poise, beyond reproach.

He puts his arms around my shoulders. "The big news is: You'll be singing this aria at Maison Sakura on your birthday this June. It's going to be your first big test, Sofia. Then there will be no stopping you. You will sing it for the first round in the contest at the Met, and your future will be set." His gaze is on me, a fiery stare that frightens me.

"Do you have anything harder? I mean, "Ah, non credea mirarti" is a six-minute aria filled with crazy high Fs. I'll probably fail, Didier. Let's not take any chances."

"You won't fail." He pulls a chair out for me. "Please have a seat." He turns on the television and plays a video clip. "Did you forget that you won the Queen Elizabeth of Belgium Voice Competition in 2009 singing this very aria? How come you never told me?"

"I forgot to mention it. I'm sorry."

I see myself standing in the Brussels Opera House right before singing the aria in the finals. I'm dressed in a golden gown with black lace roses over the bodice and a single shoulder strap covered by the same motif. I begin to sing the sad, yet exquisite aria. My eyes well up just knowing that right after that competition, upon our return to Brazil, Eli was killed, and I didn't last another year in opera.

"How can such a small person have such an incredible voice?" He clasps my hand. You have such a gorgeous instrument. I'll make you shine. All I need is for you to fall in love with me and everything will be perfect."

I smile, but don't say a word. Memories come rushing into my mind of me and Eli in Brussels. We made love at the hotel after the finale. I was still in that gold dress. I was still wearing the green emerald necklace presented to me by the queen. But when I lost him, it felt as though all the opera houses in the world had collapsed.

Didier pops the champagne and pours me some. "Drink and be merry before the hard work starts. Madame Prunier will be coming tomorrow to turn you into the perfect diva. You're young, fresh, sensual, edgy. You're like a drug. People won't be able to get enough of you, but you must leave your past behind. Please let Dr. Lev know that you won't be as available and give him my number so that he can call me instead."

I take a sip of my wine and pick up my chopsticks. I eat a fugu sashimi, thinking that not talking to Dr. Lev was easier said than done. "I will give it my all, Didier, but I can't let go of Dr. Lev; without him, I wouldn't survive being so far away from everything I love."

"You'll get used to it when the real work begins." He clicks on the aria again. "With you, we'll make opera sexy, young, and breathing. Even people who hate opera will love you."

"I think you're exaggerating."

He pours me a glass of Vinho Verde. "You are the future of opera, Sofia, and I'm going to make you a very rich woman."

"Thank you for the compliment, Didier."

I refrain from telling him that I'm probably already a rich woman since my father invested most of my money. But that kind of "rich" interests me very little, unless it comes with another sort of richness that will replenish my soul. I continue to eat the delicious food while watching myself sing in La Sonnambula.

"Are you sure I can win the contest?"

"I'm sure you can, if you work hard to close the gap in your career." He puts his chopsticks down. "To celebrate this marvelous voice, I worked on a surprise for you. It has taken me months, and it will prove how much I care about you."

"May I take off the clogs? They are a bit uncomfortable. Besides, I feel a bit foggy. I also need to write a quick email to Dr. Lev. Totenkopf is behind bars, and it's all thanks to him."

"Don't think of any of those things tonight, Sophie. This dark story of yours has nothing to do with your brilliant future. Forget about Dr. Lev. And by the way, he's in love with you."

"You're out of your mind, Didier. For your information, he's engaged, and I'm going to sing at his wedding. You know nothing about this man. Unlike you, he isn't obsessed with women who pretend to be someone else, who never reveal an ounce of their true selves."

"That's what's fascinating about you, Sophie. You can be as conceited as you want to be, and yet, you aren't. Rare."

I hope he means that I am true to myself. My grandmother would tell me that the underside of the Blue Nestira is brown, which is what sets her free because it camouflages her. She would tell me that I can be a free woman as long as I remain brown and down to earth. The glimmer and glow of the blue crest should be reserved only for the stage.

He reaches out, clasps my hand, and kisses it. "When you are done, please join me back in here, darling. I have some Moet and Chandon and a special cobbler of the forest with Gran de Meniere raspberry peach."

"I don't think I can drink another drop of alcohol, Didier, but I'll taste the dessert. You didn't have to go through so much trouble."

"All for my butterfly. I want to make this night memorable, dear. Your new life is just beginning."

He has a look that scares me; it's a bit imposing, but I know he means well.

He wants me to shine. He is right when he says that I won't be abandoning Eli if I move on with my life. I must wake up if I am to have the courage to testify in court and help Dr. Lev win the case. I must wake up if I want the minister of culture to regret turning down a contract of mine four years ago. Time to wake up, Sofia, and show Brazil the great artist you are meant to be.

Chapter 5

I enter Didier's bedroom. With his blue comforter and geometric shams, the king-size bed seems to shimmer. I tear my focus from it and notice his long desk between two built-in bookcases. A magenta Laelia orchid in a golden pot has six blossoms that tilt to the left. I feel like I'm tilting. I concentrate on the order in his room. The smart TV across from his bed, his organized desk. Everything in its place, day in and day out.

"I'll show you something that will make you forget all your regrets," he says, guiding me across the room. He slides the glass doors open and leads me inside a long, green room filled with orchid plants. They remind me of a cascade of multicolored blooms I left behind at Capella.

It's such an arresting image. In the center, there is a blue Mystique orchid, its blooms overflowing from a wicker basket. The Spice orchids are as fragrant as roses. They have dozens of large, lovely flowers with deep-purple tinges. The pansy variety are small, with soft, lacy leaves. They are velvety and vivid in shades of red and purple. The Laelia has blossoms in ravishing shades of white, yellow, lavender, and a fusion of these colors.

"I've never seen anything as astounding as this." I turn to face him. "Since when have you been nursing them?"

"Since I read in your file that you have a special love for them." He puts his arms around my shoulders. "I know how much you love nature."

"This makes me so happy. See? No more sorrow."

He holds me tight. "That's the goal, my Carmina Burana. I looked up the descriptions of hedonistic medieval paradise in the *Codex Buranus*, especially the Latin poetry of the Goliards from which your beautiful aria 'In Trutina' comes."

I gasp. Eli did the same thing. Because of his love for the texts, I learned Latin to comprehend the mourning songs for the dead and the scores of verses of love. I'm completely stunned that he knows about the manuscript, a secret Eli and I shared.

He touches the screen on his computer and the wallpaper displays the Wheel of Fortune, which is the cover image book binders placed on the *Codex Burana*: a pair of lovers, scenes from the story Dido and Aeneas, and even people playing chess. There is also a yin/yang circle, which isn't on the cover of the original volume.

Very few moments in my life have rendered me speechless, but this is one of them.

"You're beautiful. Tell me why you became so emotional when you saw yourself performing "Ah! Non credea mirarti?" You seemed so sad and vulnerable. What pains you?" He looks concerned. "I care a great deal about you, Sophie."

"Opera singers carry a lot of pain that does not belong to them." I smile. "Plus a great deal of pain that does belong to them, plus a great deal of pain that doesn't belong to any one person in particular."

"You're clever. Yet, I sense vulnerability, a dark aspect that I like. Don't tell me it's also a peculiarity of your profession?"

"Partly." I laugh. "It's the diva in me. Sad, triste, gloomy."

He clicks on a PowerPoint presentation showing a series of divas.

Charlotte Church, the American singer, begins to sing "In Trutina." She has a lovely voice, and I usually like her take on songs, but not this one. She sings at full volume all the way through.

He leads me toward the bed. I don't resist. "I love your French braid." He puts his arms around me, swings me around, and snaps the Blue Nestira hairpin open. "I love your scent of crushed Sakura blossoms." He puts the hair ornament on the bedside table and then motions for me to sit on the bed.

I'm so drawn to him. Perhaps because of the orchid greenhouse, or because of the copy of the *Codex Burana*, or perhaps the recollections. Also, everything feels a bit foggy. Maybe it was the fugu, or the wine, or the memories. Whatever it is, I want something new, something that will make a difference. Maybe I do want to get romantically involved with him. But what do I fear?

He kneels down in bed behind me and begins to undo my braid. He unties my obi and my kimono. He gently pushes me down on the bed and leans over me. He kisses me on the mouth. His passion rekindles emotions that have lain dormant for years. His touch feels warm, tender, and tense, all at the same time.

"In Trutina" plays in the background. I recognize my own voice. Maybe I should run away from him, from his desire, from his touch while I have a chance. "Let's take it slow, Didier, please. I need to find my balance before I get romantically involved with another man. I'm full of uncertainties."

He continues to run his fingers over my hair.

"You're a mystical, emotional, and artistic woman who believes she came from a star far away and will go back there after this life. Honestly, I wouldn't worry about being balanced. You're a goddess of love who should be worshipped and fed what I have to offer."

He gets up and brings back a tray with the dessert and champagne. "In Trutina" continues to play. He feeds me spoons of peach cobbler and sparkling wine, and I take a plunge into a world so dazzling, so thrilling, so magical that nothing else matters now.

I clutch him in my arms. I want him close. I breathe in his scent of Blue de Chanel.

"When I was a child the flowers were my toys. I used to walk on fields of marigolds, gardenias, and saudades, the flowers of the dead. I ate the flowers, too. Have you ever eaten flowers?"

"Nasturtiums," he says. "I make a salad at Maison Sakura with melon and drizzled with black currant balsamic." He kisses my cheek. "You're my path of flowers, my darling." He kisses me on the mouth, and I kiss him back. He begins to slowly take off my dress. Then he pours me more champagne from a bottle he has in a bucket on the bedside table.

"In Trutina" is filled with depth, pathos, and passion. It's heartbreaking. It conveys the heroine's desire for steadiness, yet it also conveys her passion and how vulnerable she is when trying to choose between chastity and desire. Like her, I'm a woman of two minds.

"Please, Didier, stop. It might be too soon." My voice is a whisper.

"Don't be scared, Sophie. It's okay to feel wanted and cherished. Just let go of the past."

The aria grows louder. I remember the stage, the lights, the applause, the calls of Brava! Bravissima!

I recall the fugu. Maybe I'm slightly poisoned. It feels as though I'm seeing smells, smelling colors, hearing textures. I hang onto him. I sense a slowing down in the passage of time, impaired distance, wavelike motion, euphoria, and surreal visual effects.

I feel a stunning luminosity, as if the Capella star had replaced the sun, banishing darkness forever and bringing about yellow, brown, and reddish marigold blooms. There are billions of blossoms falling out of the sky. I enter an alien state of mind and seem to be running into neon avenues like the ones in Rio.

The shadows in the room remind me of another night in Rio, another time filled with gloom. I recall my voice saying: "Stop. Stop. Stop." I shut my eyes and roll over to the edge of the bed. I feel the world reeling around me and try to stay put. I toss and turn. I watch the numbers on the iPod dock flip. Another one flips, then five more, then ten more. I fall into a weird sleep like the one in Rio in which I had been slightly poisoned.

The hazy glow of pre-dawn darkness jars me awake. I lie immobile. It feels as though I've woken up from a disturbing dream. Unable to fall asleep, I get up, put my kimono back on, and rush out of Didier's room, sobbing, realizing that something isn't right, at all. As I hurry down the hallway, I nearly fall, thinking that I'm four thousand miles away from Rio. I enter my room, sit down on the swivel chair, and turn on the desk lamp. I call Dr. Lev on Skype. It rings, rings, rings one more time.

"Sofia, are you okay? It must be the middle of the night in L.A. What's wrong?"

"Hello, Dr. Lev. Sorry to call you so early," I say, choking on my tears. "I need to talk. I'll even risk losing you because I know you'll probably lay the blame on me and hate me for what I did."

"What happened to you, darling?" He lowers his voice.

"I had dinner with Didier, ate fugu, and had some wine, then he showed me the beautiful orchids he raises in his greenhouse next to his bedroom—they are just like the ones I have at Capella. I missed my flowers. Then, the next minute, he was playing clips of me singing "In Trutina," which was Eli's song for me, and then he was undoing my braid and then unzipping my dress. And somehow, I guess I was caught up in the moment, and the touching led to sex, and then at some point I tried to extricate myself, but I guess it felt good to be held, pampered, and handled with care. Oh, I don't know! Eli will think that I've betrayed him. Oh, I'm so mad at myself for being so dumb."

"Listen, Sofia, carefully take a deep breath and then another, and then another please."

I do as he tells me and keep breathing, at first heavily and then, little by little, my breath isn't so labored anymore. I begin to feel more and more relaxed, and then I stop crying. I reach out, grab a tissue from the box on my desk, and wipe my face.

"Good, darling. Are you calmer now?"

"Yes, thank you. Sorry to drag you into this, but I was desperate to talk to somebody. I'm sure you probably think that I'm just a stupid girl. I guess I was a bit paranoid. Do you think I suffer from some kind of mental illness? Did you notice anything when we worked together at the clinic? Or do you think I'm just a crybaby? I guess I was having a good time, but I wanted to stop because I thought it was too soon to get involved sexually."

"May I please say what I really think?"

"Yes, please, but go easy on me. I won't be able to take it if you think low of me."

"You're about five-foot-two and weigh one hundred ten pounds. I'm certain that a small person like you can't tolerate too much alcohol. How much did you drink last night? Do you remember?"

"My memory is fuzzy, but I think I must have had three glasses of wine and champagne combined—I'm not sure. I feel kind of fuzzy, if you know what I mean, kind of sick."

"That's a lot for a person your size. You were at least intoxicated, if not drunk, and I think this is the problem. I don't think you were crying only because you were missing Eli when you listened to "In Trutina," or because you felt that you betrayed him, although those things may have played a role. I don't think you have any mental illness. But I do think you need to understand that you weren't able to fully consent to what happened last night, and you yourself said that at some point you wanted to remove yourself from the situation, although parts of it felt good. Most important, even when people consent, people can change their mind at any point in the process and the other person must do the right thing and stop. Did you ask Didier to stop?"

"Yes, Dr. Lev. I suppose I must have changed my mind, but I guess, I didn't know I did, or at least, I didn't let Didier know for sure that I did. Oh, it's so confusing. He was so kind to me." I break down crying again. "You know, I never told you, but when I was twenty-one, Officer Almeida raped me. I don't think that Didier was the problem last night. It was just the bad memories coming back. I was thinking about that night in Rio. It felt as though I was in a dream, a cloudy and cold one. In the middle of Almeida's attack, I must have entered an altered state of mind. It seems I was sleepwalking through it, and fading away, fading... I never looked down to see myself lying below, or maybe I was just a bit high and imagined all that. Almeida was so vicious. I can't believe I never told anyone about that before. I'm so ashamed. Do you understand?" I sob. "Oh, it's so crazy. Maybe I just want to come home."

"Yes, it must feel overwhelming and confusing, but I just want you to be calm, okay? Can you do that for me? Just breathe, sweetie. Deep breaths. Good. Keep breathing. It all shall pass. Tomorrow, everything will look different, and we'll talk again and look into this whole thing with fresh eyes. I'm here, and I'm not going anywhere."

I take deep breaths and begin to feel almost serene. "I wish I were near you now so that I could reach out and hug you. You're so good to me. Even though you have to deal with all my baggage, you still don't think badly of me." I fight a wash of tears. "I miss you a lot."

"I miss you, too. I, too, wish I were near you so that I could hug you. Please never worry about venting 'all your baggage.' It's an honor to be of some help. I care a great deal about you, Sofia, and it will never change, regardless of what you share with me." He gazes at me. "You look peaceful, now. I can send you a ticket in twenty-four hours if you decide to return. You'll be safe. I promise. Do you trust me?"

"Yes. Thank you. You're such a wonderful guy. I don't know what to say. I still feel confused, but safe now, thanks to you."

"May I play something for you?"

"Yes, please. I'd love that. Music makes me feel peaceful."

"Hang on." He gets up and picks up the laptop.

I continue to breathe deeply, trying to keep myself together.

He sits at the piano. "I think it's one of your favorite songs, and you said we would perform it together someday." He brings me back to the moment.

He begins to play the Bachianas Brasileiras No. 5. As he continues with "Aria Cantilena" by Villa-Lobos, he brings Brazil back to me. His intonation reminds of the lullabies my mother used to sing to me. The tempo reminds me of the sounds of the mesmerizing rain and the wailing winds of Capella. His solicitude reminds of the warmth Brazilians are known for.

"Gorgeous, Dr. Lev. Thank you, thank you. You're hired."

"May I hang up, now? I need to go to the clinic to see Julia Trina. She isn't doing well, but as soon as I return home, I'll call you, and we'll straighten this all out."

"Please send my love to Julia and the others. You're the greatest."

"Maybe. Get some rest for me." He hangs up.

I get up, let the kimono fall to the ground, and walk to the bathroom so I can take a shower. I continue to think of Dr. Lev and realize that I must get my priorities straight. I should have at least given him a call last night after I read his email about the indictment of Officer Almeida. I'm filled with regrets. He has never let me down. He puts up with me even though I'm trouble. Shame on me for neglecting him when he is doing everything to help me get my life back on track and convict the man who robbed me of Eli.

I need to get a grip. Maybe I should return to my land, even though there is a target on my back. If I do return, I know I must give up my opera and go into hiding. Tears run down my face. It's so sad to think that all this glamour has just caused more pain and sorrow. I'm no different from Madam Butterfly. Like her, I've turned away from all I care about to shine on the stage again. Maybe the right thing would be to catch a plane back to Brazil soon.

Chapter 6

Morning has come. I barely slept after I talked to Dr. Lev. I'm still confused and disheartened that I gave into Didier's demands. But today is the day. I'm meeting Madame Prunier, and will be singing to her for the first time. I've got to get my act together and do my best so she will want to work with me and help me win the contest. I'm focusing on this thought alone to keep moving ahead.

I walk inside the closet and pick up the red, strapless dress Didier chose for my singing today. Chiffon feels like it's melting on the skin. I have no idea how he knew all my measurements. I guess he had an app for it and was able to have the clothes made without a hitch. I put on my red high heels and then walk to the vanity. Since my hair looks disgraceful, I start braiding it. I think a low bun will do. I'm growing very nervous as time goes by. The clock is ticking, and in twenty minutes, I'll have to sing an aria I haven't sung publicly since 2010. It's been six years since I won that competition in Belgium. The world seemed perfect then.

I apply the concealer Alondra gave me to hide the dark circles below my eyes and put on some makeup. Didier still insists that I must tattoo my eyebrows, but I won't do it. I've got to have a say on a few things if I want any part of the old Sofia to survive.

Didier walks up to me. He's all dressed up as well in a black suit, a blue shirt, and a red tie. "Madame Prunier is here."

"I'm ready, but before we go, I must tell you that I'm not sure I really wanted to have sex last night. I think I wasn't able to fully consent."

"Of course you consented, Sofia. You were having a great time. I would have stopped if you showed any signs of discomfort. You told me that you still felt guilty about Eli's death, and you also mentioned a rape from the past. I think you were having a flashback, but I promise not to touch you again unless you want me to. You can trust me."

My eyes well up. "I guess you're right. It's all a blur. But Dr. Lev said that

I was intoxicated, at best."

"Dr. Lev wasn't in that bedroom last night, and he will always take your side. I told you he's in love with you. From now on, I'm limiting your contact with him even further. He isn't good for you. For one thing, he's making you need him more and more so that he can have you all to himself."

I raise my voice. "Never, ever, say anything bad about that man. All he does is fight for my right to have my day in court, and for justice for Eli. He's a better human being than the both of us combined. Unlike you, he'd never make me need him to gratify his own desires. If you ever accuse him of anything as nefarious as that again, I'll go back to Brazil."

"No need to get upset. You look stunning in red. I love the hair and the makeup, my diva. Let's go, my Amina, but first, let me put this on you." He takes a ruby heart-shaped pendant necklace out of his pocket and puts it on me. "Now the outfit is complete." He takes me by the hand and guides me toward the attic studio.

Suddenly, I want to run away from all that constricts my heart. It feels as though it's being squeezed smaller and smaller, like Chinese foot-binding, but it's too late. I've made up my mind: I want my opera back, and Didier is the only person who can give it back to me. Madam Prunier is an expert and will make my dream come true. I might as well forget that old Sofia ever existed.

Didier guides me inside the studio. "Mademoiselle Sophie Morpho is ready to sing "Ah! Non credea mirarti." His voice is deep, and he sounds a bit emotional.

"Excellent choice, Monsieur Guisan. Very brave, indeed. Please sit at the piano. I'd like you to accompany her."

"Certainly," he says. He sure looks the part.

I approach the piano, fearing that I'm going to ruin this entire beautiful aria. Maybe I should just sing "In Trutina."

"Welcome, Mademoiselle Sophie." Madame Prunier is a small, blond, elegant woman. Her French accent is lyrical. She, herself, is a great diva and has travelled all over the world singing Bellini, Rossini, and other brilliant composers.

"Thank you, Madame." I walk to the music stand next to the piano and position myself behind it. There are two tall flower arrangements of red roses and blue cornflowers. The room looks even bigger and more intimidating with the ceiling lights on.

"Monsieur Guisan says you're a real treasure, and I can tell already that you are. What a doll."

"Merci," I say, but all I can think about is my desire to learn to curse in French because I saw Piaf do that in the movie about her life. I'll ask Didier later.

"Begin, s'il vous plait." She motions for Didier to start.

He plays the first notes, and I'm suddenly transported to a world I left behind long ago. It feels right to go back to it. I feel a deep emotion as if I'm about to break down crying. I continue to give my best despite my fear. The lights take me back to the stage in Brussels when I sang the aria. I sing the most difficult part and then finish after holding the high F at the end for quite a while. I take a deep breath.

I hear applause. "Brava! Bravissima," Madame Prunier says. "Le timbre est trés beau…et la diction parfaite. My goodness, such a great voice! Your mother would be very pleased with her, Didier." She looks at her music sheet. "Now, I'd like to talk to you about the more exposed passages so that you'll be able to do smooth transitions. There is too much pressure in the beginning. I want it softer and a bit faster, Mademoiselle. Amina is sleepwalking, remember? She walks about town in her sleep. She is not aware of her singing."

She turns to Didier. "Please, Monsieur, again from the beginning." She looks at me. "Just one more thing, 'mirarti' is in one long breath. Go on."

"Ah! Non credea mirarti…"

"Stop, Mademoiselle Sophie. Remember to use less power, softer, but not low. Control your breath. It's a bit all over the place. And a bit more movement, please. Start over."

Didier begins to play.

"Oh, I never thought you would die so soon, sweet flower…"

"Yes, so beautiful. Continue, but don't hold back. Just a little more tristesse, grief, sorrow. Remember that the flowers are dead." She motions for me to stop. "The breath is getting in the way. How do you hold your breath, Sophie?"

"Ha, ha, the spot somewhere…I don't know how to tell in English. Ha, ha." I smile nervously.

"Show me, sweetie. Where, how…go on. Don't collapse your chest."

"Ha, ha… I keep forgetting. Sorry, Madame."

"Monsieur, she has to practice how to support her breath." She makes me stand up straight and fixes my posture. "Yes, there. Now from the beginning again."

I continue to sing, but images of the night of the rape in Rio come to mind. I feel a deep sadness and it shows in my singing. All the flowers died at Capella. The land was left barren for months, and only my music brought my flora back to life.

I hear applause. "Brava, darling Sophie. Bravissima!" She turns to Didier. "Her voice is just like Genevieve's, lyrical, dreamy, and it has enough pathos to sing this. Go on, now sing everything again from the start."

I begin from the start, knowing that it will take infinite work to get to sing this piece alone. But I'll never give up. I'll work every single hour of the day to get it just right. I'll never let go of my opera again. To think that I almost lost it forever fills me with anguish. I continue on, forgetting about the pains and sorrows of the past. Singing is all that matters. I sing each phrase. She stops me. I repeat. I continue. I won't stop until she tells me to.

"It's almost perfect. I'm giving you a break, Mademoiselle Sophie, but please return in an hour.

"Thank you Madame. I promise to be on time. Merci."

I return to my room. It has been two hours of work, and I am exhausted—and yet so filled with happiness. Didier does so much for me. He is making my life complete. He couldn't possibly have taken advantage of my state of mind last night. I committed a serious error and must make it right. I'm sure it was the rape in Rio that made me feel raped all over again.

There is a large box on top of the desk. I open it to find a traditional Japanese kimono. It's royal blue with Blue Nestira butterflies feeding on a cherry blossom. It is silky, glossy, and it feels like it's melting in my hands. It's a piece of art, indeed. I pick up a note left on the bottom of the box and begin to read it.

> Dear Sophie Blue,
>
> If you don't already know, the colors of the Blue Morpho's wing are generated by nanometer-sized structures on the wing's scales, and the reflected light from them is what creates the iridescent blue color. It's more like an illusion, and yet, it's real. That's true about your voice, as well. It's something real, but the iridescent light it emits is immaterial, dreamy, and magical. You and the Blue Nestira are as rare as they come.
>
> Anyway, the obi is made of stylized symmetrical hollyhock

from polished amethyst and jade scales. The flower motif was used as the seal of the Tokugawa family in Japan when the family ruled the country. I brought this with me from Japan even before you decided to sign the contract. I knew you would come and sing my favorite aria at Maison Sakura on your birthday. You'll look perfect as Madame Butterfly, I promise.

Love,
Your Didier

I feel as vulnerable as Amina. Will I be able to get my voice to the same level it was before? He sure has high expectations about what my voice can do. I dread letting him down.

I reach for my phone and begin to compose an email. I must right a wrong.

Dear Dr. Lev,

Sorry about the call last night. I'm ashamed about telling you things that weren't true about Didier. He told me that I did consent. I really think it was a flashback of the rape when I was twenty-one. Officer Almeida was brutal, and I kept that secret for too long. My father would never have believed me. He always said that I was asking for it because I wore skimpy clothing and showed too much skin. That's the reason he gave me a gun in the first place, so that I could shoot any bastard who dared to take advantage of me. Well, I wasn't even good at that. My own mother told me that I was a cheap slut when I got pregnant by Eli at seventeen. See, I don't think you should trust my word over Didier's.

For one thing, I slept with a man I've known for just a month. They say women are different, but I think we crave the same intimacy men do. If there is love, it's the most awesome thing in the world, but sex can be great, too, when a person feels lonely. And I feel so alone in America. I hope I'm not wrong. I hope you won't judge me. I can't afford to lose you. I know you're only thirtyish…but I don't know if you're old school. At the clinic, the interns say you are a straight shooter who runs a tight ship. Well, you know, interns talk, but we love you a lot, okay? I think it was the alcohol that made me think it was rape. Thanks for explaining about the consent thing. I've learned my lesson. No more alcohol-fueled sex from now on. And I told Didier that I'd be the one to let him know if I want it.

I saw the ticket attached to the text you sent me. Sorry about the trouble. SO ASHAMED! I'm staying. I'm bad news, aren't I? I've got to grow up and get my act together if I want to be Brazil's number-one diva. Good thing he put me on birth control, because there is a 'no pregnancy' clause in the contract.

Sorry, but he said that I won't be able to contact you as often because I keep bothering you when you have so much work to do. He says you are an honorable man, and I'm kind of a spoiled brat. I think he is right and won't be troubling you too often.

You're as lovable as a teddy bear—I mean, a big one. So sweet. I have a beautiful surprise for you, but I'm saving it for when I get to Rio to testify. It's something that is one of a kind. There is only one of it in the whole entire world, just as there is only one Dr. Lev.

Thank you for everything.

Xoxo

I click Send, get up, walk to the end of the room, and open the door that leads to the balcony. The rain has stopped, and everything looks washed clean. Since Didier has driven a wedge between nature and me, the beautiful trees give me some comfort He has created an artificial world in which I dwell, deprived of green. It's a dull world, however glamorous. He makes me stay indoors hours on end, warming up my voice and going over *La Sonnambula* and other scores, as well as watching several divas sing different arias so that I can see how they do it. He upsets me when he gets very critical of some of them, especially Anna Netrebko. He says he has no idea what all the hype is about her. Besides, he says that she ruined her voice by having a child. According to him, it has grown much darker and heavier, which will permanently keep her from singing bel canto. I disagree and tell him that she now has a fuller, richer voice that makes her bel canto even more mesmerizing. And Gruberova, he says, can't sing one good note and should have retired thirty years ago when her voice was still magnificent. He's so critical that I dread to hear what he'll have to say about my performance later tonight.

Slowly, he's giving birth to a new Sofia that has little to do with the Sofia I've known for twenty-six years. He also hired a publicity coach for me because he thinks I must learn to deal with the press or they'll eat me alive. Maybe it is better having everything I say rehearsed ahead of time so he doesn't have to "fix" my "bad interviews."

I look down from the balcony and notice that the Sydonie roses are plain gorgeous. Their flat, quartered blooms are elegant. I love their petals, which are often arranged in distinct groups of four. They produce a fragrance much like that of the damask, intense and sweet. I have a big garden at Capella. The flowers make me happy. The only thing crushing my heart is the upcoming demise of a jacaranda tree I grew up with. The gardener says that it is too close to the foundation and will have to be cut down. Earlier, I sent an email to Dr. Lev asking him to help me do a ritual for the jacaranda via Skype so that I can thank her for all she has given us and to say a proper farewell.

I get back inside the room and focus on Genevieve Guisan singing "Ah! Non credea mirarti." His mother was indeed matchless in this role. She absolutely nailed the pathos and longing in the aria. It's heartbreaking. He wants me to be just like her. I'm afraid I'll let him down, because I want to be more like Anna Netrebko, the People's Diva—so cutting edge; but he says that she's not refined enough, not cultured enough, and as proof of that, he cites the last interview she gave, when all she did was eat the tacos she prepared for the publicist at her apartment on Fifth Avenue. He said that it was the most unmannerly thing he has ever witnessed in the world of opera, which he considers the Holy Grail. May he never know that once I gave an interview in Brussels and couldn't resist eating the Belgium chocolates the hotel provided. Actually, I was starving after singing for ninety minutes and wished I'd had some tacos to chow down on—and some vodka, since it had been cold as hell.

I exit the bedroom, looking forward to the soothing tea Didier has prepared for me before I begin to work with Prunier again. I soon realize that cherry blossoms perish as quickly as Amina's flowers do.

Chapter 7

Alondra enters the parking lot of a restaurant called Suspended Gardens. The name makes me think of the opera Nabucco, which touches me deeply because it speaks of the oppression against Jews in Babylon. Subjugation is never right. Dr. Lev is right when he says that Officer Almeida must pay for all his crimes, including the ones against Jews in Brazil. No wonder I promised Eli I'd convert to Judaism—a promise I intend to keep.

The two old-fashioned lamps by the entrance stand like sentinels.

"Valéria has been working here for the past two years as a hostess." Alondra opens the restaurant door. "She likes the people and the atmosphere. Too bad she's off tonight, but you'll see her tomorrow." Her scarlet lipstick lights up her whole face. She is beautiful and sexy.

The hostess picks up two menus and leads us to a table by the bar.

Suspended Gardens is filled with plants. It has many individual rooms. The scent of cilantro and other fresh herbs and spices permeate the air. We sit down. I see an elderly customer drinking a clear beverage. The clear liquid reminds me of cachaça, the Brazilian rum Papa loves.

I still don't understand Papa's denial of Officer Almeida's role in Eli's murder. Before he took control of the BOPE, he was a different father. He made sure all my needs were met and used to sit with me and talk about whatever was important to me. He was engaging and witty. It was only after the BOPE that he became impassive. Power brutalizes, and that's my conclusion.

The plants make me think of Capella. I miss my farm. I used to run beyond the bamboo grove where I heard voices of the children-spirits. Dr. Lev sent me photos of my marigolds, and they're simply gorgeous. The filter he uses makes the pictures seem ephemeral, yet still substantial. To repay him for his kindness, I sent him a DVD in which I performed *Rusalka* in Brussels. He loves the aria by Dvořák.

"Meet Sofia, Ana," Alondra says to the hostess.

"Nice to meet you, Sofia," the blonde woman replies. "I'm glad to see you, Alondra. I'll get Molly for you in a moment." She walks away, her floral dress swaying as she moves.

"It must be nice to work at a restaurant. You get to see new people all the time. I spend so many hours indoors that I feel like a prisoner in a plexiglas house." I think of my Blue Nestira, and I'm gloomy. One day I will see one flying free in the rainforest.

"Did you tell Didier we were going out after the spiritual women's group?" Alondra puts her purse down on the chair next to hers.

"I left him a note." I blush. "I told him I was going to your house to get a Reiki treatment because I needed to relax my vocal chords." I play with the steak knife in front of me. "If I told him the truth, he'd get mad. He wants me to practice seven hours a day and then watch videos of major opera singers. I'm sure he will complain about my long break, but I just wanted to do something different."

The waitress approaches us. "What are you having tonight?" Molly asks in a bubbly tone. She has burgundy hair and wears burgundy lipstick. She's tall and thin, and her black nail polish makes a statement. She's probably what Didier would call Goth.

"Meet Sofia, Molly," Alondra says. "She's my girlfriend from Brazil."

"It's nice to meet you." She has a very young voice. She's probably no older than twenty-one. "Brazil is hot!"

"Nice to meet you, too," I say.

"Please bring us two glasses of Rodney Strong Cabernet. I want Sofia to taste Jose's guacamole. Send him to our table so she can see how he prepares it." Alondra hands the menu back to her.

"Sure, girls. I'll be right back." Molly walks away.

"This is a beautiful place, Alondra. I love the plants hanging down from the ceiling."

"I love hanging gardens, too." She leans over. "There is a guacamole-making contest going among the waiters. You'll have to come back to try out the others."

"If I can sneak out again. Didier keeps a watchful eye. I suppose he turned out to be like my father."

"Here we go, girls. This wine is phenomenal," Molly says, putting the wineglasses down.

The way she talks reminds me of Nurse Stephanie, who was the queen of slang at the clinic back home.

A waiter pushes a cart filled with bowls and fresh ingredients. He stops by our table. He chops onions, tomatoes, and cilantro. He squeezes the lemon juice into the mortar, peels an avocado and mixes everything together. "It's ready, Señoritas." He sets the mortar on the table. "Enjoy."

I dip my tortilla chip into the avocado puree. I never thought of eating avocado as a vegetable. In Brazil, we eat it with sugar, as a dessert. In Brazil, I did many things I can't do in America. But in America, I can do many things I could never do in Brazil, like feeling free from the watchful eyes of my father. I used to fade against the strength of his compelling ways. How can he not believe his own daughter? I owe my freedom to Didier, and for that, he deserves all my gratitude.

"Do you feel lonely in America?" I ask Alondra. "How does it feel to live alone?" I wipe my lips with a napkin. "Brazilians live in herds. It's cultural."

"I felt lonelier in my marriage, Sofia. My husband used to put me down, and he was also abusive. Now it's a lot better, though. I have to work hard to support my children. My youngest son is growing like a wildflower. Still, I'm happier now. Do you like your guacamole?"

"I like this guacamole, but Didier doesn't let me eat it at home. He says it has too much fat."

"He's too controlling, Sofia." She signals Molly. "Are you sure you want him running your career and life in such a way that he has a say on everything you do? He's kind of odd."

"He does much for me. Madam Prunier is preparing me to perfection, and I feel confident that I will win the contest if I follow his program." I take a sip of my wine.

"Are you sleeping with him? Is it a part of the contract?"

"Yes, but of course it's not in the contract. The sex is good and comforts me. He wants things to become more serious, but I really don't feel love for him. I don't know…he's so good to me, even though he's tough on me when it comes to opera. Today I needed to get away, and I hope he'll forgive me. I've seen him angry, and I dread to see it again."

"Don't let him run your life, Sofia. You have rights, too. There is a contract, and he must abide by the rules, as well." She sprinkles salt in her guacamole.

She's unknowingly breaking Didier's rule Number 33, which says that it's impolite to put extra salt on the food at the table. Or is it number 43? Besides, we use some organic, no-salt seasoning at home.

"He wants me to give it my all, and he's right. My American dream is very expensive. It takes thousands of hours to prepare myself to sing at the Met, but when the time comes to sign the contract, I'll have my own say on a few issues."

"I understand." She sips her wine. "Watch out, darling. Better yet, get yourself a lawyer. I can't believe you don't have one."

I sip my wine. Dr. Lev told me the same thing. He said that he did his residency in California and knows people here, but I told him that I trust Didier and feel he has my best interests in mind. And Didier might be right when he says that Dr. Lev worries too much about me. I wish Dr. Lev would treat me more like a woman, but he sees me more as a daughter or something, even though he's only seven years my senior. I guess he's just overprotective.

"If you ever need to talk to me about anything, please feel free to call me. Or just come by the Hive." She smiles. "I like you a lot, Sofia. Let's go out again some time, to a club or something. Los Angeles can be exciting if we dig the right stuff."

"I'm glad you're my friend. I love you, Alondra. You're also super-funny."

She reaches inside her purse. "I have more mail from Dr. Lev. He called and said that he believes Didier continues to intercept his letters to you. He also sent you two thousand dollars you can use in case of an emergency. He asked me if I would help you open a bank account so that he can keep sending you money. All you need is your passport."

"Dr. Lev is crazy. I'd love to have my own bank account, but Didier has my passport."

"Sofia, that's dangerous. You should get it back as soon as possible. Don't sign the contract unless he gives it back to you." She gets up. "I have to use the ladies' room. I'll be right back." She walks away.

I open the FEDEX envelope and then Dr. Lev's letter.

> Cara Sofia,
>
> I'm sending you this express letter to let you know that Vento is sick. Do not despair. The veterinarian said that he is suffering from anemia. It is not life-threatening at this point, but he wants to start treatment soon. Vento has been a little

lethargic and depressed. He doesn't have as much appetite, and his hair has no luster. I'm on top of things and promise that nothing will happen to him. It took me a while to write because I was waiting for all the blood tests. Do not fret, darling. All will be well, I promise. I've enclosed the blood work for you to see and wrote down my own notes so that you can understand what's going on. Sorry, we haven't been able to communicate as often. But I'll send express mail as many time as needed.

The money is for emergencies. I worry about your safety, but Alondra is more than willing to help me be in touch with you. Still, I won't stop trying to contact you electronically.

Be very well for me, Sofia.

Um carinho, Lev

I'm stunned that Vento is ill. I feel like running to Rio right this minute. Tears drip down my face. As soon as I get home, I'll get my electronics back and call Lev. No, in fact, I prefer to Skype. I want to see his face when he tells me about my dear horse. I pick up a napkin and wipe my tears.

Alondra comes back. "What happened, Sofia? Why are you crying?"

I hand her the letter and put the rest of my things inside my purse, still crying hard. I'd die if I lost my horse.

"Oh, darling, don't worry. He'll be okay. Let's go so that you can talk to Dr. Lev. He said that he's on top of things, and I'm sure he is. He never lets you down." She looks at the tab and puts the money on the table.

I take the letter back and follow her out of the restaurant, still crying.

She drives out of the parking lot and onto the empty street.

The defroster clears the windows. The heater warms the vehicle. She turns into our dark street. We drive past a construction site. An orange sign says Men Working. The electrical arrow flashes, pointing right. Orange cones in a row show the way.

I wish I could be at my farm with Lev. He'd know how to calm me down. I miss him so terribly. Didier has forbidden me to Skype with him as often as I want, but only he can comfort me in times of distress. I have so much to tell him, so much to say, so much I want to share with him that I don't know which words to choose.

Alondra parks by our front door.

I see Didier's Hummer parked in front of the house. I wonder why he didn't park in the garage.

"Thank you for the fun night." I kiss her on both cheeks. "I hope we can do this again. Sorry we had to leave in a hurry."

"Don't worry, Sofia. I understand. Call me if you need me. I hope everything turns out all right with your horse. I love you."

I scramble out of the car and run towards the door, unlock it, and rush inside.

Didier grabs me by the arm, drags me in the kitchen, and throws me in a chair. "How could you lie to me? I've been looking for you all over town. You said that you would be in Silver Lake and then at your publicist's house, but you weren't there. You get home late, wearing jeans with holes and smelling of cheap wine. I can't believe I had to look for you."

"Alondra and I decided to go out to dinner. I needed a break." I rub my arm and get up. "I got a letter from Dr. Lev. My horse is sick; I've got to call him, now." Tears drip down my face. "Give me my electronics."

He grabs my arm. "You're not calling anybody. You lied to me, Sophie. You're going to practice now. I'll play the piano." He tightens his grip.

"Let me go." I raise my voice and try to escape his grip. "I need to talk to Dr. Lev. My horse is sick, and I need to know what the risks are."

His face is livid. "How about practicing your aria? You ditched it today. Call him after we practice for one hour."

I raise my voice even louder. "Let me go call Dr. Lev—now!" I punch him on the chest.

He grabs me with both hands. "Don't ever do that again, do you understand?" His grip will leave a mark, I'm sure.

"I'm sorry, Didier. Please, let me call and see what's going on with my horse." I'm choking on my own tears. "I beg you. I promise to practice afterwards for as many hours as you see fit."

The screensaver on his laptop shows a scene from Phantom, when Christine is being led to the underworld by her dark lover.

"Okay, but be prepared to work until late tonight." He lets go of me. "I'll bring your computer to your room. Get a hold of yourself."

"I will." I run to my room and into the bathroom. I wash my face. The cold water makes me feel more alert.

Didier comes in and hands me my laptop. "You have thirty minutes."

"Thank you, Didier." I follow him outside the bathroom, sit at my desk, and call Dr. Lev on Skype.

"I'm glad to hear from you, Sofia," Dr. Lev's voice is low and even.

"Dr. Lev, please tell me how Vento is. Please tell me the truth. Is my horse very sick? I'll die if he doesn't make it."

"I'll tell you everything I know, sweetie. Breathe." His voice is just above a whisper.

"I'm calming down. It's just that I can't do right tonight. I've made so many mistakes. I even punched Didier when he grabbed me and told me I couldn't call you because I skipped my practice today. I'm so sorry. Please tell me about Vento. I'm ready."

"All the blood tests are in, darling, and it's not so bad. I promise you that with the right treatment, he'll be just fine. I'm sorry I had to wait a while to tell you, but all is well. Do you believe me?"

"Yes, thank you. I love you. I wish I were by your side now, and you could hold me. It feels very good to be in your arms. I know I shouldn't be saying these things. I mean, it's so childish of me. Sorry. I meant to say that you always give me hope. Don't worry, I'm a big girl and can take anything thrown at me." I break down crying. "I'm such a mess. I miss my mom."

"You are a remarkable woman who is strong and perceptive. It would be an honor to be able to comfort you. I hope you know how much I care about you, Sofia. And trust me, there is nothing childish about you. Child-like, yes, because you have this open mind and seem not to worry about what people think of you. You're so confident."

"But I care a lot about what you think of me. I'll be your friend forever. I took an oath, and I'm sticking to it."

"You can also count on me, darling. I'll be in your life for as long as you want me to."

"Are you sure?"

"Yes. By the way, I've invited your mother to come over to my parent's house on the day of your debut at Didier's restaurant on your birthday. She wants to see you sing, and we'll have a little celebration. She'll Skype with you."

"Really?"

"Yes. You don't say much about your mother."

"Unlike millions of Brazilian mothers, she's cerebral, steadfast, and averse to emotional extremes. Like most Brazilian mothers, she is loving and generous. She is strict about hygiene. It is not okay sitting on your bed with your street clothes on, is not okay leaving bags and purses on the floor, or leaving newspapers on the couch. I think is her German heritage, although I know most Brazilian mothers are neat, but she is obsessed. I never managed to tidy up my room the way she wanted, so she told the maid to do it for me. Unlike me, my sister can do no wrong in her eyes. But she does say I'm perseverant."

"Rest assured that your mother loves you. We've spent time at Capella taking walks and playing the piano. She's very proud of you."

"You're most kind, Dr. Lev. I must do something great for you. I need to know the date of your wedding so that I can fly to Brazil to sing at the reception, as promised. Do you have one?"

"Sorry, but I don't have one. Cristina and I decided to put things on hold for a while."

"Once you said that I was a great listener. Do you want to talk to me about it?"

"You are indeed an amazing listener, but I think I have to figure out this one all by myself, Sofia, and then I'll share my feelings with you."

"I'll listen carefully, I promise."

"I know you will."

"Thank you for the money. I might need to use it to travel to Rio to testify. I'll repay you someday, I promise."

"It's not a loan, and I mean that."

"Well, I'm going to repay you big time. Are you going to watch me sing, too, or do you have to work at the clinic Friday night?"

"I will be in attendance. I told my parents and my grandmother that they will be treated to a night of beauty and passion and a voice so astounding that they'll be hooked and wanting more."

"You're so biased, Dr. Lev."

"Of course I am. And it's Lev, if you don't mind. I've been telling you this for a while, but you haven't caught on yet."

"Sorry, Lev. It's just that you're so above me."

"No. You know, Sofia, I wish you'd give yourself a bit more credit, darling. You're such a gifted artist, but not only that, a brave woman and a compassionate human being that few of us can claim to stand as tall as you. So, no more Dr. Lev."

"You exaggerate, but I'm too tired to argue, Lev. I love you."

"I love you, too. Are you going to sleep, now? You need to rest after such a difficult evening."

"I have to practice or else Didier will get mad. I'll ask him if I can work for just an hour. Have a great night."

"You, too, Sofia. Boa noite, querida."

"Boa noite, querido." I hang up.

I put the phone down, wondering if Lev has romantic feelings for me and not just admiration. I know he is a fan, but I wish he were more than that.

As I walk up to my studio, I realize I'd better never punch Didier again. I open the door and walk up to him. "Ready to work?" I ask.

"Yes, my diva. Get settled. We'll go over "Ah, non credea mirarti."

"Sorry I punched you. I'll never do it again."

"Thank you. You actually have a mean punch."

"Remember, I must have strong muscles to be able to sing. I exercise a lot so my lungs will be able to handle the work ahead."

"Good. I promise not to hurt you again. I nearly went out of my mind when I thought I had lost you. I never told you this, but my mother killed herself two years ago. She left me a message, and I didn't come to her aid until it was too late. I just can't lose you."

"I'm sorry, Didier, for your loss." I reach out and give him a hug. "I promise to never let you down again. Ready to work?"

"Yes. Let's get you ready for the Met."

He sits at the piano, and I hear the first notes of the aria. I concentrate on the task at hand. I'm worn-out, but I do my best to make him proud.

Chapter 8

It has been four months since my arrival to America. Another birthday has come. Twenty-seven makes me old when it comes to being ahead in the opera world. Tonight, I'll be singing to an American audience for the first time at Maison Sakura. I'm a nervous wreck, having to sing "Ah! Non credea mirarti," even though I've practiced the piece for months. I have spent several hours a day training my voice and working on my breath. It takes an astronomical amount of work to accomplish an artistic goal, but I'll never give up.

I sit down on the bed and open a letter from Isabella. My best friend from Brazil never forgets my birthday. We're kindred souls, and I miss her dearly.

> Rio, June 13, 201-
>
> Sofia,
>
> I'm a bit lazy nowadays, and that's the reason I haven't written more often. It must be excess of work, but not lack of love for you. I'm involved with the psychology of propaganda. It's very interesting. But I still work at the clinic and at my practice (mostly in the evenings.) All Dr. Lev does is talk about you and your singing. Rodrigo left without an explanation. Better this way. There was nothing left to be said. He didn't want to deal with living together. His loss.
>
> Well, I'm ready to go out to see an Oswaldo Montenegro show. It's a reunion with friends. I uploaded his new song to your timeline. I'm going with Daniela. She's still the same, so organized and with such aversion to emotions that everyone doubts she's really Brazilian. Culture survives in spite of our ignoramus minister of culture. This whole month, museums are free and the philharmonic will give concerts at the opera

house for ten reais, like five dollars. Anyway, querida amiga, be very well and return to sing to us at the Teatro Municipal. We can use a great, young, gorgeous soprano to breathe new life into the art. I'm sure that when you win the Met competition, Brazil will be begging you to sing in our opera houses.

The black statuette candleholder is the figure of your favorite Afro-Brazilian orixá. May Goddess Oxum sprinkle you with her sweet waters. Think of me whenever you light a candle. Happy birthday, darling. I love you forever!

Please write, woman!

Um grande beijo and a lipstick smooch,

Isabella

She's so kind and special. I truly miss her and the clinic. Only opera could make me give up the company of those I love dearly.

Next, I open a large FedEx box and find a card from Dr. Lev. Van Gogh's sunflowers are bright yellow and luminous.

Feliz aniversário, Sofia!

I sent this package overnight. I hope you get it on your birthday. My mother sent you the brigadeiros. I told her how much you miss the Brazilian chocolate treat from your land. She made them herself. My grandmother sent you the *Rusalka* babushka nesting dolls, and the Belgium chocolate bars are from me. You said that you don't have much access to sweets, so I decided to surprise you. I hope you enjoy. Your real present won't be revealed until later when we Skype. *Veja Magazine* has a fantastic report on your grandmother's Indian nation and their fight against the Brazilian government, which wants to build a dam near their reservation that will certainly flood their land. Hope the editorial will inform you about this important issue. More news later.

Have a great day!

Lev

The cover on the magazine has the Greenpeace logo. They are helping the Aruaques fight their new oppressors, the Brazilian government. It's the saddest thing in the world to think that they might lose their land so that Brazil can profit.

I open a large, golden box Didier left on the desk for me and nearly faint when I see a black mink coat inside. It's so disheartening. There is no way I'll ever wear something that has caused other beings such pain.

Skype is calling. I put on my red robe, sit on the swivel chair, and answer Dr. Lev's call.

"Happy birthday, Sofia." He has a big smile on his face. "Did you just wake up?"

"Yes, I just showered and took a nap. Sorry, my hair must look like a beehive. I was too tired to dry it. Please don't hold it against me."

"You look as beautiful as ever. I have someone here who wants to talk to you." He gets up and moves to another chair. My mother appears on the screen and then sits down in front of me.

I break down, crying. "Mãezinha, Mommy, I've missed you. You look so beautiful with your hair in layers and your shiny green eyes. Eu te amo tanto. I love you so much."

"Calm down, Sofia. No more crying. Feliz aniversário, meu bem, minha linda. Even though your hair is such a mess, and you're still in your robe, you look gorgeous."

I wipe my tears with a tissue. "Do you still love me, dear Mama, even though I left without saying goodbye? Or are you still hurt and angry?"

"Yes, of course, I love you," Consuelo said. "Stop doubting my love. I understood your actions after Dr. Lev explained everything to me. You're still my baby, and your father's, even though he forbade me to get in touch with you and even forbade me to watch your performance tonight. But Dr. Lev said that I could be loyal to you as a mother without being disloyal to your father. I'm here at his parents' house to watch the show and have dinner."

"Papa is just unforgiving. He still defends that evil man instead of his own daughter."

"You know your father. He's a tough man, and he has to be. He deals with hardcore criminals every day. I can't rest until he comes home at night. But then the other day he called me at work to say that his dog died, and he was crying. Yes, that big guy was in tears."

"Major died? Oh, he'll never get over it."

"That dog was a hundred years old. He won't get over you leaving, Sofia, that's for sure. You're his pride and joy, and you left his house. You're going to testify against his right-hand man, the man he has treated like a son. You are defying the commander of the BOPE, and you want compassion from him? I understand my husband. He's not evil, although that man Almeida certainly is, and I always hated to see him around you, but your father was grooming him to be his successor. It's not easy to be in his shoes. You've got to grow up."

"See, Dr. Lev? She always takes his side. That man threatened to kill me, Mama. How can you defend Papa?"

"See? You're still behaving like a child. I told Dr. Lev how your father spoiled you, and he seems to agree with me."

"Is it true, Dr. Lev? Are you taking my mother's side, now? I thought you were my friend."

"Listen, Sofia. I'm not taking anyone's side. Actually, I am going to leave you two alone so that you can have the freedom to speak to each other without worrying about what I think or feel. I'll talk to you later, darling."

"Please don't betray me."

"Never. I'll never betray your trust, regardless of my relationship with your mother and the conversations we've had and will have in the future. My opinion of you is mine alone. Do you believe me?"

"Yes."

"Okay. See you in a while. Feel free to talk to Sofia for as long as you wish, Consuelo."

"Thank you, Dr. Lev."

He walks away.

"Stop being childish, Sofia. Don't upset this man. He does everything for you and deserves your respect. Besides, his grandmother told me that he broke off his engagement and caused a big upset in the Jewish community, which has cost him a lot. She said that when he was at Capella taking care of your horse, Dr. Cristina demanded he return to Rio, even though he invited her to stay with him at the ranch during the time he was there. His grandmother thinks he's in love with you."

"What? Are you sure? He was so in love with Dr. Cristina."

"His grandmother says he made up his mind shortly after returning from Capella." My mom pauses. "Do you love him? He's a great man."

"He must be devastated. How can you think about him being in love with me when he just broke up with his fiancé? They were such a lovely couple. I'll bet he's torn. He's an honorable man. It must have been difficult for him to do that to her. She adores him. I'll bet they only had a fight because she got mad at him for staying there."

"There is nothing you can do when a man falls in love with another woman."

"Even if this is true, which I doubt, it's not easy to break up with someone you've dated for two years, Mom. He must have regrets. Please, don't say anything about what his grandma told you. Promise?"

"I won't, but if his mother talks to me about it when we have lunch again, I'll give her my opinion. Every time Dr. Lev and I spend time at Capella, all he does is talk about you and your singing. He plants things for you and takes good care of your horse."

"You had lunch with his mother? How in the world?"

"Yes, I met her at Capella. Dr. Lev took her and the judge there for the weekend to see your farm, and we had a great time together. She's lovely, and she adores you. By the way, I should be going. I'm their guest of honor. I'm so proud of you, darling. We'll be watching you and sending positive thoughts, okay? You are such a star."

"I love you, Mama."

"Happy birthday, again. We'll talk a lot when you come to testify. We'll straighten out this whole thing between us. Like I said, don't feel bad about Dr. Lev falling for you. It's not your fault, and he can handle it. Bye."

"Tchau, mãe. Eu te amo."

"Te amo. Bye."

My mother gets up and leaves. She is still the same mother—lovely, yet practical, and always stirring things up. I've got to keep her from interfering in Dr. Lev's and Dr. Cristina's situation.

"Happy birthday again, darling," Dr. Lev says after he sits down. "Did you receive the brigadeiros my mother sent you? And my special chocolate?" Dr. Lev's killer smile makes my heart skip a beat. I had never noticed how handsome he is when he is relaxed. He was always very busy at the clinic, and his professionalism didn't allow for idle time. His button-up cobalt-blue shirt makes his eyes even bluer.

I break down crying. "Sorry I've caused you so much pain, Dr. Lev."

"What's this about, Sofia? Why are you so upset?"

"My mother said that I'm too dependent on you. You do too much for me. Stop being so good to me, Dr. Lev, when I've offered you nothing."

"May I disagree? It's true that I help you in many ways. I promised I would, and I will continue to do so unless you tell me otherwise. But you've given me so much more. Because of you, I discovered nature! Instead of just going to Capella to take care of your business, I choose to go there to immerse myself in peace and quiet. Not only that, but you furnished the bedroom with a piano, so I started playing again. I discovered that I do love my music and want to pursue it again with the early passion I had for it. Then, you made me realize the meaning of trust, real trust. You gave me power of attorney without hesitation and seem to have complete confidence in me. It's so rare. That's why I told you that you should never doubt my loyalty to you. I talk a lot with your mother and understand her concerns, but I'll never betray you. Do you believe me?"

"Yes."

"That's important. Nothing will come between us. I promise."

"Do you trust me, too?"

"Yes."

"I'm your friend, and I'll never betray you. I'll never hurt you on purpose. I'd rather die."

"I know. When you arrive in Rio, we'll talk for a thousand hours, and everything will be crystal clear."

"I have to tell you something. Every time I get on the stage, at first I feel my blood turn to ice and look for a person to make eye-contact with and sing for them. I guess I don't have to keep looking for someone tonight. You'll be there with me even though you're four thousand miles away."

"I'm honored." He holds some photographs of a horse. It's not Vento. "Meet Diva, your new horse. I got her for your birthday. She was seized by animal control with a bunch of other horses that were being starved and neglected. She was in the worst shape of all and went to rehab. She's now doing nicely, up to a good weight, and very happy at Capella." He holds up a closeup of a sorrel horse. She is magnificent. Her brownish-red coat gleams.

"You're crazy, Lev, like any other psychiatrist, but I'm thankful you are. She must have suffered so much. Tell me more about her, please."

"She's heavily muscled, compact, and can run a short distance over a straightaway faster than any horse I've seen. Her best blaze was 440 yards in 21 seconds. She's a diva, as I said earlier. She's won many prizes in the past. I'm telling her all about you so that when you come to prepare for the trial, she'll know pretty much everything. I got her a trainer, as well."

"Not only have I got a new horse, but a beautiful animal has been saved, too, and is now in the hands of the most caring person I know. That's so cool! You just made me super-happy, and I have no words to thank you. Please, let me help with the expenses, at least that. Didier will pay me for my performance tonight."

"Not a chance. Diva is a present to you, and I'm paying for everything, including the trainer, for as long as she needs one and I need one. Just so you know, I'll be riding her until your return. Naturally, I won't neglect Vento. Last week, I went to town and got his mineral block so that he can get what he needs. The salt in it is from the Himalayas. He seems a little jealous, but I showed him some of your videos and he smiled, I swear. Just write down everything you need me to do on your behalf, and it shall be done."

"I'm really glad you enjoy Capella. I wish I were there today to ride the horses with you. I feel so free and unafraid when I'm on Vento. He takes me far away from all my cares."

"We'll do a lot of riding when you come to testify. The trial has been set for the seventh of August, but even though you won't testify until the very end, you need to be here at least two weeks earlier to give a deposition and be updated on everything so that we can take care of your safety. I'm taking time off to assist you during your stay. Dr. David is going to sub for me at the clinic. Do you think you'll be able to come? I know how busy you are, but your testimony is essential for a conviction."

"I'll be there. I'll talk to Didier tonight. I know he'll be a little unwilling to let me go, but I'll tell him that you're going to help me practice my arias so that I'll be ready for my audition in September. Are you still up to it? I'll bring the scores to Capella."

"I'll be very happy to help you with that. Just let me know soon what arias you're doing so I can practice on my own while I wait for you to arrive."

"Didier hasn't decided on all of them yet, but I'm sure that "Ah! Non credea mirarti" is one, and also the cabaletta in Amina's opera. He also wants me to sing Susana's aria. But I need four more as backup."

My phone rings. "Sorry, Lev, I have to get this."

"Go ahead. Do you want to me call back in ten minutes?"

"No need." I answer and put on the speakerphone. "This is Sofia."

"It's Didier. I'm heading home to get you in a couple of hours. There's a lot of traffic, so I need you to be ready on time, 100 percent ready, Sophie."

"I'll be 200 percent ready."

"Make sure you lock everything. Yesterday, I came home and found the back door unlocked, the milk on the table, and the door of the fridge open. You must pay attention before you leave the house." He sounds annoyed. "You're twenty-six years old, not ten."

"Your dog asked me to take him for a walk. He brought me the collar and a Frisbee, so I took him to the park. I barely had time to get a sweater. If you walk him more often, he won't be so anxious."

"You've been forgiven. How do you like your birthday present?"

I take a deep breath. "Sorry, Didier, I don't want to hurt your feelings, but I'd never wear a mink coat. I'm sure that about a hundred animals were skinned and left to die so that a woman could look pretty. I'm sorry, but I'll never be that woman."

"I wanted to keep you warm in New York when we go there for your audition, that's all. You should have told me that on the questionnaire I sent you." He seems even more annoyed.

"There wasn't a box there for me to check it. Sorry for all the trouble. Would you please return it? You've given me so much already and in such a short time. You've been generous enough."

"You can choose something else."

"Anything?"

"Yes, it's your gift. I want to make you happy."

"Would you donate to the group that is trying to save the Indian nation my grandmother once belonged to? They could use this money to help their cause."

"You want me to give three thousand dollars of my money to save your indigenous people? That's insane, Sofia. You look so inoffensive, and then you surprise me with your big political agenda."

"Actually, it's my money. You said I could choose anything I wanted."

"Touché! I don't know how to deal with you. You can't change the world, Sophie."

"I know that, but even if my ideals seem absurd and impossible to carry out, I won't relent. Any little bit helps."

"How about being a bit more materialistic and shallow? It would help me." He gives a little laugh. "Never mind. I'm going to be there in two hours."

"I'll be on time. Thank you for the gift. I'll make you proud tonight."

"You'd better, my beautiful diva, however idealistic. See you soon." He hangs up.

I look at Lev, who had little choice but to listen. I try to explain. "He's thirty-something. That's why he's a bit grumpy at times."

"Oh, is that how people in their thirties behave?"

"Except for you, of course. You're never cross." I smile. "I have to go, Dr. Lev. I'll email you as soon as I discuss my trip with Didier. I'll be there when the time comes, I promise."

"Thank you, Sofia. I know it will be difficult for you, but I'll do anything in my power to help you with the trial and your opera."

"I'm so grateful. Thank you. And remember, I'll be singing for you tonight. Você é um amorzinho, Lev." I can't help telling him that he's a sweetheart.

"E você Também, querida. Soon, I'll be able to show you how grateful I am to have you in my life."

"Ditto." I hang up.

I hear the doorbell and walk to the door.

Alondra stands ready, her red case filled with beauty products that will turn me into the glamorous woman Didier wants me to become.

"Hi, Alondra! Please come in."

"Hi, Sofia! Ready to do your hair and makeup?" She kisses me on the cheek.

"Yes. Didier wants me to be on time."

She follows me into my room, opens her handbag, and hands me a CD. "This is for you. The singer's name is Lila Dawns. Her Spanish music is great. I think you'll like her very much. Feliz Cumpleaños, chica."

"Thank you, gracias, obrigada. Let's put it on." I take the CD out of the case and slide it inside the slot in my laptop. The first notes fill the room with warm chords and complex rhythms. She reminds me of Marisa Monte. The Brazilian pop singer has the same kind of warm, full voice.

"All I need is Lila, the moon, and a bottle of tequila to get in the right mood." She laughs. "Do you think you can sing songs like that?"

"No. My friends in Rio say that when I try to sing pop or jazz it's just horrible. Only opera sounds good."

She picks up the box of matches from my desk and lights some sage. "Let's purify this room, too." She finds a plate and puts it underneath the little bundle to do the smudging.

May Didier never find out about these things, or he'll forbid me to hang out with my friends. He told me to stop evoking spirits and the like so that I can be more normal. He's such a white man. The smoke rises as she walks around with the small burning bundle.

I sit down at the vanity, and she begins to work on my hair.

"Put your head down, Sofia. I don't want to burn you. Didier wants your hair to be impeccable tonight. It will look sleek and silky with the oil I'm applying to it. You'll look sophisticated and ready for the limelight—a new Sofia."

As she tames my hair, I think that, little by little, old Sofia is fading away. This new woman I'm becoming is the blue of Didier's Nestira. She seems flawless and she must be if she wants to fit in into his unblemished universe. She keeps giving up one thing after another to realize her dream.

Lila Dawns continues to sing in her warm, dark, and sexy voice. The song, Cielo Rojo, evokes a crimson sky and nearly lulls me to sleep. I reach a deep place where magic and reality fuse. The soft beat of drums reminds me of my indigenous people trying to survive extinction. It reminds me of my forest being slowly decimated. But it also reminds me of a steady heartbeat, the beat of the universe, promoting life. Maybe when I become known on the world stage again, I'll be able to help advance important causes, and that will make everything worthwhile.

Hopefully, I'll shine tonight and finally get to sign the contract.

Chapter 9

Maison Sakura is a two-story restaurant. It has several separate, large rooms. I've been in the Orchid Room since I arrived this evening. Didier has created a fantastic scene here. A night sky appears to be drenched with thousands of stars, and a full moon lends a sense of mystery to the universe he has created. Soon, I could be sleepwalking like the heroine in the aria, lamenting the loss of a great lover. Except—I'd prefer to be alone.

Tonight, he's serving us many types of sushi, but the star dish is nigiri and shiso leaf, astringent and clear, with pistachio miso on top of homemade mochi. It's nestled under a slice of sea bream and then wrapped around pickled lotus root.

I haven't spoken to him since he brought me to the restaurant. It's better that way. Before a performance, I prefer to be alone. I focus better if no one is telling me what to do. I still hear Madame Prunier's voice reminding me to sing with less power, or let out less breath, or make a word more nuanced, or anything else that would make my singing as perfect as it can be. In ten minutes, I'll be called onto the stage by Noah Lasky, the Master of Ceremonies and my accompanist. We've been working together for three weeks on this piece alone, and we have a great rapport. He's a Jewish man no older than I am. His curly hair and large brown eyes remind me of Eli. He's funny and makes me laugh when I'm nervous, just as Eli used to do.

I hear people quieting down in their seats at the tables, and I'm feeling stone-cold. I think of Dr. Lev. I'm singing this to him. Even from afar, he makes me feel centered. Maybe it's his ability to accept me as I am; maybe it's his solicitude. Maybe it's his sense of compassion. Even though he's in pain after breaking up with Dr. Cristina, he still takes care of my needs; but that's who he is—his impeccable ethics make him singular.

I stand up and breathe, close my eyes, and make a little prayer to Goddess Oxum. Her sweetness is everlasting. I touch my jaguar bracelet and feel the presence of my grandmother. She always told me that opera was my calling and that I should never squander my gift. Tonight, I'm the blue side of the Nestira, and I'm supposed to glimmer and glow.

I hear Noah's voice talking to the audience about the opera. I feel a special connection with "Ah! Non credea mirarti"—maybe because I have a deep love for ravishing Gruberova. She reinvented Bellini's aria. Whenever I listen to her, I feel her singing from the bottom of her soul. I try to convey the same thing, but I don't know if it comes across with as much strength as I desire. Being a small woman is a bit of a disadvantage because I don't have the large lungs stereotypic of opera singers. Besides, even when I get the tempo and the lines right, I still have to open up and bare something on the stage for all to feel the extent of the sadness of the aria. Amina's lover has broken up with her, and all the flowers are dead. It takes grit. The mental focus alone can derail a singer.

I take a deep breath and walk out into the open area. The bright lights blind me for a second. Noah takes me by the hand and guides me to the center of the stage. He stands next to me. I put my right hand over my chest and bow to the audience a couple of times.

The set is staged perfectly with the flowers to which Amina sings as she sleepwalks under the shining moon. They are supposed to be dead, but they still are full of an eerie, shimmering life under the silvery stage lights. The small bouquet of purple petunias in my hands feels wet and alive. It sizzling up here onstage. The air is electrified. Cameras live stream the show. The house is packed. I feel my hands grow cold. It is always that way when I'm performing, and no matter how much I practice, I still feel nervous. I know it's not about tossing out high Fs with perfection, but about conveying a whole story in a foreign language with all the emotions, the sadness, the opera implies. The aria is demanding on the body and the voice, but I can't blame anything or anyone if I fail. I have to be careful with my gestures so I won't distract the viewers, yet I have to convey Amina's passion even when she is sleepwalking.

People begin to clap loudly. I bow from the waist one more time. All of a sudden, the room is quiet. Noah walks to the piano, which is next to me. I turn my head to face him and make eye contact. He nods. I turn to face the audience. I hear the first note and think of Dr. Lev. I begin to sing the aria. In a moment, the world ceases to exist, and I'm standing all alone singing each note with all I've got. I'm unafraid. I've been trained to use my voice to convey all kinds of complex emotions. Opera unites my heart and mind, and I fly high.

There is perfect silence. I take a breath. I begin to sing.

Images of fields of flowers at Capella flood my mind. Eli comes to mind. He is offering me the forget-me-nots so blue. I take them in my hands and smell them. He smiles, but then he fades away. Extending my arms, I offer the flowers to him, but now he's just a memory. The fields of flowers grow distant, too, and all I have are the silver rays of moonlight flooding the stage as I hit the high F, and the note floats in the air. Petals of yellow roses begin to descend upon the stage as I hold the last note for as long as my breath allows.

The audience erupts immediately into shouts and screams, calls of "Brava!" and all kinds of noisy chaos. "Brava! Bravissima!" echoes—the place goes wild. As I hear applause, I snap out of my trance. I put my hand over my heart and bow once, twice, three times. The audience is still applauding as I turn and signal for Noah to join me. He walks up to me, stands by my side, and we both bow.

Didier comes to the front of the stage and hands me a bouquet of red roses. I smile at him and touch his hand. "Thank you. Obrigada. Merci." I laugh. "I pulled this off, after all."

The audience is still clapping.

"I'll meet you in the Tea Room." He walks away.

I throw kisses to the audience and bow once more. I exit the stage, walk through to the back of that room and go upstairs. I open the door.

Everything is set for tea on a low table. There are two deep, hand-thrown black bowls of green tea with matcha powder. The imperfections of the bowls give them style. The cast-iron teapot is sheer elegance and mystery. There are two silky red pillows facing each other and two bento boxes with honey sticks and purple motchi balls. There is a pink cherry bonsai. I sit down on the pillow and open a note from Didier.

> My Geisha,
>
> Your version of the aria has a perfection that makes it unique. I can hear Bellini applauding. You sang with your soul, my darling, and your technique is outstanding. No wonder you win my heart over and over again. You blew many a diva to dust. Ah, the clarity…resonance… nuance, simply intoxicating to hear. Magnifique voix. There is also grief, a sense of utter

solitude in your voice that makes you unsurpassable. I felt something nearly beyond my grasp and comprehension. You haven't as yet said that you love me, but I'll patiently wait for your love, my geisha. You are my pride and joy.

Your Didier

I fold his note thinking that I might be his ultimate luxury item. I'm probably no different than a famous painting he might acquire. I'm his art. And I might as well be. He has given me my opera back. But he won't have my deepest secrets, my core. I've built armor around me that will never break open.

He comes in. He's handsome in his black tuxedo. He's blond hair is impeccable, and his smile makes him look on top of the world. There is no stopping him.

"That was extraordinary, darling. Now all you have to do is let go of the past. Forget your pain and the hurtful memories. Eli has been dead for five years. It's time to let go."

I gasp. "I can't believe you just said that. I knew you weren't the most compassionate person in the world, but what you just said was callous, and even cruel. Take it back and apologize, or I'm leaving right this minute. You don't even have to drive me home. I'll take an Uber. Alondra downloaded the app on my phone."

"I'm sorry, Sophie. I just want you to be happy, to snap out of your sadness. The world is ready for you, but you must leave this pain behind. I'm sorry, but I'll always tell it to you like it is."

A tide of feelings overwhelms me. I feel an urge to run far away. "Please don't tell me what to feel. My grieving process is mine alone, and no one can tell me when to be done with it. It's none of anybody's business. I need to get justice for Eli before I can let go. Maybe after the trial, it will be possible."

He approaches me, sits down next to me, and picks up a folder from the low table. "Here's the contract and a pen. This is your big moment. If you sign it, I will do everything in my power to help you win the competition and become Brazil's number-one diva; however, you must agree not to fly to Rio to testify. You must stay in America and continue your daily work with Prunier and Noah."

"No deal. I must testify. Officer Almeida's conviction hinges on my testimony, and I promised Dr. Lev I'd be there. I must keep my word." I put the pen down.

"I'll hire a lawyer, and you'll testify via Skype. Don't forget that there is a target on your back and that the defense will tear you apart. They'll destroy your reputation and your dream will be over. The best way to accomplish your goal is to do your part from here."

My eyes well up with tears. "I can't betray Dr. Lev—or Eli's memory."

"You'll be betraying no one. This doctor should be concerned about your safety. You're well known in Rio, and that officer and his neo-Nazi ring are evil. They might kill you even though Almeida himself is in jail. In your country, there are no bars to imprison criminals of such caliber. You must be realistic, Sophie."

"I need time to think it over."

"No, you don't. You'll testify from afar and continue your work. You've come so far, darling. You'll be such a star. Dr. Lev will understand if he really cares about you and your career. He wants you to be happy and achieve your dream, doesn't he?" He hands me the pen. "I'll call him myself and explain the situation. I'm sure he will see things differently after we go over my plan. I promise you it will work." He looks "in charge," as always. He seems to knows what's best for all concerned.

I stare at the contract, wondering if Dr. Lev will understand, wondering if Eli will forgive me, wondering if Didier is right when he says that I might get killed even though Dr. Lev says he can guarantee my safety. But it's true that the defense will tear me apart, and my reputation will be in tatters.

Once more, I feel caught between my duties and my dream. No wonder I only find myself whole in opera—in the land of passion gone awry, unrequited love, suicidal lovers, murder, specters, and destructive forces. Someday, my voice will dim and my performances will show little exuberance. The world will fail to remember my art. Some might mention my days of glory, while others will see only a pale shadow of what I used to be, but I know, I will have lived my dream.

"I have one request, Didier."

"What is it?"

"I don't want our sexual relationship to continue. I'm sorry, but I'm not in love with you."

"But you will be, Sophie. I know you will. I will wait."

"Are you going to comply?"

"Yes."

"Thank you."

He hands me the pen and then pops a bottle of champagne. "This calls for a celebration." He pours me a glass.

As always, his world is bubbly, hypnotizing, flawless. It's an intoxicating universe that will prepare me to return to the glamour of opera. I must risk everything to be able to sing on the big stage again, and he holds the key to that door. I might as well do as he tells me.

I hold the pen, my fingers tense and tight, still wondering if I should turn my back on Lev. He will hate me, for sure. He has showed me such kindness. How can I possibly betray the man who has stood up to my own father to fight for justice for me and Eli? Tears drip down my cheeks. But it's true that if I stay in the U.S., he and Dr. Cristina might still have a chance to get back together. I feel terrible thinking that I might be the reason he has broken up with the woman who loves him so dearly. Maybe what he feels for me isn't love, after all, but admiration, and in the future he might regret giving up his fiancé for a woman who can only put him in harm's way.

I sign the contract that will bind me to Didier for a long time to come. I give the document back to him, aware that I've just turned my back on Eli, Judge Daniel, and Dr. Lev. Like Amina, I feel I am sleepwalking through life once again.

All I know is that I keep giving up one thing after another to fulfill my greatest desire.

"You won't regret signing the contract, Sophie." He looks unwavering. "You'll soar, I promise."

I take a sip of my sparkling wine. "I hope you're right."

"We'd better get going, darling. Tomorrow, you have a full day of practice. Madame Prunier wants you to work on Madam Butterfly." He hands me a book. "I bought the Royal Opera House version of the opera for you."

I hold my copy of Madam Butterfly close. I am going to read the libretto all over again. Even though I know the story, there is always something new to learn about a character as complex as Cio-Cio San.

Chapter 10

From my desk, L.A. looks gray and filled with gloom. The sweetgum tree is losing her leaves, but she is still the most elegant tree in the world. Between the two mighty oaks, she looks fragile, yet sweetgums are resilient and offer protection from the Santa Ana winds, which made a comeback last night. The winds are mild compared to the tropical gales overrunning Rio de Janeiro during the summer months. My city is as fragile-looking as the sweetgum tree, as resilient, and as stunning.

I click on my tablet and check my email. My heart skips a beat when I see a message from Dr. Lev. He hasn't written me in three weeks. I open it right way and rush through his words.

> Cara Sofia,
>
> Sorry that I haven't been in touch for nearly a month. Before I tell you what happened, I want to assure you that I'm recovering well. There is no other way of saying this, but I was shot as I was leaving the clinic. I was injured near the heart. It was a serious hit, but I was taken to the hospital immediately, and the surgery went well. I'll be out in a couple of days. My mother has been playing your music, and your art is the only reason my patience isn't fading. It has been a great part of my recovery and a remarkable source of happiness. My heart beats in tempo with your voice.
>
> If anyone ever asks me what "haunting" means in relation to music, I'll just play the DVD of you singing *Rusalka*. Beautiful lady...beautiful voice...beautiful scenery. Effortless, faultless, perfect. I love the strong sunlight streaming through the window, shining bright. You killed it, sweetie. I hope you'll sing it in person when you come to testify. Thank you for all this, and please don't worry about me.

I hope that I am missed, as well. I'm giving you my mother's phone number if you want to call her. She's a surgical nurse and actually works at the hospital where I'm staying. She will be home by the time I send you this email. I just want you to know that there is no reason to panic. I'll let you go, darling. I hope you know that I'd never abandon you. I'll try to keep in touch as much as possible. If you have the time, please email back.

Love, Lev

I take a sip of my mineral water, too dumbstruck with the news to call Dona Larissa right away. There is complete silence. I wish I were in a bad dream, but it's true that some evil person tried to take his life. I remember Captain Almeida's weapon against my skin; cold, metallic, and hard the day he raped me. I watch the numbers flip over on the digital clock. I watch them flip over. I watch. I'm terrified of making the call and learning that Lev's life may still be at risk.

He never puts himself ahead of others and might not be telling me what's really going on, so I don't panic. Now I know how great my love for him is, as if I had been touched by a razor-sharp knowledge of what it is to be a woman without a mask to shield my innermost feelings. I feel naked before him: no disguise, no camouflage, and yet, I'm not afraid. I don't fear this fire that burns and blazes inside me. I'd do anything in my power to diminish his suffering.

At once, I feel an urgency I never felt before. I get online and search for a flight to Brazil. I still have the ticket Lev sent me three moths ago when I was uncertain about staying in America. I must fly to him right away. There is no time to waste. He needs me, and I will be at his side, with or without Didier's consent. I type in the number on my ticket and make a reservation for the flight leaving LAX this evening. It doesn't matter if I have to pay three hundred dollars more in fees. I must get out of here today and run to the one I love dearly. I must show him how much I care. I log off, pick up the phone, and dial 01155215545672.

It rings, and rings, and rings one more time. I shiver. Maybe he died and his mother is making funeral arrangements.

"Alo," a female voice answers.

"May I please speak to Dona Larissa?" I take a deep breath.

"This is Larissa. Who is this?"

"This is Sofia de Menezes, Dr. Lev's friend in America." My eyes well up.

"Sofia! I was expecting your call, querida."

I begin to cry. "Is he going to be okay? I've just got an email from him, but I couldn't Skype him. Please tell me the truth."

"We are expecting a full recovery, honey. He's stable and his surgery has been a success. Don't be so upset, okay?"

"Do you know that he has never let me down? A thousand unknowns are better than the certainty of him not making it. I feel so much sorrow and remorse for telling him about Eli and getting him involved with Officer Almeida and the likes of him. I can only imagine how disappointed you are in me."

"I'm not, sweetie, not one bit. One thing I know about my son is that he'll fight for anyone who has suffered an injustice; it's in his DNA, and you shouldn't feel guilty. He cares deeply about you, and I wouldn't blame you for what happened to him, not even for a minute, nor would his father."

"Please tell him that he's very dear to me. Tell him that I wish I could be there right now to see him and care for him. In fact, I've just booked a flight to Brazil leaving LAX tonight. I'll be there in twenty-four hours due to a stop in Georgia. Please tell him that I received the new passport he sent me and the extra money."

"I'll let him know tonight when I return to the hospital. But tell me, will Didier let you come?"

"I'm not telling him. He works late tonight. I'm supposed to go to the opera with a friend. I'd never abandon Dr. Lev. Please tell him that. I regret I wasn't going to testify in person. I should have fought Didier on that, but please let him know that I will be at his side soon."

"I'll tell him. Thank you, Sofia. I'm sure he'll recover much faster with you in Rio. That's such a kind gesture. I'll be forever grateful. No wonder my son speaks of you with the utmost admiration."

"Thank you for raising such a special person, Dona Larissa. Your son is unique. I'm glad we'll meet soon. I have so much respect for you and Judge Daniel."

"We feel the same way, sweetheart. Be careful, please. Até breve."

"Ah, I'm buying some things online as soon as I get to the airport to be delivered to his place. I'm a certified Reiki Healer and want to give him treatments.”

“Send them to my address and I’ll take them to his apartment. I’ll email you my address. Have a safe flight.”

“Have a good night.” I hang up.

Rusalka’s aria begins to play.

“Song to the Moon” is a howling aria in which the love of a water nymph for the prince she worships is doomed from the start. The English horn solo after the second verse is the “death” motif, as Rusalka will became a death spirit in the bottom of the lake when her Prince rejects her in her human form. Only those who have known unrequited love can feel it to its full extent. I will sing it to him alone, and I hope my performance will be spot-on so that he will love it.

I wonder if Lev has feelings for me, as my mother said. Does he love me? Does he see me as a woman or just a friend he has vowed to protect from harm? Even though I Skype with him often after my practice, and it isn’t enough. There is only so much technology can do. It leaves out the sense of touch, the closeness, and the warmth that only face-to-face communication can offer.

I click on compose and begin to write him an email.

> Dear Lev,
>
> Not all of us have the ability to come up with the right words and gestures to offer another who matters to us a great deal. At times, I felt the need to be of use to you, somehow... I didn’t know how, but I felt it quite deeply. “Também, você parece até um caracol.” I mean, you say so little while I talk a lot. You’re always so collected, while I make such a fuss about everything, and you’re always so measured while my feelings are all over the place. Maybe when I see you in Rio, you’ll tell me more about yourself...what makes you happy, what makes you dream, what keeps you up at night...I know at least one thing: “Song to the Moon” is your favorite aria, and I will sing it to you as soon as I land in Brazil. Your mother has all the details.
>
> Anyway, I’ll be thinking of you, hoping that my vocal gifts will come through when I sing to you, so that I’ll finally give you something of true value, something that comes from my core, my innermost being, something that you bring out of

me with your kindness. Because of you, I want to be a better person and do more to make the world a bit better for others through my singing.

I'm hoping you get well soon. It hurts me deeply to think that you're in pain. Just so you know, I'll always have your back. Have a good night! See you very soon.

Love,

Sofia

I walk to the closet and grab my carry-on. I begin to pack my things, hoping that Didier won't call until I'm already out of the house. He is constantly checking on me and my whereabouts, but hopefully, he'll remember that I'm supposed to be in the salon with Alondra and then at the opera with her tonight. Still, he might inquire, and if he does, I hope to be on the plane to Rio where he won't be able to stop me. I know this might be the end of my dream, but I can't let Lev down. Still, I pack my scores and librettos since he promised that he would practice my pieces with me when I come down to Rio to testify. Besides, I can always Skype with Prunier and work hard from Brazil. But will Didier forgive me for running away? He will surely be enraged. He'll probably rip the contract apart, but I must fly to Brazil. I'll ask Alondra to help me out in case he looks for me.

The unusual clock on the wall marks 1:11 pm. The transparent machine has an emerald background and small golden parts moving together—the first wheel, the top one, the second, third, and the escape wheel. I wonder what kind of a brain would come up with such an ingenious idea; most likely, somebody who wants to know what's beneath, like a psychologist probing the mind.

I pick up my handbag and begin to pack my passport and ticket. I put on my jaguar bracelet. My grandmother told me that I have the spirit of the jaguar, that I'm strong and free. She told me I have to be ready for anything if I want to live like a daughter of the Aruaques. I text Alondra, telling her that I'm skipping the visit to her salon this afternoon. I'll call her from the airport and explain everything. I grab my luggage, my handbag, and walk away, maybe for the last time.

Chapter 11

I stand at the window in the guest room in Dr. Lev's apartment. Ipanema Beach is nearly empty on this winter day. The South Atlantic seems unsettled. There are red flags on the shore, signaling maré cheia. I remember whirlpools and undertows hiding beneath jade-green waters. It has been two weeks since my arrival in Rio and a week since I've been caring for Lev.

The crimson drapes allow just a bit of sunlight to trickle through a slit. The maroon fabric sofa and the burgundy of the bedspread with its flower motif on a golden band make me feel like I'm in a Russian castle where the tsar has all the power. Maybe Lev has a dark side I haven't seen yet, but I find it hard to believe he has a mean bone in his body. He is a gentleman and such a loyal friend that it hurts me to think that he had to go through such a horrible ordeal.

The tapestry on the wall across from the piano has a yin-yang mandala on a textured blue watercolor background. I wanted to add a soothing color to the bedroom before starting his Reiki treatments. While in America, I ordered a massage table and other items to use during these few days before we head to Capella to work on the trial and my music.

I've burned some bundles of sage smudge sticks, just like my grandmother used to do at the ranch. The flute in the music I'm playing is uplifting, soaring, while the staccato strings add just a bit of tension for awareness and increasing concentration. The aqua table runner on the rectangle stand against the wall is smooth and shiny. I've placed Reiki black stones with gold inscriptions on a black tray and charged candles with intention. There is one for protection made of frankincense, sandalwood, rosemary, and clove. I want him to have a soothing experience and feel the strong energy of life that surrounds us.

My long, button-down, gauze tunic over my cream slip feels comfortable. I wear drops of rose of attar. This extract is said to capture the healing qualities of the Damask rose, and I want to use it to make the session even more powerful. I sit down on the sofa and shut my eyes. I breathe slowly to calm my mind, body, and soul so that the energy of life will flow from me to him.

There is a knock on the door.

"Come on in, Dr. Lev."

He walks in. He wears a white cotton shirt and dark-blue linen slacks. Even though it has been a week since he left the hospital, he still has not regained all his strength.

"How was your night, Sofia? Did you sleep well?" he asks. "And please call me Lev."

"It was lovely. I slept like a rock. I guess I just feel blissful being near the ocean and in your home. Just knowing that you're in the bedroom next door makes me feel happy. I was terrified when I heard about what happened, and we were four thousand miles apart. I had to come to you that very same day."

"I'm glad you feel at home. I love to have you here. These last few months have shown me that you are, as I suspected, a lovely woman."

"And I've found out that you are a very caring man. Thank you for having me. I really don't want to stay at my father's house, and I do want to care for you. Are you ready for your treatment? It's just a 'massage' for the soul. I know it's not the kind of hard science you're used to, but it will help unblock the negative energy that results from trauma. It's just going to be a transfer of the life force energy that surrounds us flowing from me to you. There are no side-effects. I want so much to do something good for you, to give back, and to show you how much you mean to me."

"I'm looking forward to it. Thank you for all the preparation. Everything looks so inviting."

"Great. I love doing this work. Please lie down here on the massage table and just relax."

"You have a client for sure." He lies down.

"You haven't tried it yet. You have to experience it first and then tell me if I have a client. And I want you to use your scientific language and be very honest. Don't praise me just because you're my friend."

"I'll be very honest and try to be unbiased. You know that I love everything you do and this, I'm sure, won't be any different."

"Try to think of me as if I were a stranger you've just met so that you can be objective. The treatment will feel like rippling waves and won't hurt at all." I walk to the end of the table and stand facing his head. "I'm going to cradle your head in my hands and begin the healing. It's all about transferring my highest energy to you to get your body and spirit into balance." I'm speaking in my softest voice. "It's also going to boost your immune system and remove toxins." My hands are cupped over his head. It's a gentle touch.

I think of a path out of a thick forest into a clearing where a carpet of orange poppies extends for miles. I hear calming, healing sounds. I remember the reservation by the Xingu River where the remaining Aruaques live. My grandmother's ancestors are wise and kind. I listen to their drums in my mind, their way of communicating, their ways of taking care of the earth and using only what they need, of being thankful for what they have, for the life force that has been given to them and for the benevolence of nature. I feel a jolt of warm energy and my whole body seems to be pouring out the Ki energy that the universe provides. I feel it flow from me to him with all the love my heart can muster.

I walk a few steps and put my hands over his thorax as gently as I can. That's the most sensitive spot, the one where he took a bullet. I focus on the music and remember diving in the cool waters of Cabo Frio Beach, where once I found mother-of-pearl. It was hard to open the shell, but once I did it, I found seven small pearls in it.

In my mind, I see an array of blue, green, and yellow electrified waves, as if I had fit LED lights to his body. It feels as though I'm seeing over a hundred million stars circulating overhead. I feel healing taking place and thank the universe for allowing me to facilitate it. I slowly remove my hands from over his chest and breathe in deeply.

"I'm ending the treatment for today," I whisper into his ear. "You're welcome to just lie here while I prepare some healing tea for you, Dr. Lev. Thank you for allowing me to do this."

He seems to have fallen asleep. I walk away from the table, pick up my iPhone and iPad from the desk, and leave the room. I walk down the hallway, thinking it's such a shame that a man like him was victim of such violence, but I will show him so much love that he will heal in no time.

I enter the kitchen. The cabinets are made of Brazilwood. The reddish dye is lustrous. It is the most beautiful wood there is, great for making cello bowls, refined closets, and elegant jewelry boxes. Unfortunately, those trees are on the brink of extinction. I pick up a black teapot and fill it with filtered water. Being back in Rio is cool. I have been missing coconut water, suco de manga, black coffee in demitasses, tropical rain, and Portuguese. I have missed the crowds, flocking to lines and eating rice and beans every day. The beach is stunning, and the inner forest is sacred. Rio is gorgeous. It has charisma and fits my temperament. There is rain in the making, and I'm sure there will be flash flooding and mud slides, and the city will be a mess. I'd better do my errands before the downpour.

While the water boils, I set the table with sea-green placemats, black teacups, and a bowl of honey sticks. I'm brewing him some sakura-yu tea, even though it is supposed to be served only at weddings and other auspicious occasions. But he deserves the best. I've also gotten him some sakura-mochi, dumplings containing sweet bean paste wrapped in a salt-preserved cherry-tree leaf is also reserved for extraordinary occasions, but what could be more special than his recovery, the celebration of his life? I want him to feel special, loved, and cared for. I whisk in the sakura-yu and dip a honey stick in each cup. I let the tea steep.

The Laelia orchid plant in the center of the table commands attention. She displays a host of shades of green. Although small, she looks majestic. She has three broad petals; two that are similar to each other, and a third that features various markings and spears. She has a frilly margin and is sensual both in feeling and character. There is nothing fake about her.

I hear my own voice singing, "Qui la voce sua soave," the love aria of Elvira. I remember singing it in Prague when I was seventeen. It was my first major competition. Winning it was the beginning of my career on the international stage. I sang it with all my heart and soul because Eli was by my side, and I had just found out I was pregnant with his child. I feel a mix of pride and regret. I just hope that Didier will reconsider and continue to support my efforts to win the competition at the Met.

We've talked on the phone. He is still hurt that I left without saying a word. I promised him that I'll continue my studies with Dr. Lev and later with Madam Prunier via Skype, but he hasn't said if he is okay with that. I told him that I will accept his decision and take responsibility for my actions.

"May I come in?" Dr. Lev's voice sounds low and mellow.

"Of course, please. It's your house, your kitchen. I'm just the tea brewer."

"But I know that a certain lady gave me precise instructions about what she was going to do to help me heal faster. She said that the tea drinking part was a ritual and she'd need to prepare everything with much tranquility. So, I don't want to disturb her."

"Your presence is tranquil, but thank you for taking my efforts seriously.

Especially for a psychiatrist like you, my healing methods might appear so unscientific that I don't even know how you came on board." I pull a chair out for him.

"Well, medicine is all about trust in the practitioner. It doesn't matter if you have years of rigorous training to meet high scientific standards if you don't have the client's trust. Although I'm not yet schooled in your methods, I trust you entirely. Thank you for the treatment. I feel very relaxed, and I am looking forward to the next session."

"Thank you, Lev." I sit down across from him. "I'm going to write down a few things I need to do to make the sessions even stronger as we progress."

"I'm certain of that, especially because the practitioner has such a luminous soul, which is reflected in her sparkling voice and dramatic operatic style. This is sheer grace, Sofia. You're a true artist, and I am ecstatic to have you in my life. And by the way, my mother is impressed with your nursing abilities. You don't miss a beat. You wake up at two a.m. to give me my meds and make sure that my vitals are taken three times a day. Thank you so much."

"I told you I was going to repay you for all your kindness. Being in the States alone for months was crazy-making; without you to talk to, I'd have died. I'll do anything to show my gratitude. This is just the beginning. In fact, later, I'm going to the market to get some more fruit to make smoothies for you. I got you a juicer."

He drinks his tea and eats his treats. He's so special in so many ways that I want to be at his side for as long as he needs me and longer. It's going to be tough to leave him behind if Didier agrees to continue supporting my opera.

"Speaking of going places, your father called last night, Sofia. He wants to provide you with a bullet-proof car and two BOPE officers so that you can move around safely. Would you be willing to accept his offer?"

"No, thank you, Lev. I don't want anything from my father. You said that there is no immediate threat to my safety, and I believe you. I'll just take my gun with me. Do you still have it?"

"Yes, it's in my safe, but I worry about you going out by yourself. I would like to drive you around if you allow me."

"Certainly not. You've got to rest. I'm here to ensure that you put your health first, and I'm not budging. You'd better get used to this new Sofia who is devoted to you. You never thought I could be this tough, did you?"

"I've noticed a few traits that have led me to conclude that you can be stern when it's called for."

"Then, you've been warned. I'll make sure you're brand-new before I'm done with you. By the way, I have something special for you in my room. I've been keeping this a secret for the longest time." I get up.

"I can hardly wait to see it." He gets up and follows me inside the bedroom.

I reach inside the drawer in the desk and take out a black square box and open it. "This is an emerald necklace presented to me by Queen Mathilde of Belgium when I won the opera contest in 2011. I'd like you to have it as a payment for all the hours you've put in this case without charging me one cent. And now you nearly lost your life from a bullet that was probably meant for me. I have a certificate of authenticity, and I've never worn it because Eli told me that I should only wear it in his presence since he'd be jealous otherwise." I hand the box to him.

"Wow, it is fabulous!" He turns it over in his hands. "But I can't possibly accept this, Sofia. I've been playing the piano since I was five, and I know how much sweat and tears went into earning this. Besides, I have a stake in this case. Officer Almeida and his ring have been committing crimes against Jews for a while now. May I put it on you? Let's see what it looks like on its rightful owner. I'm sure Eli would be happy knowing that you've been fiercely loyal to him all those years, and I believe he would want you to be happy with someone else."

"If you say so."

He puts the box down on the desk. He places the necklace around my neck. His faint scent of musk reminds me of some of the trees at Capella. He stares at it, and I see awe on his face. He lets my hair down and smoothes it with his fingers. "Perfect."

Our eyes meet. There is so much I want to tell him, but the words don't come to me. I reach out and put my arms around his waist and lean against his chest. He puts his arms around my shoulders and holds me tight.

I remember the garden at Capella the last time I was there. A wispy wind was blowing. The petals of the coral Sydonie roses were falling to the ground, and I was like them, shedding parts of me I no longer needed. My mind fluttered above the ordinary. There was a pulse that beat in unison with my heart, and I turned into the petals themselves and left my spent blooms behind. He inspires me to leave the sorrows of the past behind.

"I'm really glad I came here, and it doesn't matter if Didier stops supporting my singing. I'll find another way to achieve my dream."

"You will have your opera, Sofia. I said I was going to help you practice for the time you stayed in Rio. Should we begin?"

"Are you well enough to play? I feel you are still a bit fragile."

"I can do it. I'll do anything for you, but first, may I take a picture of you? You look too stunning not to save this image."

"Go ahead. You can use my iPad."

"May I record this session? My grandmother would be delighted to see you singing, darling. She's your number one fan."

"Please."

"Would you like to do *Rusalka*? I've been practicing it for weeks in anticipation of your arrival."

"Perfect."

He reaches out, picks up the iPad on the desk and then takes a picture of me. Then, he sets it down on top of a bookshelf next to the piano. I walk closer and stand by the instrument. He puts the score on the music rack and lifts the piano cover.

Rusalka's fate resembles that of a cherry blossom, as her happiness lasts only a week. I hope the happiness in store for us will last beyond my time in Rio, but there is so much at stake, so much I'm not sure about.

"Ready?" he says.

"Ready." I take a deep breath and hear the first notes of "Song to the Moon."

I focus on the task at hand, knowing that perhaps in a matter of weeks I'll have to leave him behind and return to America in pursuit of my dream.

Chapter 12

Evening falls in Rio de Janeiro. The room is semi-dark, and I can hear the ocean. It's one of my favorite sounds in the world. It has been two weeks since my arrival. It fills me with happiness that Lev's health has improved so dramatically. We've been practicing my music daily and have grown even closer. Didier has accepted the fact that I'm staying until the end of August when it's time to testify. To think that I almost let Dr. Lev down fills me with anguish. He has stood by me in countless ways and it hurts me that I betrayed him.

My little black dress dates back to the time when I used to sing at the conservatory. I have to rely on the clothes I've left behind, since I brought very little with me when I left Los Angeles so unexpectedly. I put a drop of rose of attar behind my ears and comb my hair.

Lev stands at the door. "May I come in?"

"Please, Lev."

"Wow. You look dazzling." His gaze is on me. He walks up to me and kisses me on the cheek. "I'm glad you're going out tonight. You've been so adamant about staying at my side and taking care of me. Your loyalty is priceless."

I burst out crying. "I'm so sorry I told you I wasn't coming to testify the day after I sang for the first time at Maison Sakura. I regret it, Lev. What a betrayal."

He puts his arms around me. "Listen carefully. You didn't do anything wrong. You were under pressure, and Didier manipulated you. I knew it all along and didn't hold it against you at all, darling."

"You should have." I lean against his chest. "I let you down after all you did for me. Please forgive me."

"There is nothing to forgive, only things to love and admire." He picks up a tissue from the box on the desk and wipes my tears and then holds me even tighter. "I'm so happy you're here. You left everything behind to come to my aid, and it's because of you that I'm almost completely healed. No more talk of sadness. I missed you so much when you were away." His voice is just above a whisper.

"Me, too. I nearly died when I learned that you had been shot. I wanted to run all the way here and hold you close and never let go. I'll do anything for you, just ask."

He buries his face in my hair. "This is the same scent I smelled on my pillow this morning. Was it a dream or were you in my bed last night?"

"Well, I heard you scream something about being shot, so I got in bed with you and crooned you a lullaby my grandmother used to sing to me when I was scared. You went back to sleep, and I went back to bed."

"I wish you had stayed the night, Sofia. Did you want to stay?"

"Yes, but I didn't know if you wanted me to. Besides, Dr. Cristina called me yesterday, and she was very upset because she learned I'm staying here. She blames me for your breakup, even though I told her that I'm not really your type and what you feel for me is admiration and some pity. Oh, Lev, she's so devastated."

"Listen, Cristina shouldn't have called you in the first place. I broke up with her two months ago because I was certain that a marriage between us would not work. It isn't your fault, Sofia."

My phone rings once, twice, three times.

"I'll let you get that." He releases me.

"It's probably Isabella." I reach out and grab the phone.

"This is Sofia."

"Are you still coming, woman?"

"Yes, running a bit late, but I'll be there in no time. Leaving Leblon in five minutes."

"That's where you're staying? With Dr. Lev? I've been trying to track you down for a week now."

"Of course not. I stopped by to pay a visit. Who do you think he is? He wouldn't want to hang out with the likes of me. Psychiatrists have a reputation to protect."

"Well, the ones who actually have a reputation, which isn't the case with Dr. Rafael. You know that he made a pass at Rosangela last Friday? She was in tears. By the way, did you ever tell Dr. Lev what Rafael did to you?"

"Of course not. You know how Dr. Lev is: he gets angry about little things and then makes a big deal out of them. But I told Dr. Fleetly, and Dr.

Rafael was disciplined. End of story."

"I still think you should have told Dr. Lev. He was your supervisor and would have done more."

"It's over, Isabella. Actually, I'm leaving now, sweetie. Let's have some fun tonight, okay? I don't want to think about bad stuff."

"Do you need a ride?"

"No. I'm riding in a BOPE car, courtesy of my father. My father says my life might be in danger so I accepted his offer after refusing to have anything to do with him."

"Great. At least your motherfucker father is good for something. See you soon."

"Bye." I hang up and put the phone down.

Lev stares at me. "What was it that I was never told about because I make a big deal about little things and get all angry when people tell me about them?"

"Nothing important. See? You look very upset, now, and that's why I didn't tell you, Dr. Lev. I knew you'd make a big deal about it. I took the matter to Dr. Fleetly, and everything was resolved. Case closed, okay?" I soften my voice. "Remember that you are my big, lovable teddy bear and that you shouldn't be stressed out. Please, don't be cross."

"Will you tell me about it tomorrow?"

"If you insist, but I still think I'm a big girl who took matters into her own hands." I grab my purse and phone.

"It's important, Sofia. Please."

"Okay, Lev, if you promise me you are going to sleep and forget about this tonight. When I return I'll check on you, give you your meds, and sing to you while you sleep if you have another nightmare."

"May I pick you up? I want to bring you home. I still worry about you out there."

"No. The whole reason I accepted my father's help is so that you don't have to drive me around. I want you to rest. I worry about you even more when you are out there."

"Hang on. I'm getting something I put in the safe so that you can wear it tonight." He walks away.

I check on the tray I've left for him with his meds and the vitamins I've gotten for him. I hope he will be just fine until I return. As much as I want to be with Isabella, I'll miss him terribly.

He returns with the emerald necklace. "Let's put this on its rightful owner." He places it around my neck. "Now it's complete. Be safe out there, Sofia. Tomorrow I've arranged a special day for you. I'd like to talk to you about some very important things."

"Can hardly wait." I kiss him on the cheek. "If you need me, please call me and I'll come back to you right way." I walk away before I have a change of heart.

As soon as I open the door, I come face to face with one of the officers my father provided for me.

"Boa noite, Dona Sofia. I am Captain Sergio. Where are we taking you?" he asks.

"Ipanema. Here's the address." I hand him Isabella's card.

"My pleasure." He escorts me inside the elevator. He is too much of a reminder of Officer Almeida, and I think of the night Dr. Rafael behaved in a creepy way. I shiver as I buckle up in my seat.

I remember that Christmas party at the clinic when I was suddenly summoned into Dr. Rafael's office. He smelled of hard liquor. He told me to sit in a chair across from him and suddenly took off his red tie and wrapped it around my wrists and told me to speak, which I was unable to do. He told me not to be scared, that it was just a game because I gesticulate so much that he knew for sure that I wouldn't be able to utter a word. Then he traced my lips with his index finger and said that the experiment was over for the time being, and that it was a secret. I was terrified. A month later, I decided to talk to Dr. Fleetly. I hope Lev won't bring this whole thing to light again. It's so embarrassing.

I come out of my reverie as the car stops in front of my friend Isabella's. I get out, open the gate, and walk up the cement path. Her garden is still adorable, just the way I left it five months ago when I planted the hyacinths and heliotropes. I ring the bell.

She opens the door and smiles. "Hey, girl! How good to see you. You look so gorgeous, and that necklace is out of this world. How do you protect it? Do you have a gun on you?"

"Yes, it's inside my purse."

"You're funny, Sofia. Come in, please. Tell me everything about your fairytale romance with the Frenchman and your life in Los Angeles." She guides me to the sofa.

She wears a red maternity dress that shows her pregnancy bump. I feel a twinge of regret. I might never wear one. My career will ask much of me, and the contract says "no pregnancy."

I sit on the couch. "There is no romance. It's strictly business; he manages my career and I make him money."

"But I thought it was different. It's the sex, isn't it? He's not good in bed."

"I'm just not in love with him, so all the rest doesn't matter."

"Okay, Sofia, but I thought he was perfect for you. He understands your opera. It's going to be tough to get a Brazilian man to appreciate your art. You're just unequaled, yet edgy at the same time. "

"Don't worry, okay? I'm committed to my singing, and everything else has taken a back seat. My training is grueling. It's hours on end of warming up my voice and practicing one aria after the other."

"I think it's your grief over Eli's death that prevents you from committing to a man. You start dating them, and then when you feel happy, you back down. It's okay to love again, you know."

"I still maintain that it's my opera that occupies my entire life."

"Okay, baby doll. Can I take your coat?"

"Sure." I remove my black fleece coat and hand it to her.

Rio is very cold for a change. The wild wind blowing outside will certainly bring a lot of rain.

"So, are you sure you're not staying with Dr. Lev?"

I skirt the full truth and answer while putting my purse down on the side table to avoid her eyes. "I offered to give him a Reiki treatment. As soon as I settle down, I'll do just that."

"I miss him at the clinic. He is the best supervisor. Do you know that he broke up with Dr. Cristina? No one saw that coming."

"I'm sorry to hear that. They seemed to make such an ideal couple." I feel my heart drop, remembering that she put the blame on me for the breakup. I'm still not sure it was me, but she said that Dr. Lev changed when we started working on Eli's case. Maybe she is just too heartbroken to accept his decision to break off the engagement. Still, I feel guilty somehow.

"Are you hungry? I have sashimi salad, your favorite, and your favorite wine. I challenge you to drink a whole bottle since I won't be able to drink tonight." She gets up. "Everything is ready, baby doll."

She shows me the table, which is impeccably set with black chopsticks, and all.

"I'm ready whenever you are. Can I help?"

"No need. Please have a seat at the table."

I take my phone out of my purse and check my messages. There's one from Lev telling me that he'll be able to pick me up any time after eight if I change my mind. I notice that my phone is about to die.

Isabella returns with a red bowl of sashimi on a bed of spinach and a bottle of Vinho Verde. "Hey, girl has anyone ever done hypnotherapy on you?" She pours me a glass of wine.

"No, why?"

"I need a subject. I'm taking this thousand-hour course, and I need to practice."

"Okay. I'll help you." I text Lev, telling him I don't want him out on the streets.

She returns with a tray of sushi rolls and a bottle of raspberry sake.

"Are we playing Scrabble, too?" I spot the game at the end of the table.

"Yes. I know how much you like the game." She sits down across from me and helps herself to some salad. She picks up the controller and turns the iPod on. "I downloaded new songs by Zizi Possi, your favorite."

"Perfect." I help myself to some wine. I hear the first notes of "My Heart Comes Apart."

I love the song about a lover describing what the love she feels for her man does to her. It seems as if she's describing my feelings for Lev. Maybe I should just tell him tonight what I feel, and how I wished I had stayed in his bed last night. I am afraid to get involved with him because I know it will be hard to return to America without him, but I don't think I can stop what is about to happen between us.

Isabella pours me a glass of water. "Finally, I get to spend some time with you. I've missed you so much. You're my best friend, Sofia, and no one understands me so well."

"And you are my best friend—more like a sister who went through a lot with me when Eli passed. I'll never forget your kindness and support. I love you."

Zizi continues to sing. Her song "Perigo" is one of my favorites of her repertoire. Perigo, danger, describes exactly what I feel for Lev. Just as the song says: "If I have any bit of a chance, the night will say." Yes, tonight, I'll let him know how I feel and see what happens. A rejection would be crushing, but if he feels the same way about me, it would be out of this world. I feel tears start.

Isabella puts her chopsticks down. "Where are you staying?"

"No more lies. I'm staying with Dr. Lev." I blush and play with my chopsticks.

Isabella immediately picks up on the moment. "Sofia! Are you sleeping with him?"

"Of course not, Isabella. I'm caring for him since he took a bullet for being involved with my case. He's not the kind of man who will sleep around with anybody."

"Except that you aren't just 'anybody,' Sofia. I'm sure he's in love with you. He talks about you often and shows me all your YouTube videos. How about you? Do you love him?"

"All I know is that being around him feels like getting an extra supply of oxygen. He's such a beautiful person and so thoughtful, and hot, too. He is so stylish and intelligent."

"So, why don't you tell him how you feel and get a whole tank of oxygen?"

"Ha, ha, funny. Don't forget that my father is like Wally's father from the opera by Catalani. He's controlling and has a record of every man I've been involved with. Dr. Lev is a Jewish man, and I can't seem to be able to have those. If I start a relationship with him, he's a marked man all over again."

Zizi sings the song about a lover's jealousy just because her man comes home late one night. She can't tolerate the thought he might have been with another. I feel exactly like that when I think Lev might still love Dr. Cristina. I feel bad for being happy, knowing he broke up with her. I'm a very callous person.

Isabella refills my glass. "Do you like Los Angeles? Because I really think you should stay in Rio and reboot your career here in your city so you'll be here when my baby is born."

"I need to be there, although I miss Rio so much. I don't know. I'm so conflicted. But I must sing at the Met, and Didier is my ticket to realizing one of my dreams. Except that he is still pretty mad about my sudden departure. Maybe I'll just stick around, but I know that Brazil will never make me into the diva I'm meant to be. And I myself don't have the confidence."

"That's where hypnosis comes in." She gets up and walks around the table to sit down on the chair next to mine. "Close your eyes, darling. I'm going to get you relaxed enough to give your mind a few suggestions about going for what you want without fear. So, breathe, breathe slowly and deeply, slowly and evenly, as many times as you need to get into a state of mind that is receptive to accepting my guidance."

I breathe more and more deeply, and as I continue, I begin to enter a trance. I still hear her soft voice, but it's growing fainter and fainter. Maybe it's the wine, but I seem to be relaxing and letting go of all my cares. It feels as though I'm at Capella, riding Vento in the soft rain. I hear Isabella's commands penetrating a deeper spot in my brain. I begin to imagine myself walking on stage and facing the judges. I feel a bit anxious, but as her voice reaches the recesses of my brain, I begin to feel warm and tingling. I see myself singing Butterfly's aria like that geisha from Nagasaki would. My voice is clear and crisp, and my emotions spill over the stage, and my performance touches the hearts of those around me.

"Your face has such luminosity. Open your eyes slowly, slowly, and look at me."

I open my eyes and take a deep breath. "This stuff really works." My voice is barely a whisper.

"We can do it again a few times more while you're in Rio. Next time, we'll go deeper."

"Can we play some Scrabble, now?" I take another sip of my wine.

"Let's play." She returns to her place, pushes the dishes away, and picks up the box. As she sets up the game, I pour myself another glass of wine. I feel a bit fuzzy, but it's better than sad, afraid, or blue for not knowing if Lev sees me as the woman he wants to spend his life with. I pick up my phone to text him, but I realize that it's dead. Good thing it is, since I feel like asking him to pick me up right this minute and take me somewhere where I'll forget about all my sorrows and drama.

Zizi begins to sing "Noite." "Night" describes exactly what I feel at this very moment. I won't be able to sleep tonight if he's not by my side. My passion for him is far too great not to have him in my bed tonight.

"My first word is H-O-R-S-E," she says and then pours me a shot of sake.

I think of Vento, my Wind. He is probably missing me a lot. I smile thinking that in a few days I'll be at Capella for at least three weeks before the trial. I look at my tiles and feel a bit out of focus, but manage to spell the word H-A-C-A-T-E. I'm very fond of the Goddess of the Crossroads. She was the adviser of Persephone in the underworld and can see in three different directions. I wish I had her vision.

"I've got A-S-U-N-D-E-R," she says.

That's exactly how I feel, as if parts of me are scattered everywhere, just to think that, eventually, I'll be back in Los Angeles and far away from Lev.

We continue with the game as we listen to Zizi. Even though I told her I was going to finish the whole bottle of wine, I think I'll stick to three glasses only. I'm feeling a bit tipsy. "I got T-A-T-U-A-G-E-M," I say. I've just gotten a tattoo." I think of Lev and want to go back to him. I feel like getting a new supply of oxygen. Or, I think as I get up and feel the world reel above me, maybe I'm just plain drunk and really losing brain cells.

"I've got to go, sweetie, but before I do, tell me where you're having the little tyke."

"I haven't decided, yet. I wanted to have the baby in that birthing center in Leblon, close to Dr. Lev's house. It's great, but it's too expensive, even with insurance." She gets up.

"I'll pay the balance. It's my present to you and my nephew."

"Are you crazy, Sofia? It's a lot of money."

"I'll have it in four more months. My pleasure." I kiss her on the cheeks. "I love you. Do you mind calling the BOPE officer? He's at the bar next door. Here's the number." I hand her a piece of paper.

"I'll do that and get your coat."

As she steps out to make the call, I fight a wash of tears. Maybe it's the thought of never having the baby I so much want. Maybe it's the wine, or the sake, or even the hypnosis. I guess I'm just going out of my mind. It's crazy to be in love with someone so out of my league.

She returns and hands me my coat. "The officer will be here in five minutes, beautiful."

"You're my beautiful momma. Take good care, okay? I'll see you before I take off to Capella. I'm dying to go to my farm, but I have to stay in Rio first." I kiss her on the cheeks and then put my coat on. I walk away thinking that it's going to be nearly impossible to leave my ranch behind again. I step out the door and walk the path that leads to the gate as the heavy rain falls hard. I rush to the sidewalk and run to the BOPE car.

I get inside, thinking that Officer Almeida won't rest until one or even the both of us are dead. As soon as his doctor gives Lev the green light, we'll go to Capella, and that will make me feel more relaxed. After the trial, I hope my father will realize his mistake, will see how brave Lev is and how much he has done for me, and will grant him more protection.

The car drops me off in front of the apartment, and I rush inside the building. I get inside the elevator, thinking that I can't leave him behind again. The night is gelid. I get out of the elevator and walk toward his apartment as my brain cells continue to die for lack of oxygen.

Chapter 13

I fumble for my key and unlock the door to Lev's apartment. I get inside the foyer and smell the sandalwood oil I burned before I left. He might be thinking I do witchcraft or something with all the rituals, candle lighting, and smudging. The digital clock on the credenza marks 9:39 PM. I hang my drenched coat on the hanger by the door. I stayed longer than I planned at Isabella's, but it was so much fun to be with her again. The wine also helped.

I tread lightly on the wooden floor. "Elvira Madigan" from *Mozart Concerto 21* still plays, and I recall that I left the iPod on repeat. The haunting theme song of the movie about a real tightrope walker makes me love classical music even more. Her illicit affair with Lieutenant Sixten Sparre didn't end well. I'll always mourn them, although the tragedy happened in the 1900s. I stumble a bit as I enter the living room. It is ill-lit, except for a lamp that sheds light where Lev sits reading the newspaper.

"Sorry, I didn't know you were here. I should have used the kitchen entrance."

"You can come in from anywhere you want. I've been catching up on some reading and waiting up for you. I couldn't get a hold of you, and I was a bit worried." He puts the paper down and stands up. "I thought you might need a lift." His graphite tie dangles down his neck.

"Sorry, my phone died. The BOPE officers were waiting for me the whole time." I walk up to him. "How thoughtless of me not to call from Isabella's; I guess it was all the wine. I mean, I'm not drunk or anything, just a bit tipsy. She dared me to drink a whole bottle of Vinho Verde. Well, I managed three glasses. We listened to Zizi Possi and played Scrabble. I spelled T-A-T-U-A-G-E-M. I have a real tattoo. Sorry for leaving the music on." I can tell that I am rambling on.

"No need to explain or apologize for anything. I like listening to Mozart and took the liberty of using the piano to practice the score to play it for you, if you want. It's a beautiful piece."

"You look handsome with your tie hanging down your neck, your white button up shirt and black slacks. And your dense black hair. And blue eyes." I clasp his tie. "May I please wear it? I always wanted to do that."

"Most certainly." He undoes his tie and puts it on me." His scent is a mixture of citrus and musk. "It looks good with your black dress, black gloves, and stunning necklace. You look absolutely striking tonight." He touches an emerald. "You're as prized as this stone, actually more, and no wonder I missed you so much. I wanted to pick you up and bring you home. This place was lifeless without you, and, I, utterly lonely."

My heart skips a bit. I reach out and put my arms around his waist. "This is the most touching thing I've ever heard, Lev." I cry through my laughter. "I'm a bit of a mess. I guess it's the alcohol."

He takes my face in his hands. "How can you be so beautiful? It's going to be nearly impossible to lose you again. I'll do anything in my power to keep you in Rio. I need your love. Say you'll stay in Brazil."

"Poor baby, don't hurt so much. You have all my love and more. I'll do anything for you." I laugh through my tears. I lean against his chest and begin to unbutton his shirt. "Do you want to make love to me? I think you need some cuddling."

"You have no idea how much, Sofia, but I'm afraid you had a bit too much to drink." He puts his arms around me. "Let's just cuddle tonight."

I release him and take a step back. "Why are you rejecting me, Dr. Lev? What did I do wrong? You just told me that I look stunning and that you'll have a hard time losing me again and that I'm as prized as my necklace. Earlier you said that you wished I had stayed in your bed last night. Do you still have feelings for Dr. Cristina? You said that you're torn about having to break up your engagement."

"I'm not rejecting you, and you didn't do anything wrong. I want you, but it would be a mistake to make love to you when you're not entirely sober, darling. I don't want you to later regret doing something you weren't ready for. I can't afford to lose you. It's an impossible thought."

"I'll never regret it. I know what I want, and I know you'll never take advantage of me."

"I hope not, because if I did, I'd have to do a lot of soul searching to figure out who I really am, since your well-being is of the utmost importance to me." He holds me by the hand. "You're quivering. Please have a seat." He leads me to the sofa, and I sit down. "I'm going to get a towel to dry your hair and some hot cocoa for you. You look so fragile." He kneels down in front of me. "May I take your stilettos off? I want you to lie back and unwind."

"Thank you." I half-lie on the couch. "I do feel a bit weary. I worried about you the whole night. I wanted to just come home and take care of you."

"I'll be right back." He gets up and walks away.

There is a painting by Leonid Afremov hanging on the wall. The foliage of slender trees surrounds a pond. The mirror-like surface reflects the yellow and green of the trees and the light of the blue sky. A distant bridge is thrown over the space between the onlooker and the painting itself.

I wish I'd never have to say goodbye to Lev again. He is the most caring person I know, the most honorable, and the one I truly love. But I have to audition at the Met. I'd better get used to having to say farewell. Maybe he is right and we shouldn't get involved any more than we already are.

He returns and hands me the hot drink and then sits on the sofa next to me. I have my legs crossed on the couch and my back to him. He begins to dry my hair with a royal-blue plush towel. I take a sip of the drink and feel warmer. I love when he clasps strands of my hair and dries them tenderly.

"When I was a child, Doralice used to make hot chocolate for me every time it was freezing at Capella. It was so yummy. Thank you for getting me this. It always makes me feel loved."

"That's the whole point. I want you to feel cherished. I bought you some treats from the same place since you told me you were missing Brazilian food."

"Thank you." I slip closer to him. "When I was a child, my father used to dry my hair and then braid it before I went to sleep so that it wouldn't be like a bird's nest in the morning. I grew so lazy and eventually fell asleep. I sure miss that father."

"You can fall asleep if you want, and I'll take you to bed and tuck you in."

"Thank you, Lev, but I'm in a talking mood. I like telling you about my happy memories. I feel free to talk to you about anything, even when I don't make much sense." I take a sip of the hot chocolate and feel more alert. "I feel that I can say anything to you and not be judged."

"I'm glad."

"When I was a child, my mother played the piano for me as I sang Brazilian folk songs my native Brazilian grandmother taught me. She worshiped me. Oh, I do miss her so! She was so good to me and spoiled me rotten." I lean against his chest. "How about you? Why are you so good to me and do all these nice things for me?"

"Because I, too, worship you. Because you're my type. Because I love you, Sofia."

"Please, do tell me what you like about me."

"Your black, thick hair that falls perfectly down to your waist, your eyes, which are as green as the emerald in your necklace, your smile, your huge laugh, and your sienna skin of the native. Actually, everything, including your scent of rose of attar." He puts his arms around my waist. "I was at my office at the clinic a couple of hours ago and came upon that picture I took of you when you first sang at a Christmas party for the patients. I was impressed by how remarkable you looked. I mean, not only your physical beauty, but a certain je ne sais quoi that draws me to you. There is something about you that I long to understand."

I turn to face him. "Did you have an emergency at the clinic? I thought you weren't ready to return to work, yet."

"I went to talk with Dr. Fleetly about what happened with Dr. Rafael. I looked at your complaint in his file and told Dr. Fleetly that if he didn't fire him, I'd quit, because I'd never work at the same place where a sexual predator practices. What he did to you is intolerable." He looks grave and aggravated. "Tomorrow, I'm reporting him to the Board of Behavioral Sciences, and hopefully he will lose his license."

"What? Why? You can't keep doing things like this, Dr. Lev. This is crazy. The clinic is ground zero for you. Now, all the bad memories will come crashing down on you. I took matters in my own hands, but then you go ahead and solve my problem for me." I stand up.

He gets up. "He committed a crime against you, and I thought just disciplining him wasn't enough. I'm sorry, Sofia, but I can't stand it when vulnerable people are harmed, especially you. It's impossible for me to not do something about it. I'm afraid you'll have to accept that about me."

"Look at you, Dr. Lev. I'm sure you got shot because you were trying to get justice for me and Eli. Isn't that enough pain for you? You may be a great forensic psychiatrist, but you can't see that I'm your blind side. I'm a liability for you. I'll find another place to stay tomorrow, and if you excuse me now, I'll go devise a plan to shoot bad guys and then crash and burn all the alcohol." I walk away in the direction of my room as he follows behind.

"I hope it's a very good one, Sofia. I've just learned that a hundred men from your father's battalion did a sweep at the favela and captured the two men responsible for what happened to me. When they were booked, they vowed that someone from their ring would harm you. Your father called and asked me to convince you to go back home where you'll be safer." He hands me the newspaper.

"And what did you say?" I glance at the headline and put it down on the desk.

"I said that I wouldn't dare, but that I was going to ask you to go to Capella sooner. We've got to take you out of Rio where people can recognize you. You need protection."

I open my handbag, draw out my gun. "Don't worry, it's locked. It can discharge eighteen bullets per minute. I'll make sure there won't be any other Dr. Rafael or Officer Almeida, and that you never get shot again. I'm the one who's going to protect you. You'll never get hurt again—not on my watch."

He looks stunned. "I'm a little sensitive to guns right now. Please, let's put it away if you don't mind."

I put the pistol back in my purse and put the purse inside a drawer of the desk. "Sorry I upset you. I'm just angry that they did that to you. Every time I think of it, I feel such rage. When I learned you got shot, I felt helpless, and so livid that I wanted to make them pay for it. Oh, I feel so distressed right now! It feels like that time when my father threw my blanket in the trashcan as if it were a piece of garbage. I can't stand seeing you hurt, Lev. I love you too much."

"I got you something, and I was going to wait until tomorrow, but I guess this is the just the right time. I'll get it and be right back." He walks away.

The lamp on the desk quenches the darkness. The stargazers he gave me yesterday have blossomed inside a tall lapis lazuli vase. The smell of burned cherry oil suffuses the air. I'm thrilled that my father caught the criminals who shot him. I walk inside the bathroom, take one of my gloves off, and begin to brush my teeth. I must be crazy to show him my gun when the ordeal is still fresh. Tomorrow, I'll double up on his Reiki treatment. I want to get rid of the Prozac that he prescribed for himself. I feel a little lightheaded, go back inside the room, and crack open the window just enough to be able to stick my head out and get some fresh air. I shiver.

The marine layer has fogged up Rio de Janeiro. The neon-lit street looks surreal. The full moon peeks from behind the clouds.

He returns and hands me a thick patchwork quilt. "You said that you always wanted one to use at Capella where it gets mighty cold sometimes."

It's a scrap-quilting pattern with a free-form design. The scraps vary in size and are mostly square or rectangular in shape, with a few triangular pieces grouped into color families like in a color wheel; there are light and dark hues, warm and cool tones and a variety of fabrics that add texture to the blanket. The reverse shows a music themed fabric with musical instruments and notes. The music cleft squares, the violins, pianos, and clarinets make it very elegant. I wonder about the cuts and snips and the scars left behind to be able to make something so remarkable.

"It's gorgeous, Lev. Thank you so much. It's just stellar. The hand-stitched appliqué is flawless."

"I'm sorry I stepped over some boundaries about the incident at the clinic. My love for you gets the best of me, but I know you are smart and courageous enough to deal with your own problems and make the best decisions for yourself. I promise not to interfere in the future."

He puts the blanket around me and holds me close. I feel a wave of heat, something kindling, and then slowly flaming. I feel the warmth of his breath and hear the throbbing of his heart. I hear my blood pumping through my veins. I bring my hand to his face and caress it with my palm. Our eyes are fastened. He kisses me on the mouth. I kiss him back, and then I undo a couple more of the buttons on his shirt and kiss his chest above his heart. The moment is charged with subtle electricity, something silken, yet gritty. He lifts me off my feet, carries me to bed, and drops me down carefully. He lies down next to me.

I continue to unbutton his shirt and kiss his chest. I run my fingers over the long surgical scar beneath his heart. I lean closer and kiss it as lightly as I can. I try to suppress a sudden wash of tears.

The andante begins again. The strings are blue, the wind is green, and the piano black; a thread of exquisite notes that blend together in perfection. To think that Mozart wrote this all in one night after coming home drunk justifies my drunkenness. If I sang now, I'd be at my best.

I hear the notes in the concert and see Elvira running free in a green field in the direction of Lieutenant Sixten. I want that green to heal his scar once and for all. I remember the poultices my grandma used to make out of marigolds to heal the wounds of others. I'll make them for him at the farm.

"Would you like to kiss my scars? I have several. Growing up at Capella was as beautiful as it was rough."

"I'd love to do that, but can you tell me the stories behind them?" He sits against the headboard and then cradles me in his arms.

I show him a tiny scar over my eyebrow. "I don't know how I got this one. It was so long ago."

He clasps a few strands of my hair and pulls them off my face. He kisses the star-shaped scar. His lips feel smooth and warm like the patchwork quilt around me. I remember the passion fruit flesh my grandma used to make maracujá mousse, tarts, and jams that filled me with tingly sweetness, as Lev's touch does.

"What else?"

"I have to take my stocking off to show you the one on my leg." My eyes are focused on his.

"Allow me."

As he takes off my pantyhose, I want to pull back, to stop myself from getting even more involved with him. I know that, soon, I'll be leaving him again to be alone in a foreign land, separated from all I know and care about. I know I'll feel the crippling sorrow of separation, but it's too late to cleave myself from him.

His fingers glide like silk over the scar.

"I was scaling a jabuticaba tree at Capella when I was thirteen and fell on a sharp object. I got nineteen stitches."

As he kisses it, I remember the thousands of gorgeous, white, fluffy flowers all over the trunk and branches of my beloved tree. I breathed in their honey-scented perfume. Then, a few weeks later, thousands of the grape-size glossy black fruits began to smother the trunks and all the branches. I picked the fruit and took a bite through the stringent skin that covered the white flesh. It stained my lips, fingers, and clothes. I filled a whole basket and continued biting into the soft flesh of one, then another, then the rest.

"Anything else?"

"I'll have to take my glove off for this one, the one on the left arm."

"I'll do it." He begins to peel my black glove from my arm.

"My iguana got really mad whenever I put her back in the terrarium, and once she foamed at the mouth and scratched me pretty deeply. After that day, I let her go. The first few days were hard, and it took me great effort to give up my desire to get her back. Sometimes I still imagine her roaming around at Capella. It wasn't easy to set her free, and I feared for her safety day and night. I knew I couldn't keep her from being hurt, and I also knew that letting her go was my only option."

He takes my forearm and traces the long, curving scar. I clasp a few strands of his hair and kiss his face feeling the hardness of his cheek bones but also the smoothness of his skin. Then I kiss him on the mouth, and it's like the deepest notes in the andante, reverberating inside with great intensity, but I remember that intensity can be soft.

"Any more scars, darling?" he whispers.

"Not really, but I have a tattoo. It's a Blue Nestira on a very green leaf." I look into his vivid blue eyes and take a dive in warm waters. "You're gorgeous, Lev."

"So are you, Sofia." His touch is stirring, light and tingling at the same time. It tastes like the cherimoyas I used to eat as I crossed a field of sunflowers that led to the waterfall.

I let go of the quilt, unbutton my dress, and then pull down my bra just enough to show him the tattoo on my left breast. "How do you like it?"

"It's stunning." He begins to kiss the tatuagem and I shut my eyes.

I think of the invisible scars within, the ones that curve, the ones that branch out, the ones that run as deep as a well. Some still throb, others sting, and a few still bleed.

As he makes love to me, I remember walking the tightrope of life without a net, looking at the ground, putting one foot in front of the other. I almost fell three times before I made it to the other side. I climb on top of him and cleave to him as if he were the safety net beneath me, but I know that there are no guarantees.

"I'm so in love with you, Lev. Do you love me back?"

"You have no idea how much I love you, but I'll try to show you."

The music is more resonant than I've ever heard it. It unfolds slowly and evenly. It's a bit more delayed than the usual pace, which makes it even more stunning. The cadence is short, but perfect, with non-legato passages that are maestroso. The individual melody lines are pure magnificence. The pianist has a crisp, light, articulate touch that is gorgeous in nuance, interpretation, and phrasing. Haunting. The orchestra is whispering something almost inaudible, more like a mantra that sets the piano soaring above the violins and cellos. It is music of the highest class. In the end, the piano and orchestra fuse in perfect unison…and then…complete silence, and no more rustling of sheets. There is a world without end outside.

I lie next to him with my head on his chest. He has his arm around me.

"My hair might look like a bird's nest in the morning. Don't freak out." My voice is barely a whisper.

"Do you want me to braid it?" His voice is deep and mellow.

"Oh, yes, please. Sorry for all the hurt I caused you tonight. I blame it on the wine, or maybe the high tides, or it could be the hypnosis session. Isabella's a novice and probably messed my head up."

"No apologies needed." He sits up and begins to braid my hair.

I realize that we just had unprotected sex and that I might get pregnant, which would complicate everything. For one thing, Didier would cancel our contract. Besides, Lev might not want to father a child and, in the end, I'd have to shoulder the responsibility all alone for the pregnancy. In any case, after the trial, I'll be returning to the U.S. to audition for the contest at the Met. I must get out of Rio for my sake and his. I must get started on Plan B in the morning.

He finishes braiding my hair as I begin to fall asleep, thinking that someday I'll travel to Sweden to see the famous grave of Elvira and Sixten on the cemetery of Landet. I hope he'll come with me.

Chapter 14

I finish packing my suitcase at Lev's apartment and put it by the door. I pick up the box with the emerald necklace in it, open it, and put his house key inside. I put it back on top of the desk. There are five unanswered messages from him on my phone. I texted the BOPE officer to pick me up. In ten minutes, I'll leave for Capella and he'll never see me again.

I look outside. The beach is nearly empty as the day ends. The South Atlantic is very green from here. Red flags on the shore signal maré cheia. The ocean is rebellious today. Undertows and whirlpools hide beneath dead waters. It's as dangerous as Officer Almeida and his team of lawyers. I nearly broke down during the deposition, but my desire to get justice for Eli made me strong.

I shift my gaze upward to the gray sky where there is rain in the making. It won't be so bad to go to the farm. I have fond memories of being outdoors at Capella when the rain falls as hard as a wall. One day, after a deluge fell, I ran through green fields, searching for four-leaf clovers, and then I played in the stream. The green forests and the rolling grassland had spread green everywhere. I ambled through the orchard, eating a ripe, juicy peach I picked from a tree. The sun and the wind lingered on my face. The azalea lacewing bugs looked like fancy needlework with their blue, aqua, and purple tints against the leaves. At least, my natural world will bring me peace of mind.

From the speakers, I hear myself singing "Addio del Passato" and turn slowly to see Lev standing at the door.

I gasp. "You're here."

"Shouldn't I be?" He steps closer, his gaze still on me.

"Of course. It's your house. I'm the one who should be gone. Actually, I was just leaving." I nudge my chin to the necklace box on the desk. "Your key to the house is in there."

He steps closer yet. "It's your key."

"Stay in your lane, Dr. Lev." I pull away from his touch.

"Okay, but just tell me why I was stood up? I was at the Russian restaurant, waiting for you. I tried to call you, but you never answered, even though I left numerous messages." He looks perplexed.

"I put it on silence during the deposition, and then I forgot to turn it back on. In any case, I wasn't going to talk to you. I was hoping to get out of here before you stepped in. Actually, my ride is here, if you'll excuse me." I pick up my purse from the desk and step forward, but he blocks me.

"Please don't go before you tell me what happened. I think I deserve to know why you're leaving me without a warning."

I answer the call and let the driver know that I'm not leaving, yet.

"I just realized coming back from the deposition that you were right when you said that I wasn't sober enough to decide to get involved with you. It was a mistake, and I'm sorry if I led you on." I suppress a wash of tears. "You're not the right kind of lover for me. It's better to end this whole thing, now."

"That's not what I heard last night or even this morning. No one had any regrets. You told me you never wanted me to let you go. What's really going on, Sofia? Please tell me."

"My father was there, and he told me that you worked out a deal with the prosecutor—that if your father didn't testify for the defense, he'd get immunity from obstruction of justice for not turning in everything about the investigation done by his agents. How could you take my father's side? Please, step out of the way."

"I can explain if you give me a chance."

"I won't believe a thing you say from now on." I blink back tears.

"You may choose to do that, but I'm telling the truth when I say that I thought it would be too devastating for you to have your own father go against you when it's already so difficult to go through this trial and face what happened all over again. You've been so hurt in all this, including by your own father, that I just wanted to make things a little less overwhelming. I can't stand it when you hurt so much. Besides, if he testifies for the defense, the people who are plotting against you will be emboldened."

I raise my voice. "Stop treating me like a little girl. Lev. I'm a grown woman and can protect myself against my own father or anybody else for that matter. Just so you know, I was the one who went into Eli's apartment to decide what to do with his things because neither his parents nor his brothers could do it. Officer Almeida was the one who let me in when the police tape was still blocking the door. He wore his Gestapo-like uniform and gear. I scrubbed Eli's blood off the walls and carpet. I knew then I could go through anything in life and survive. I can't be with a man who will always try to prevent me from falling or facing pain and sorrow, even when he has to go against his own principles and let a man like my father off the hook."

"I didn't go against my principles. Your father had to pay a high price for not testifying. I demanded he make his platoon's psychiatrist turn in Officer Almeida's records, and I was sifting through it this morning in my office while you were at the deposition. It's a sure way to prevent his lawyers from using the Insanity defense and putting him behind bars for life. I promised you I'd do that, and I will keep my word, Sofia, but you have to trust what I'm doing."

Tears drip down my face. "Still, you've got to stop protecting me from getting hurt, Lev. Why didn't you tell me this before I heard it from my own father?" I soften my tone. "I'm a full-fledged woman, even though it may not seem that way. I know I may seem naïve, but I've been all over the world and have met heads of state and sung at their palaces. I may have been sheltered and escorted everywhere I went, but I'm still a woman who goes after what she wants and is not scared of losing more than she already has. All I asked of you was to treat me like an equal, but apparently, you don't see me as one."

"I never meant to make you feel less than you are. You are my equal and more. I've told you—you're way out of my league, and I respect and admire you a great deal. I love you more than I've ever loved anyone else. I'm sorry. It won't happen again. I promise to consult with you before I make decisions involving you, even if it will hurt you as I suspect it would. Will you give me another chance? Please. I'll let you decide what's best for you."

"Okay, but you must keep your word, or it will be over."

"I promise, darling, but please don't even think of leaving." He peers at me. "I need you by my side."

I step closer. "And I need you, too. I can't see my life without you. You are like no other."

"How was your deposition? Were you able to state everything we went over?"

"I managed. I mean, I went through it without breaking down, even though Officer Almeida's lawyers were merciless. But I stood my ground. I've never felt so strong, so capable of doing anything. They tried to break me, to bend me, but I thought of Eli and I stood firm. They'll never defeat me."

"I always knew you were a remarkable and resilient person, and I'll help you accomplish all your goals if you stay by my side."

"It will be nearly impossible to say goodbye to you."

"You don't have to leave. We'll figure something out that will work for the both of us. I'm not going to lose you. Impossible." He steps even closer and doesn't stop looking at me. "Not after last night." His intensity makes me nearly panic.

I'm torn. I want so much to stay by his side, but I have no choice but to pursue my opera.

"What's buzzing tonight? Do you have any good food in this joint?"

I shrug.

"I got you stroganoff from the restaurant where I was stood up, and a whole chocolate cake from Confeitaria Colombo since you said you can't eat any of this stuff in Los Angeles. Do you want to eat, now?"

"Sorry, Lev, but I have to run to the pharmacy to get a prescription before I forget."

"Are you sick? What do you need a prescription for?"

"Nothing, really. Just a migraine. I've been getting a lot of them lately. Maybe it's all the tension leading up to the trial—or the alcohol last night."

"Why didn't you ask me?" He looks puzzled. "Actually, I have something in the house that's pretty safe."

"My doctor called it in, you know. I don't want to waste his time."

"Which pharmacy did he call? I'll get it for you. There's a hit on your life, Sofia, and your father says we might have to leave for Capella at any time."

"Please, I don't want to feel like a prisoner in my own city. I promise you that I'll go to Capella in a few days and stay put. I think you worry too much. I'll drive the bullet-proof car."

"Okay, but take your gun with you, since you insist on going alone. How about I ask one of the officers to get your prescription."

"I'll let the officer drive me there. Hey, didn't you say you were going to show me something in your room? I'm dying to see it."

"Yes, I've kept it under wraps for a while." He takes me by the hand and leads me out of my room and down the hallway and into his bedroom.

It is spacious and bright. A cherry-colored couch sits across from the large bed. The Brazilwood furniture is a sad reminder that my beloved trees are now endangered. Two solid bronze pots sit on the handsome antique table against the wall. They have been engraved with a wealth of graceful flowers, fruit, and foliage in a naturalistic style. They are only surpassed in beauty by the red-and-white orchid plants they hold. A bookcase filled with books on classical music, the brain and pharmacology, and forensic psychiatry.

Detail from the Wheat Field, by Van Gogh, hangs on the slate wall. The vivid yellow wheat and the contrasting colors disguise the shadows underneath. The unpredictable and uneven juxtaposition of colors speak of my own mismatched feelings. Being back in Rio brings conflicting emotions, especially knowing that I'll be leaving for Los Angeles eventually.

The rain falls outside. The deluge will cause a lot of damage. How I wish we'd never be worlds apart now that we've become so intimate.

"Before I show you the real surprise, I want you to look inside this." He hands me a metallic green gift bag lined with golden tissue paper. "I got these things for you this afternoon."

I draw an umbrella out of the bag. I open it and gaze at the motif, The Woman in Gold, by Klimt. I gasp. "This is exquisite, Lev. Thank you." I recall the story behind the painting. The sitter's niece was a Jewish refugee who escaped Austria and years later recovered the stolen art. I put it down on the floor and pull out a box of Godiva dark chocolate. "How did you know I was craving it?"

"You told me that Didier doesn't let you have any for reasons beyond my understanding, so I got you this. Go on, get your next gift."

I draw out a book on braiding hair. "This is so cool. I've always wanted one."

"Now I can do a different braid every time you're about to fall asleep after you make love to me."

"I really like your vibe." I reach out and kiss him on the cheek. "Thank you for this. It's so special." I put the book down on the desk.

"Now, the second big surprise," he says. He pulls a sheet off a wall hanging above his desk, revealing my own portrait. It's from the photograph he took of me the first time we practiced together, the one in which I wore the emerald necklace for the first time.

"This is stunning, Lev. Still, I look very much like my late grandmother, just a brown woman from the Amazon Rainforest. I guess the expensive jewel doesn't hide where I come from and what I am made of." I turn to face him.

"No wonder it's warm, earthy, sensual—and yet sophisticated. Your raw beauty is as classic as it is distinctive." He reaches out and lets my hair loose.

"It looks perfect, now." He steps closer and puts his arms around me. He buries his face in my hair, and I feel his breath on my neck. "You're my goddess of love, and I'll treat you like one."

"You're so biased." I feel my heart beating fast and my blood pumping through my veins.

"Is it true that you made a mistake last night or is it not? I think I deserve to know."

I wrap my arms around his waist. "Last night I didn't want to be left alone, and I didn't pretend to be something I was not. I knew that I could pull through no matter what, that I could use my magic to make bad guys weak. Last night, I was a woman who could do anything. I could catch or kill anything, had special powers and abilities, and I became addicted to making love to a man who braided my hair in the most careful way. And I promise, it wasn't the alcohol."

"That's the very reason I'll restructure my whole life around yours and support your art," he says in a matter-of-fact voice. "You'll have anything you want because I'll be at your side and make sure it happens." He speaks more softly. "I'm sure it took hundreds of millions of years of evolution to create a woman like you. Just the musicality you were born with is astonishing; it makes you so supple. At some point, there is perfect order. And then, it shifts, and there is something disquieting about you, maybe the eyes that appear soulful and yet daydreaming at times, upsetting the balance you yearn to achieve. But this skewed balance is very attractive to me." He takes me by the hand and leads me to the couch.

"Please, you are the one whose nature took thousands of millions of years to make, and I am lucky to have found you."

We sit side by side. "Do you still want me to be your accompanist? I promise I'll work hard for you and get you to where you need to be, darling, if you stay with me."

"I know you would, Lev, but Brazil isn't good for opera, right now. The quality of our music has decreased considerably, and besides, the country is falling apart because of all the corruption. There is even the threat of impeaching Dilma Russeff, which is making things extremely unstable. I've got to pursue my opera elsewhere." I kiss him on the cheek. "I'm so sorry to have to go. I guess I was over my head last night, thinking that I could stay in Brazil. I hate myself for having to leave you behind. I must win the competition. Didier says he'll get me there."

"I'll wait for you to return, and then we'll work together and be together at all times."

His fingers run down my face. He kisses me on the mouth, and I kiss him even harder.

He takes a green jewelry box out of his pocket, opens it, and shows me a striking diamond necklace. "This jewel came from my Grandmother Lyudmila's heirloom necklace. She managed to hide when she was in Auschwitz. She made a shorter one by removing one of the six strands. She gave it to me so that I could make something out of it to give to the woman I'd one day marry. A month ago, I took it to a jeweler and asked him to add one more layer so that it looks like the original owned by my grandmother, as well as the one worn by Adele in the The Lady in Gold portrait.

I blink back tears. "I can't possibly accept this, Lev. It's too much of a responsibility. I can't even think of damaging or losing something so precious. And besides, I'm not worthy of it."

"Please accept it. It belongs to you." He fastens it around my neck.

I lean against his chest and feel his breath. I recall his scar and the danger he faces by being involved with me. I touch the necklace, and my heart breaks to know that it has such a poignant history. A tide of feelings overwhelms me, and I feel an urge to run a whole league. I want to tattoo him onto my skin. But if it could cause him any harm, I'd rather harm myself. He invites me to reach deeper and isn't a bit concerned with my impetuous style; in fact, he welcomes it. He has impeccable tolerance for my imperfections. With him, there is no drifting by on the surface.

"I love you so much, Lev." I reach out and kiss him. "With you, it feels like I'm on the verge of something I can't name."

He kisses me back with the same passion as his first kiss.

The objects in the room eavesdrop, certain that our love for one another has been bound by the peril we face every minute of the day, which makes me doubt my choice of getting involved with him all over again.

"I can't stand being the culprit of the crime committed against you. This love I feel for you goes against you. If I stay, you might pay the ultimate price, and I'll be damned if I let it happen."

"Love is never a crime," he says. "We belong together. We'll figure this whole thing out."

There is pouring rain outside, but I can still hear the ocean, the waves surging and fading away.

"I'll get you some dinner, if you want."

"Yes, please, I'm starved and parched."

"It won't take long." He gets up "Would you like some wine?"

"No, thank you. I'm still under the inauspicious grip of a hangover." I half-lie on the couch.

"Just stay put while I fix everything." He walks to the desk and turns on the iPad. "Just listen to yourself singing *Rusalka*. Later, I'll play the piano and you sing to me. Deal?"

"Yes. Thank you for everything, Lev."

"You bet." He walks away.

It is extraordinary how after all he has been through—a bullet aimed at his heart and two weeks in the ICU plus one more in a regular hospital room—he still faces everything with such courage and optimism.

I get up, walk to the window, and look at the sea. Blue. Familiar. But the familiar is fading since I left my father's house. Didier wants me to adjust to my new culture, and I feel ever more attracted to the unfamiliar. I no longer want "old Sofia" to be in charge of my life.

Maybe Didier is right when he says that Brazilians are far more reliant on each other than Americans. But it feels lonely to be too independent. In Brazil, we live in clusters and talk to each other even when there is nothing to say. Or maybe I don't know how to be autonomous. Mama didn't raise me that way except that my love for my opera is making me break free from my own culture.

Still, even when I was a girl, everything I ever thought or did had fire in it, if not fire per se, something of a blazing quality, as if a great fire could burst forth at any time. All I know is that I'm running in many different directions, and it's hard to say where I will end up when my career reaches a magical plateau and one of my greatest desires is fulfilled. Will I still be the Sofia that I know? I wonder if I'm going to wither on foreign soil. I wonder if anything Brazilian will be left of me where Didier commands. But if I win the Met competition, Brazil will be forced to give me the credit I deserve, and I will be able to spend most of my time performing in my own land so that I can be near Lev.

With him, I feel that I'm diving into a healing ocean, and I want to stay put until the last tide of my day has gone out, until I have mended the broken pieces of my life. With him, I begin to revert to my original state and find the way back to myself. With him, everything is as it should be.

Still, I'll have to leave all that he has to offer so that I can become the opera singer I am meant to me.

"Sofia," Lev calls. "Are you ready to have dinner, now?"

I turn to face him. "Yes, thank you." I walk to him and we both head to the living room. I think I could get used to it, but I better not. I must remember to get my Plan B at the pharmacy later. There may even be a need for a Plan C, but today I just want to sing *Rusalka* to him and feel like the nymph from the opera by Dvorjak—I want to know human love, even if I have to become a death spirit in the bottom of a lake.

Chapter 15

Along the entry to Capella stretches at least a mile of verdant fields, gardens, an orchard, and the one-hundred myrtles my father helped me plant since I was eleven. It is late afternoon, and I'm riding Vento. It is empty and quiet on the riding trail. I see the most beautiful sunset. It is orange, yellow, and bright. I see the tall pine trees against it. A light rain begins to fall. We are trotting. It is beautiful with the wind on my face. I am one with my horse. It's kind of him to take me on this ride. If he wanted to, he could have caused a lot of damage, and in the end what could I possibly have done about that? He weighs 1,200 pounds, and there is nothing I can do to stop him. He takes me back to my core, a place where no one has a claim on me, no one treads on me, not even lightly, and no one approaches me uninvited. I feel there isn't anything that can't be solved by riding Vento.

He trots past the pond along the serpentine path. The dark greenery all around guides us further into the lush growth. A disorder of leaves from the pink floss tree blanket the ground. The hydrangeas along the way thrive despite the sudden cold spell. The red bougainvillea spreads over the copper trellises. Such winter moods evoke a combination of fragility and strength on my ranch. The field of marigolds is a carpet of red, yellow, and brownish blossoms that go on for miles. There are billions, thousands of millions of blooms; how can I leave this world behind to go back to Los Angeles and the artificial garden Didier has created for me, however glamorous?

But how I long to sing at the Met. I long to sing "Ah! Non credea mirarti." The aria from *La Sonnambula* is meant for sopranos who can weep with their voices. I can do that. First, I hit a high F and let it float, then my legato connects the notes in a smooth, even manner, and then my pianissimo is soft and quiet with some color in it, first indigo and then purple. The colors of bruises show that Amina's flowers lasted one day and are now dead. Like the lover who has gone away forever, not even her tears will bring them back. I must go back to pursue my opera.

The hardest thing of all is to say goodbye to Lev. We've become very close these past five weeks we've been together. He has been helping me practice my arias whenever I Skype with Madam Prunier. He's a gifted pianist and very patient. For the most part, Madame makes me repeat a phrase ten times to get it just right, although sometimes, I do my own thing and disregard one rest or another, tampering with the mark the great composer put there to indicate silence. Madam thinks it's outrageous. She tells me: "Listen to Gruberova, Mademoiselle; she sings it the way it's meant to be, as Bellini intended."

A week ago, Lev and I saw a meteor shower, which, according to NASA, was shooting out from its radiant point in the constellation Auguri where the star Capella is. NASA also mentioned that the universe will probably end in what they are calling a Big Crunch, a Big Freeze, or a Big Rip. They're not sure. It is a very expensive guessing game. I turn a corner. When I think of leaving Vento, my farm, and Lev behind, it feels as though my own universe is about to end in either a Big Rip, a Big Crunch, or a Big Freeze. I'm not sure, either, and like NASA, I keep changing my mind.

We arrive at the stable. The moonlight floods my hair, face, and shoulders. It spreads over the yellow asphodels with their eerie gray leaves. The sacred flowers of Persephone lead me back to my darkness. The wind has messed up my hair, and I regret not braiding it. It's getting tangled. My heart is tangled. My world is tangled. How can I leave what sustains me? I dismount and hand Vento to Eduardo. Doralice's youngest son takes care of my precious child whenever I am away and Lev is in Rio.

"Thank you for taking such good care of Vento, Eduardo."

"I like to do this for you, Sofia. Are you staying for good?"

"I can't, but Dr. Lev and the trainer will be coming on and off to ride him, too."

"I'll feed him some carrot cookies."

"Thank you." I step away and walk to the guesthouse.

The wind whispers as it used to when I was a child through the gossamer veil that separates the invisible from the visible. The melody blowing forth brings good news from the Great Goddess of Wind. Evening bird calls, chirps, and other sounds suddenly make a netherworld materialize, and I can almost see my bambuzinas, the angel spirits that play amongst the bamboo. I used to run to them, the bearer of good and bad news, and suddenly tripping on a salamander, I would scrape a knee. But soon I was feeling all better and running in the wind on the narrow path.

I wonder if there is a way to stay in Rio and still sing at the Met in September. But Didier won't agree to that. The contract says that I must follow all his instructions, and if I breach our agreement, he'll rescind it. If he cancels it, I'll lose all the connections he alone can offer and my dream will be over.

I enter the guesthouse. It is set away from the main building. It's a cottage with two bedrooms, a living and dining room, and a kitchen. It's deep-red and nearly hidden behind tall pine trees and plants that blossom all year long. The walls inside are marine-blue and the windows that open wide have deep-red sills with some gold in them. The fireplace is always lit in the winter, since Friburgo can freeze during July and August. I love the trails and the bucolic spots beyond the cottage. Everything looks rustic, but there are modern appliances and even Wi-Fi.

I enter the bedroom. A green hexagonal table next to the bookcase is filled with opera scores and librettos. The marine-blue walls have an outline of gold, which sounds grandiose but is subtle. There is a rustic wood fireplace, and above the mantel, a flat-screen television attached to the wall. A print of The Kiss by Gustav Klimt is mostly gold, with some black and a bunch of yellow, purple, and red flowers. It's a great way to interpret love. This is how a woman should be adored by her man.

I focus on the portrait of a woman. Her lilac dress emphasizes conflicting emotions. Her eyes are soft and heavy at the same time. Even though executed with steady, solid lines, her figure nearly blends with the landscape, especially the pink floss tree that serves as background. She seems to be dissolving as the sunlight filtering through the foliage floods her face.

There is a photograph of me dressed in a black coat and a cream-and-black skirt in front of tall trees with black bark. The play of light and shadow reminds me that color doesn't come easily to the life of an opera singer who is always immersed in gloomy drama and deep sorrow. This time, though, I had just returned from my grandma's funeral.

I often sit down on the small couch by the fireplace to watch videos of me and decide what needs to be improved.

There is a flower arrangement on top of the piano. It's a combination of color and form, tall willow leaves, blossoms of purple irises and lilac hibiscus. The essence of each flower, branch, or twig shows through even though they have been stylishly arranged.

The Brazilian flag on top of the piano has a constellation on it. I remember the names of the stars: Alpha, Beta, Gamma, Delta, and Epsilon. The fifth letter of the Greek alphabet means a small quantity of anything, which right now is the amount of my desire to go back to America and to Didier. I'm sure I'll never be able to become the superwoman he wants me to be. It isn't humanly possible, but that's him. He, the perfectionist, wants everything to fall into place without a flaw. Maybe I should stay with Lev. All he asks of me is that I be myself, and the more I am myself, the more he seems to like me. I could get used to that.

But I long to sing "Deh Vieni, non Tardar" from *The Marriage of Figaro*. Susana's aria is delightful. Too bad the last time I sang it, the orchestra didn't come in on time. The conductor seemed desperate and gave them a cue, and still the first violins missed the downbeat. Let's hope that doesn't happen at the Met. "Deh, Vieni non tardar oh gioia bella. Oh! Don't delay, oh joy, my love." This one I'll sing as written. It's Mozart. Every note has to be just perfect. He would be proud. Indeed, "music is mathematical perfection" as he once said. Madam Prunier will be proud. The Met will be proud. There is no turning back.

I grab a towel from the closet and head for the bathroom. In a week's time, I'll be in the courtroom, testifying against Officer Almeida. I turn on the shower. Even though Lev has gone over my deposition with me at least ten times, I still fear the cross-examination that will certainly come from the defense team. Even though Judge Levien will be presiding, I still fear having to face that criminal in a court of law. I'm terrified of making a mistake. Even though Lev will be there, I still fear falling apart and not being able to give my testimony to prove how depraved Almeida's heart is, why he is called Totenkopf. Hopefully, I'll be able to keep things together until the end. Hopefully, the prosecution will show the jury how Totenkopf destroyed, in fact, two lives. It was true that, after his death, I left the opera and put my career on hold for too long.

My red nightgown and my red challis robe with its golden-garlands motif feel warm and soft. The red slippers keep my feet warm. The temperature has gone down considerably. I hear the crackling of the fire in the fireplace. I grab a brush from the vanity and walk to the window. The rain is now falling as hard as a wall, rain of unequaled beauty, unequaled power, and unequaled ebullience.

I walk to the bed and pull the comforter off. Maybe I should rest a bit so that when Lev comes, I'll be less tired. I lie on the quilt he gave me in Rio that first night when we made love. I reach out and pick up a seed pod I brought in yesterday from a container on top of the bedside table. I hold the husk, thinking that inside it there is a tree and that I'll certainly plant it behind the cottage.

I hear a knock on the door. "Come in," I say and then put the brush down on the windowsill.

Lev opens the door and walks up to me. He kisses me on the cheek. "How was your ride?" He looks handsome in his blue jeans and black sweater. He looks even younger and full of verve. No more signs of illness or stress.

"It was the ride of a lifetime, with a glorious sunset and all." I smile. "Vento is so good to me."

"You deserve it. Do you want to eat? I got dinner ready for you. I set the table in the dining room, but I can bring your food to you, if you prefer, to eat at the table in this room." He walks up, puts his briefcase on top of the dresser, and then comes to me. He helps me up.

"Would you mind bringing the food up, Lev? I'm a bit fatigued, but I am starved and parched. I missed you so much." I circle my arms around his waist.

He holds me tight and kisses me on the mouth. "I've missed you greatly, Sofia. I'll get your food and be right back."

"Thank you for everything."

"My pleasure." He leaves.

Now that he's back, I realize how much I've missed him. He casts out the fear in me, and makes me feel that I'm strong enough to deal with the trial ahead and my upcoming audition. The competition at the audition will be fierce, but we have worked hard together, and I will prevail. But the trial…I just hope I won't fall apart when they show photos of Eli's autopsy. I have to make myself very strong for that. I walk to the fireplace and light a green candle that's on top of the mantel. I turn on the television and click on Didier's channel. I click on the clip of "Ah, non credea mirarti" and watch myself singing at the command of Madame Prunier. She is a great teacher and was able to build on my strengths. I don't know what I'd do without her.

Lev returns with a silver platter, filled with exotic fruit, green cherimoyas, orange passion fruit, reddish cashews, and deep purple jabuticabas, an edible color wheel. He puts it down on the wooden table by the window. "Please have a seat. Let's eat while listening to this brilliant rendition of one of the most beautiful arias there is."

"These fruits are so exquisite. Where did you even find them?" I sit down across from him.

"At a new specialty store in town. Once you said that, when you were on a tour, you stayed at the Hotel das Cataratas in Brazil's Iguaçu National Park. You said that before the performance, they served drinks and a platter of fruit so exotic, you could only identify the cherimoyas. You told me that the luxury was so beyond anything you could afford that you were a bit unsettled. I hope you like my version of it. I got the best Brazilian fruit I could find. And this is a mango margarita made with Brazilian rum."

"Wow, I'm so impressed. Thank you for this."

My eyes are drawn to a vase sitting on the credenza. It holds a single magenta laelia orchid. "This is stunning," I take a deep breath.

"Do you still love the national flower?" he asks.

"Yes, although she's now a hybrid called cattleya." I help myself to some fruit. "Thank you for such an indulgence."

"You're welcome." He gazes at me. "Did I mention today how much I love you?"

"Yes, but I don't mind hearing it again, Lev. I love you, too."

We sit at the table across from each other. I put my plate down, pick up a few berries, and pop them in my mouth. I remember that Mama used to give me jabuticaba popsicles throughout summer.

He pours me a margarita.

"Sorry, Lev. I'm not drinking alcohol, but I'll have some guava juice." I scoop some of my passion fruit flesh with a spoon and think of Grandma Iracema. I take a bite of my cashew fruit and remember filling a whole basket with the fruit I picked from a tree, then biting into the soft flesh of one, then another, then another, then the rest.

He picks up half of his cherimoya and hands it to me.

I pick up a spoon and scoop out the brown seeds embedded in the white milky flesh. I taste the silky pulp that has hints of at least six ambrosial flavors. I remember that night in Hotel das Cataratas when I was a bit high and filled with exhilaration, especially after we performed the *Bachianas Brasileiras No. 5*.

He scoops some of his cherimoya. "I think you'll like to know that I've just found out that Officer Almeida is affiliated with a group founded in 2002 in Santa Catarina, the Townlands. The leader is an economist living in São Paulo; reportedly, he sought to advance the group's agenda of white racial supremacy through political means as well as violence. His members in Rio carried out ten killings during the month of December 2014, reportedly targeting blacks, homosexuals, and Jews. Two of their members had a hit out on you, Sofia, but they've been arrested by your father and will be arraigned by my father. Sorry, I didn't tell you ahead of time. I was concerned about you getting anxious over it."

I'm stunned. It's as though I'm speaking to the same Lev, but he isn't the same. There is a hard edge to him I've never seen before, as if he had peeled off a soft layer. But he is still super-calm and collected. "They'll kill you, Lev." I feel a bit lightheaded.

I get up and rush to the bathroom, lift the toilet cover up, and begin to throw up. Lev comes in and stands next to me. He holds my hand and offers support. I stop, flush the toilet, and then begin to throw up again. I feel cold. I flush the toilet one more time. I finally feel well enough to get hold of myself.

"Thank you for giving me a hand. I hate this part." I walk to the sink, pick up my toothbrush and toothpaste, and brush my teeth. I swish some mouthwash in my mouth and keep it there for a long time. Then, I wash my face and dry it with a towel.

"I feel much better. Thank you for helping me." I smile. "It's over for now."

"You have more color." He follows me back inside the bedroom. "What do you mean by 'I hate this part,' Sofia?"

"I'm pregnant with your child-to-be, Lev. I'm hoping you'll be alive when I have your child in February." My eyes well up. "But I don't see how. Your obsession with crushing neo-Nazi cells will rob you from me and your baby." I fight a wash of tears. "Please stop it."

"You're pregnant? Are you 100 percent sure?" He steps closer. "You're pregnant?" He looks thrilled.

"Yes. I was three weeks late, so I took a test on Thursday and one this morning, and both came out positive."

He puts his arms around me. "This is so exciting, Sofia. This is great news. You made me so happy just now. Why didn't you call me? I'd have come up earlier, darling."

"I didn't want you to have to take any responsibility for it. I had stopped taking contraceptive pills three weeks before coming to Rio. I guess I wanted to get pregnant, and I wanted you to father my child, but it's hardly fair to you. I was going to tell you when I got to L.A. in a couple of weeks." I lean against his chest. "But the nausea is just too strong."

"I think thirty-four is way past the age of consent, don't you think? I could have said no, but I wanted you. I love you and this baby you're carrying. I'd love to be a part of it, all of it. And you did well getting pregnant by me. I wanted the same thing, and I'm glad it didn't happen the other way around, as you seemed to have wanted." He reaches inside his pocket and takes out a small box. "Is that why I found this Plan B prescription on top of the desk by your necklace? And a glass of water left untouched? Later on, I found the pill next to your necklace when I was going to put it in the safe."

"No wonder it didn't work. I forgot I hadn't taken it. It was so hard to get it out and when I did, it was flung somewhere. I was ready to sue the manufacturer. I guess my father told us to get out of Rio right away, and I didn't get to take it."

"Why didn't you share your concerns with me? I thought you trusted me."

"Sorry, Lev, but I didn't want to be influenced by anyone one way or another." I feel tears start. "I thought it would be a mistake to get pregnant at this point and asked my doctor to give me the pills, but now it's kind of late."

"I'm glad you didn't take it. Do you have a Plan C in mind, Sofia, or are we having a child?"

"There is only Plan A, Lev. I can't imagine having an abortion. I want this baby so much, especially now that I'm about to lose my ranch. My father was here and said that if I testify and lose the case, he'll sell it. It's still in the trust, and I won't have access to it until I'm twenty-eight. Oh, Lev, I love my land as much as I love this life growing inside me."

"Don't testify, then."

"Who do you think I am? I will get justice for Eli. Besides, how pathetic of me to worry so much about losing my piece of land when my grandmother's tribe might lose all of their land. Oh, Lev, I must do something about it! I must win the contest and help Greenpeace fight Brazil."

"I'll help you raise the money, I promise, but I don't think I'll agree with you returning to Los Angeles. The pregnancy is a game-changer."

"My audition is coming up, and although we have practiced a lot, I need Madam Prunier to help me solidify everything. I'm sorry, Lev, but I need Didier. I know he'll be pretty angry about you and me and the baby, but I think he'll still help me even though the contract says 'no pregnancy.'"

The rain continues to fall.

"Why don't you just rip that contract apart, Sofia? You don't need it. You don't need Didier, either. You think you do, but you don't. You're a great singer and have mastered your technique. You can do anything you want, when and how you want to do it. Please stay, and we'll both fly to New York in September for your audition. I'll take a leave of absence and be by your side."

"It's not that simple. He has all the connections I need to succeed in that world. I promise I'll keep in touch with you and tell you all about the baby."

"I don't think I can keep from interfering. Didier forbade you to eat foods you like so that he can control your weight. He is a controlling man and will not take no for an answer. He might ask you to have an abortion. If you go, you're putting yourself and our baby in danger. My advice to you is to stay in Rio and let me help you get your career on track."

I take a step back. "Even though you're so damn fine, Lev, I'd never marry a man who thinks he owns the woman in his life. Maybe it has worked for you in the past, but it won't this time. I'm not your typical Brazilian girl who will put up with her lover's controlling ways." My voice sounds brittle to my ears.

He peers at me. "I'm not trying to control you. I don't want to oppress you, but I dread the fact that Didier might hurt you in some way just because a pregnancy is a big obstacle to his idea of making you into his own diva, someone who will have no other purpose in life but to feed into his fantasy of having a version of you that isn't you. He changed your name to Sophie Morpho and expects you to become her. He decides everything for you and prevents you from doing what you want to do."

"So, don't be like him, because that's exactly what you're doing. I have the right to make my own decisions, including keeping or not keeping this baby I'm carrying, even if you are the father. I'm certain that I won't have an abortion and that I can stand up to Didier and keep my child. He is not going to do to me what my father did when I was seventeen. I'll buy back my freedom as soon as I can. Would you sell my emerald necklace so that I can pay my debt to him? It's in the thousands of dollars."

"No. You're not selling anything. I'll give you the money."

"So that you can own my body, too? No, thank you. I'll get a loan and pay it in full in June when I turn twenty-eight and will be able to use the money in my trust."

"Then let me loan it to you. You gave me power of attorney when you first arrived in America, and I can pay myself back at any time I want. Actually, I can use all your money if I choose to. See how trusting you are? You did that. You knew me as your supervisor, but not much more. Didier will take advantage of you."

"You don't have to worry, Lev. You must trust me and keep your promise of not interfering with my decision to return to Los Angeles. Don't put any more pressure on me. This pregnancy will probably be as hard as my first one was until week 12, before I lost that baby I so much wanted, but I will be able to handle it with the proper care."

"Do you know if you have *hyperemesis gravidarum*?"

"Yes. During my first pregnancy I had to be hospitalized for a week because I couldn't stop throwing up and had an aversion to food, and that's how my father found out I was carrying Eli's baby."

"I talked to Dr. Fleetly and told him that I'll no longer work at the clinic and will just wait for a replacement. This gives me more freedom to fly to you and help you in more concrete ways."

"But you love your work at the clinic! Please don't stop doing something you love because of me."

"I've made up my mind. I love you too much to stay separated for long periods of time. I told you I wanted to follow you wherever you go. I applied for a grant and will be doing research, which will allow me to work from anywhere in the world." He steps closer and holds me in his arms. "How many times did you throw up today?"

"Three times, but I drank a lot of coconut water. I will be fine."

"You look mighty tired, Sofia. Let me take your vitals. Would you please lie down for me?"

"Yes. I'm exhausted." I walk back to the bed and lie down.

He gets his stethoscope and his blood pressure equipment out of his briefcase and sits next to me in bed. He begins to take my pulse and then listens to my chest. "Your heart rate is a bit fast." He checks my blood pressure. "Would you consider changing doctors? My mother is a surgical obstetrical nurse and works with Dr. Aaron in a private hospital in Rio. She also has training as a midwife and can support you throughout your pregnancy."

"I'll think about it."

"You have low blood pressure. I want you to consider returning to Rio tomorrow if you throw up more than twice. It's not safe to be at the farm if you get too dehydrated. It can be life-threatening."

"I'm just fine, just fatigued, and a good sleep will restore my body. I'm so happy to be pregnant that it really doesn't matter how difficult the first trimester will be. I promise to take in a lot of fluids tomorrow. I want to stay at Capella for another week. When I'm in nature, there's just beauty. It is what it is. There is no right or wrong. I love to ride Vento. He's my special connection with the wild. I love to feel the rhythm and the warmth of his body."

He lies down next to me. "Let's take it one day at a time, okay? Your well-being is my primary concern. You must understand that I'm a doctor by profession."

He strokes my hair, and I feel my eyelids growing heavier. He is present, in the moment. He's always able to read my body and my breath. He offers me the gift of his presence and kindness. He seems to be grounded in the quiet confidence of one who has nothing to prove, and yet he can also be vulnerable and show me what brings him to his knees. He doesn't pretend to be someone he's not. His unquenchable thirst for knowledge makes him very sexy to me, and besides, his idea of funny syncs with mine.

"You're so damn fine that I'll never let go of you, Dr. Lev. I can't believe you love me so much, but know that I love you more." My voice is barely a whisper.

"It's Lev, okay? Let's practice. Someday, I hope soon, I'll be your husband and will be helping you raise our child. And just so you know, I love you with the greatest depth, Sofia. When I was in the hospital, my mother said that she had been the most important woman in my life until you showed up. She is 100 percent right."

"Good."

"Would you like me to braid your hair?"

"Yes, please."

I reach out and pick up a seed pod from the bedside table and hold it in my hand. He braids my hair. I hold on to the pod. I can feel the seed's energy, the life force within it. It has awakened in me a desire to nurture my own seed, the one that is growing inside me. These seed pods could grow to become thirty-foot tall pink floss trees, native to my land. They do exceptionally well on rain-prone Capella grounds. Tomorrow, I'll fling these babies in the warm and moist soil, cover them with water, and give them a chance to become the trees they're meant to be. They are throbbing with life, just as my embryo is trembling with life. I feel really emotional to know that these seeds and I are one and the same. The impulse for life is strong in both of us. I will burst forth with life. The tree will bear fruit and so will I. We are one and the same. I'm one with my land, just as they are.

"Done, darling." He kisses my head. "Now, I'm going to read a comment from a blog about you." He picks up his iPad and begins to read.

> Sophie Morpho has been living and performing in the United States for the last six months. She is an outstanding performer, this magnificent Sofia de Menezes! Brazilian pride! She is as perfect a singer as she is gorgeous. Her voice is divine. Bravissima! Brazil has yet to recognize this national treasure. Maybe when she wins the Met competition in September her land will give her the credit she is due.

"Do you see how special you are? You mustn't allow Didier to have any claim on you, Sofia. You're a brilliant artist, and people all over the world love you. Don't let him put you down. He should be the one bending over backwards to please you for allowing him to manage your career. You don't need him."

"Yes, I do. I must win the contest if Brazil is to pay any attention to me. Someday, my dream will come true, and you will be my accompanist. Are you going to follow through with your promise?"

"Yes. I'll change my life to follow you around the world. I give you my word. I love you, I want you, I need you."

"I love you more, I want you more, I need you more." I open my hand. "Lev, would you please put my seed pod on the bedside table. There is a tree in there." I mumble this right before I drift into sleep.

Chapter 16

I am taking the stand in Judge Daniel Levien's courtroom. If a pin dropped, I'm sure I could hear it. I never thought this day would come. Officer Almeida does not look evil sitting there in his black suit and tie, but I know better. Today, he will face his own brutality, and I am the mirror he will be looking into. My classic black dress makes me look more mature. I put my hair in a low bun for the same reason. The thought of being pregnant gives me even more courage to fight for justice for Eli. I'm growing a life inside me, and the father is a Jewish man who will later show this jury how Officer Almeida's hatred for Eli's heritage is what ultimately drove him to kill Eli.

Lev sits exactly across from me in the last row on the right side. He looks like his father, the judge, who is also tall and well-built. His mother sits by his side. Her Russian heritage makes her different from most Brazilians. She looks as European as my mother. I spot my father on the other side of the room from where Lev is sitting. At least he is not wearing his Gestapo-like uniform. I swallow hard, trying not to shed tears, although old wounds have been opened and are bleeding again. My mother sits by his side, although I know she's standing by me and has given me her support.

The prosecutor walks towards me. Sarah Bechara is in her thirties. Her curly hair and dark brown eyes remind me of Eli's. She is of small build, but looks as tough as she has turned out to be. Lev has kept me informed of her performance in the courtroom, and I am impressed.

"Please state your name, age, profession, and relationship with the victim."

"My name is Sofia de Lourdes de Menezes. I'm twenty-seven, an opera singer, and Eli was my fiancé."

"Thank you, Senhorita Sofia. How long did you know Senhor Eli Levatter?"

"Four years, since I was seventeen."

"That's a long time. So, can you say that you knew him very well?"

"Yes."

"Can you please describe a little bit of what he was like?" She speaks in a calm voice.

"Eli was a true artist in every sense of the word. He was an opera singer and an accomplished musician who played the piano very well. He loved and respected nature. He was a loving man, a true friend, and a wonderful partner. Every Sunday, we raced through the newspaper crossword puzzles, but it was no contest because Eli would be finished with it before lunch while I was still struggling. Even though he was only one year my senior, he was wise and a true gentleman. Yet, no matter what I say, I'll never do him justice. I loved him with all my heart and will always mourn him. Experts talk about closure, but that never took place." I blink back tears. "He will always be missed."

"Thank you. That was very clear."

"Your Honor, I'd like to play a clip of the victim and witness playing and singing together. I want to demonstrate how close a bond Sofia and Eli had. They seemed to belong together in a beautiful world they created for themselves."

"Objection, Your Honor, this is not an opera house," the defense lawyer interjects.

"Overruled. You may play the clip."

Sarah continues. "Ms. Sofia, can you please tell us where this took place and when?" She clicks on the controller and I appear, dressed in a shimmering golden dress on a stage in Brussels with Eli in a black suit, sitting at the piano."

"This was during the semi-final of a voice competition in Belgium. I'm singing "Ah! Non credea mirarti" by Bellini, and Eli is my accompanist. I won the competition mainly because of him. He knew how to bring out the best in me both as a singer and a person."

"Thank you." She clicks on a green button, and Eli begins to play the first note of the aria. He looks so sublime that tears drip down my face.

I remember how deep and heartfelt my singing was that night. My performance was greeted by a wave of spontaneous applause, but both Eli and I were able to keep going without a hitch. He played with all his talent and skills. He smiled from time to time when I put all my feelings and soul into the piece. It really was stunning. I seem to be surrounded by golden light—very moving.

The aria ends and the crowd applauds, going wild, shouting, "Brava!" and "Gorgeous!" I watch as Eli stands up and moves next to me. We hold hands and bow in unison. We had a strong connection and perfect chemistry. I still can't believe we'll never play and sing together again.

"Thank you, Senhorita Sofia, for allowing me to show this beautiful moment that illustrates how much you cared about each other and what brilliant artists you both were." She walks closer. "Can you please tell me if you recognize this ring?"

I gasp. "This is the engagement ring Eli gave me when we were in Montreal after a competition in which I finished in second place! I was nineteen, and he was twenty."

"So this ring stands for joy, love, and the hope of starting a life together and maybe raising a family of musicians and singers like you." She smiles. "But according to your deposition, this ring also brings back some painful and horrifying memories." She grows serious. "Would you please tell this jury what happened the night of August 25, 2011, when you left your friend's wedding reception around eleven p.m.?"

"I was one of the bridesmaids. When the party was over, I was feeling a bit tipsy, so I took my high heels off as I walked to my car, which was parked down the street. I opened the door, got in, put the key in the ignition, but then I felt lightheaded and decided that I was going to take a cab home and pick up my car the next day. That's when I heard a knock on the window."

"Would you please tell us what happened as if you were there, right now?"

"Yes." My heart starts racing. I look at Lev, and he holds his gaze as if to tell me that he is there to protect me. I take a deep breath and begin to speak.

"'Roll down the window,'" I heard a man's voice say.

I turned my head and saw Officer Almeida standing next to my car. My heart was pounding, but I did as he said. He was in his uniform and had his weapon on him.

I rolled down the window.

"He said, 'Please step out of the vehicle, Ms. de Menezes.' He opened the door and said, "'Would you please stand in front of that lamppost and walk a straight line?'"

"'I don't think I can,' I told him. 'I'm a bit shaky, Officer. I just want to take a cab and go home, please.'"

"'How come you have your key in the ignition?' he asked. And then he said, 'You were planning to drive under the influence?'"

"I told him I wasn't, that I was going to take a cab."

"Then he said, 'I could arrest you, Sofia.' I asked why. 'Because you broke the law,' he told me."

"I told him I didn't, that I hadn't turned the motor on and I hadn't intend to drive."

"He said if that was the case, that he could let me go with a warning and drive me home. He laughed at me then, said I looked scared, and told me to relax, that he was just messing around with me and would make sure I got home safe."

"I thanked him but said I was going to take a cab. I stepped out of the car, and I nearly lost my balance. He was holding me by the arm. He said it was dangerous, especially for a girl who was intoxicated. He told me to get my things and get in his cruiser."

"'I'm not doing that,' I told him and insisted I would take a cab. He said he'd arrest me and handcuff me and his cruiser would take me straight to jail. He was serious. Then he said he was trying to help me and I didn't have to be so unkind. Then he asked why I treated him with contempt when he was always watching out for me?"

"I didn't believe him, of course, and I asked if he was stalking me. I asked how he even knew I was there, and he said that my father had told him to come and check on me and had given him the address."

"Then what did you do, Senhorita de Menezes?" Sarah prompted me.

"I picked up my things and followed him to his car. What else could I do? He told me to get in the back and opened the door. I got scared, then, and tried to resist, told him I wouldn't."

"He showed me the handcuffs, and so I got in."

He put his hand on my head and helped me get in, said to take a nap, that I sure needed one. His tone didn't sound so harsh, anymore."

"My head was spinning. I leaned my head against the cold window and shut my eyes while he took off. I didn't know why my father thought so highly of him. Not only was he a BOPE officer who carried his mission to an extreme, but he was a known, local skinhead who hated Jews, Eli included. When he stopped the cruiser, he told me to get out. I did as I was told and realized that I was not home. 'Where am I, Officer?' I asked."

I fell silent, remembering.

"What happened then?" Sarah asked gently.

"He said it was his building and that he was taking me upstairs to sober up before driving me home. I was shocked. 'I don't want to go to your apartment! I'll take a cab and go home.'"

"He said I was under his care and that he was going to watch over me until I was sober enough to get home."

Again I fell silent. This was so difficult.

"He took me by the arm and basically dragged me through the front door, into the elevator, and up to his apartment, where he told me to sit on the couch. I noticed that his tone was harsh again. I sat down. I felt a bit dizzy. I was quite scared to be alone with him. He approached me, took his gun out of its holster, and put it down on the coffee table. He sat down next to me. I shrank away from him. He saw my fear and said I didn't have to be afraid."

Sarah spoke, bringing me back to the present. "Take your time, Sofia. I know this is hard."

"He…he took hold of my face with both hands. He got real close and said, 'How come you didn't call your boyfriend to pick you up? Did you break up with him?'"

"'He's not my boyfriend,' I told him. 'He's my fiancé. We're getting married when he returns from Sydney.' I tried to stretch out my hand to show him my engagement ring, but he gripped my face more tightly."

"He raised his voice then. He said, 'Your father won't allow it, Sofia. He told me that his daughter will never marry a Jewish man.' He grabbed my hand and tried to take off my engagement ring. I jerked away from him and got mad. I said, 'I'm twenty-one and I can marry anyone I want, whenever I want, and wherever I want. And I want to marry Eli as soon as he returns from his tour in Australia. I love him!'"

"'Don't be so sure of that,' he said and then he forcefully grabbed my hand and pulled off my ring."

The courtroom was silent, all eyes and ears on me.

"'Please, give me my ring back. I want to go home,' I said, and tried to get up, but he grabbed me and pushed me down. 'You'll get it back later if you are a good girl.' That's what he said."

My heart is pounding, and I feel tears start. I stay silent for a while.

"Please continue, Ms. Sofia. I know it's hard, but you must tell this court what happened that night. What did Officer Almeida do to you that night? Put yourself back in his living room, please, and tell us the truth."

I take a deep breath and continue.

"I begged him to let me go. I tried to get up, but he didn't let me move. He said, 'You are so sexy that I can't help wanting you' and he started kissing me on the face and lips. He told me not to be scared, that he was not going to hurt me."

I gritted my teeth and continued, determined to tell them.

"I felt the room whirling. I pushed him away hard, but I was no match for him. He pinned me down and started to undress me. I was too scared to hit him. I just kept saying: 'Stop, please. Stop,' but he didn't listen. He just kept touching and kissing me. Everything was reeling around me. I remembered that his gun was on the coffee table, so I freed my right arm and reached for it, but just as I was about to grab it, he grabbed it and pointed it at me.

"He sneered at me. 'If you're planning to kill me,' he said, 'it will have to be one fatal shot, darling, or I will kill you.' He put the gun in my hand. 'Shoot.' He smiled at me and said, 'Just like I taught you that time your father told me to take you to the firing range and teach you to use a gun.' He urged me to shoot. 'Go ahead,' he said. He was staring at me, and I could see excitement on his face."

I take a shaky breath before continuing. "My hands were shaking too hard, and I couldn't keep the gun straight. My mind was racing, but I didn't have the strength to pull the trigger. I started to cry. He took the gun back. He said he knew I wouldn't shoot him because it was not in my DNA to kill. 'But it is in my DNA.' He said he could shoot me right then but he wouldn't do it because he wanted me alive."

I twist my hands together sitting there in the courtroom, all eyes on me. "He said, 'You'll be mine one day. I have always had a crush on you.'"

"And then...?" Sarah prompted softly.

"And then he put the gun down on my chest and raped me."

I feel as though I'm falling into a black hole. "No matter how hard I fought, I couldn't escape his grasp. I couldn't break free. I felt my blood pressure drop, and I blacked out."

I wipe my tears with a tissue. I make eye contact with my father and see rage in his eyes. At first, I'm not sure if he's angry at me, but then I see that his wrath is directed at Officer Almeida. My mother is crying.

"Do you need a break, Sofia?" Sarah speaks in a gentle voice.

"No, please. Let's continue." I pick up a bottle of water and take a sip; just knowing that my father believes me gives me the strength to proceed.

"What happened the day after?"

"I packed a few things and took a cab to the station, and then I took a bus to my ranch in Friburgo where I stayed incommunicado."

"How come you didn't go to the police?"

"Officer Almeida is the police. I knew I didn't stand a chance. Besides, all I wanted was to curl up and die. I really thought that my life was over."

My attorney speaks. "That's all, Your Honor. Thank you." She looks at me. "You've done well, Ms. Sofia."

Judge Levien turns to the defense lawyer. "Do you have any questions for the witness?"

"Yes, Your Honor." He gets up and walks toward the stand. "You said that you were drunk, Ms. Sofia, so how can you remember exactly what happened that night?"

"I was intoxicated, not drunk. I've spent years in therapy trying to put this behind me, and little by little, I recovered my memories of that night."

"But your heart was racing and your blood pressure was low, so I'm assuming your brain wasn't getting much oxygen, and you must have been confused. I'm sure you were not entirely aware of what was going on."

"No." I raise my voice. "I was aware. I knew I was being raped by a man twice my size."

"Just answer yes or no." He stares at me. "You were not in your normal state of mind."

"I doubt I could have been when I was being raped by this officer sitting across from me."

"Just answer yes or no. You don't know what happened that night because you were not in full command of your faculties. You were, like you say, 'intoxicated.' Yes or no?"

I look at Judge Levien.

"Answer the question, Senhorita Sofia."

"Yes."

"No more questions."

"I have a few more questions for the witness, Your Honor." Sarah walks to the stand, holding a letter I asked Lev to give to her, along with the index card box and the ring. "Would you please tell me who wrote this letter, and when, and then read it, Ms. Sofia? We're almost done." She gives me the letter.

"I wrote this letter a few days after that night. It's addressed to Eli. I sent it to his apartment because he was still in Sydney."

"Read it, please."

I open the letter and begin to read.

Amor,

You're the greatest love of my life. I miss you. I'm here at the ranch. Love, I just watched six black swans float past me as the moon started to rise above the pretty little lake beyond the fields of Capella. The water is calm, it's not windy (so rare), and there are no mosquitoes. So, it's almost perfect, but you're not here and I'm not certain when you'll return. If you were by my side today, all this beauty would make sense, but hope is dim.

Since you're not here, I drew you a pretty picture of the lake and rock. I climbed it yesterday and wrote some more up there. It's gorgeous just looking down on the crystal-blue lake. It's a small, perfect sapphire. I'm going back to the house. I've been riding Vento for long hours. Saying goodbye is the most difficult thing in the world. I won't say much more, otherwise I'll change my mind. But things are just too painful to go on.

I'm devastated. I'm leaving this life behind, a life full of love, it's true, but there is so much sorrow. I can't tell a soul, not even you who would never have judged me, why I must say goodbye. This grief must end. Today is the day!

Your girl,

Sofia

My tears run down unchecked.

"Thank you. Now just one more thing, and it will be over. Did you act on the feelings expressed in that letter?"

"Yes. I just wanted to die, so I took a whole lot of pills. But Doralice, the woman who takes care of the farm with her family, found me unconscious and called emergency services. They gave me back a life I didn't want."

"What was your state of mind after your suicide attempt?"

"I was just in bed and ate very little, just some protein drink Doralice made me take. I wasn't able to sleep well, and I cried the whole time. I wanted to die."

"Did Eli read your letter when he returned from Sydney?"

"Yes, the very day he arrived in Rio."

"What did he do after he read your letter?"

"He called me and said that he was coming to see me at Capella, right way. He arrived a few hours later. I was still in bed that afternoon."

"Tell us about that conversation, please."

"I can't." I feel like fainting.

"You must, Senhorita Sofia. Did you tell Eli what happened that night?"

Tears drip down my face. "Yes. I shouldn't have, but I couldn't keep that secret from him. He knew I was in great pain and only he could understand."

"Why do you say you shouldn't have? He was your fiancé, the man you trusted, the person who loved you the most."

"Because, despite my begging him not to, he confronted Officer Almeida a week later, and for that he was killed. Oh, I shouldn't have!"

"Objection, Your Honor," the defense interjects. "There is no proof that rape even took place. The witness was too intoxicated to remember what happened to her that night. She lies. And isn't it true that your own father called you a slut who was pregnant at seventeen? And by the way, didn't you have an abortion so that you wouldn't have to interrupt your singing career?"

"No. It's not true, Your Honor." I look straight at Judge Levien. "My father demanded that I have an abortion. He himself took me to the military hospital despite my pleading, but he didn't want a grandchild of Jewish ancestry. I wanted my child who was conceived with love, but I was denied my baby because of my father's ignorance. I was in love with the man who was murdered by Officer Almeida when he confronted him about the rape, and I was going to marry him. This officer is a murderer." I sob.

"Objection, Your Honor. It's all speculation," Almeida's lawyer says.

"Sustained," Judge Levien says.

"Do you need a break, Senhorita Sofia?" Sarah says.

I wipe my tears with a tissue. "No, please." I take a deep breath.

Sarah speaks. "Your Honor, I'd like to show a video clip of Mr. Eli and Ms. Sophia at competition in Montreal shortly before Senhor Eli Levatter's life was taken in 2011."

"Go right ahead."

Sarah clicks on the YouTube channel.

***

I enter the well-lit room. It's crowded with people. Eli follows right behind me. I wear a red rayon dress, and he is in a black suit. We both look the part. I look at him for a while before I give him a smile, the signal that I'm ready. I begin to sing a heartfelt aria from I Puritan, knowing that he is by my side and that everything will be well. He plays with the mastery and sensibility of a true artist.

From time to time, he lifts his head and looks at me in awe and smiles in admiration. We are so perfect together that the energy in the room is electrified. At the end of my performance, we both stand side by side and bow as the audience goes wild shouting, "Brava, Bravissima!"

***

The clip ends.

In this courtroom, in this minute, I realize that there is new joy in my life, and that love and hope are blossoming as I look at Lev. He looks at me as Eli once did, full of love. Soon, we'll be a family, and that fills me with contentment. Moreover, I'm convinced that I will get justice for Eli and will continue to sing as he so much wanted me to do.

Judge Levien pounds his gavel. "This court is adjourned until tomorrow at eight a.m." He stands up.

We all stand as he leaves the room. I get down from the stand and walk in the direction of the back room to meet with Lev. I speed up my pace because my father is calling my name, but I don't want to see or talk to him. I'm not prepared to face the man who chose to believe a killer and took his side for so long. I can tell he regrets his choice, but it's too soon for me to hear what he has to say. There is still a chance evil might win if Brazil decides to believe that my father's battalion is indeed incorruptible. After all, I'm just a woman, and my word matters very little in a culture that regards a man in uniform as superior. Still, I will not be silenced and will fight back, even if the price to pay is death.

Chapter 17

Lev and I are on our way to his parents' house in Gávea. It's so green there, so pretty. It's almost like Capella, which I already miss so much. In seven days, I'll return to America, and without Lev, it's going to be ten times harder. I'm terrified to tell Didier about the baby. I'm sure he'll be very upset and may cancel the contract. He might demand an abortion. I fear that possibility the most. Lev is adamant about my staying in Rio, but I've told him that this is a decision I must make alone, although I understand his concerns.

I hope this pregnancy will not end prematurely. The nausea is out of control, and I can barely hold down any food. Actually, I have an aversion to most foods, and I'm hoping that tonight I'll be able to eat the Stroganoff Lev's grandmother is cooking for me. I wish I could talk to him about my health, but his obsession with the trial is driving him crazy. He knows that his professional evaluation of Officer Almeida must show that Eli's murder and the ensuing cover-up were planned meticulously by someone with the mind of a psychopath. He's also determined to hold him accountable for raping me. Lev is not himself these days.

He comes home late after putting in crazy hours at the trial and then seeing some clients at the clinic. When he gets in, he takes off his suit jacket and tie, and then sits next to me as I lie in bed. He asks me about my day, and I tell him only part of the story about what's going on with my body since I don't want to stress him even more. He takes both of my hands in his, and we hug each other for a long time. We make love. I love his touch, his voice whispering words of love, his attentiveness.

He puts his signals on and pulls over. "We're home," he says, parking the car in front of the two-story house painted moss green. It's more like a mansion with the astonishingly well-cared-for front lawn, gazebo, trees, and plants.

"This is like a forest with a house in it." I smile. "I love it. That's how the one percent lives." I get out. "Do you think I can afford a house like this?"

"I think so. I just had a meeting with your CPA not too long ago, and pretty soon you'll be getting a report on your financial situation." He leads me through the gate. "Actually, there is a place for sale a few houses down from my parents, and if you want, we can buy it together so that we can live and raise our children here."

"I'd love to live here. It's just like a mini-Capella with the inner forest in the background and the stunning Pedra da Gávea monolithic mountain. It's as big as the El Capitan in Yosemite. Still, I want to raise money to help the Indian nation, Lev."

"We'll live next door, and we'll help your grandmother's tribe, I promise." He rings the bell. "My grandmother is very excited to meet you, so be prepared for all the attention you'll get this evening."

"I'll love her, I'm sure, and I'll love the attention, as well."

A plump woman of small stature with long white hair opens the door. He eyes are as blue as Lev's. "Hello, Sofia, I'm Lyudmila. How nice to meet you." She kisses me on both cheeks. "You're even more beautiful in person. I have a lot to talk to you about."

"I'm so happy to finally meet you. Lev has told me so much about you, and you're also very beautiful with your long, silver hair. It's so attractive."

She gives me a big smile and looks at Lev. "She's just adorable, like you said. Please come on in."

"Do I even get a kiss or is it all about Sofia?" He guides me in.

"Of course, my lovely grandson. You deserve many kisses." She hugs and kisses him, showing all her love for her grandchild. "Follow me into the living room, please." She walks ahead of us.

We follow her through the hallway. The walls are dotted with pictures of Lev and his family when he was growing up. He was such an adorable boy. I hope that if we have a son, he'll look like him. We reach the large living room with white furniture and purple morning glory wallpaper. A black piano sits in a corner. Above it, there is a large print of Vase with Gladiolus, by Van Gogh. There is a plant, a magenta laelia orchid, on top of the fumée glass coffee table. The crystal clock on the table shows 4:39 PM. The glass cabinet displays crystal wineglasses, china dishes and demitasse cups. A menorah stands in the center.

"Look, Larissa, who has arrived," Dona Lyudmila says to Lev's mother, who sees us and smiles.

Lev's mother looks gorgeous in her cobalt-blue dress; it's the same shade as her eyes. "How wonderful to see you both." She walks up and kisses me on both cheeks, and then kisses Lev. "You look very pretty in red, Sofia. It lights up your face. It's great with your black hair, too."

"Her hair looks like my own when I was young. Don't you think so, Larissa?" Lev's grandmother says.

"Yes, Mamochka. I still remember."

Larissa hugs me, and I remember when she first told me about Lev's precarious condition at the hospital. My eyes fill up when I think I nearly lost him. I realize that I'm all thin skin and raw emotions, what with the pregnancy and the trial.

"Thank you for calming me down when Lev told me he had been shot. You were so good to me on the phone and at the hospital that first day."

"It's okay, Sofia. You were far away, sweetie, and it was hard on you. Don't be so upset."

"I'm sorry. I'm so emotional these days." I grab a tissue from my purse and wipe my face. "Actually, that's the way I am. Whenever I was upset, I would lay my head on my father's lap and cry my heart out—well into my teens." I feel cold and weak, thinking that Lev might get hurt again.

"Would you like something warm to drink? You are a bit jittery and pale."

"No, thank you. I drank a lot of coconut water before I came. I'm just nervous."

She reaches out, picks up a velvety green blanket from the easy chair and puts it around me. She puts her arms around me and I feel her warmth. I feel her love for me. Her embrace calms me down. It's a touch only a loving mother has. I'm hoping she senses that I am pregnant with her grandchild. I can hardly wait to tell her, but Lev and I agreed to tell the whole family during dinner.

"Feeling warmer and calmer, now?"

"Yes, thank you."

"Let's get you settled, darling."

His grandmother motions to me. "I have something in my room to show you. Larissa will come, too, but Lev is not allowed. It's just for girls."

"I'd love that, Dona Lyudmila." I smile.

"You can call me Savta. Savta. is grandmother in Jewish."

"Thank you, Savta, for being so kind. I miss my grandmother very much. She was as sweet as you.”

“Thank you, dear girl. You are lovely, too.”

“Your father is in his office, Lev. He would like to speak to you, and then we’ll have dinner,” Dona Larissa says.

“Okay, I’ll see him now. See you later, Sofia. He kisses me on the cheek. “Be sure not to forget about me. Some people are quite enthralled by your presence and might not want you to leave their room.” He winks.

“Some people are so adorable,” I say.

“Let’s get going, Sofia.” She takes me by the hand and guides me through the spacious living room. I follow her, and Dona Larissa trails behind.

We enter her bedroom. It’s large and painted a forest green. There are pictures of her on the walls, large portraits of her playing the violin. There is a large poster of St. Petersburg with its tall castles. There is a collection of dolls inside a glass cabinet.

“Sit on my bed, Sofia. I want to show you some photos.” She grabs an album on top of the desk and brings it to me. She sits down and opens it.

I sit. It feels great to be around strong, loving women. It makes me feel less troubled. I miss my mother, and being with Larissa soothes my pain a little. I hope I get to see her before I leave for Los Angeles.

She hands me a Russian doll that sits on the bed. “I got this in San Petersburg. She’s a Sasha doll. You can have her. She looks like you with her black hair and green eyes.”

I hold the handmade doll. “Thank you. What a fine porcelain doll. ”

“You’re welcome. It was made by the artist Sasha Morgenthaler.” She points to the album. “This is Larissa, dressed in red, when she was four, lighting a candle to begin the Shabbat. We had just immigrated to Brazil. I’m standing behind her next to my husband, Dimitri. When he was in his twenties, he was a Russian soldier during the war. In 1945, he came up to me as soon as he entered Auschwitz on Liberation Day and told me that he was a Jew. He was my hero.”

“What a beautiful story. Dona Larissa looks just like her father.”

“Yes. He adored his only child and his grandson.” She turns a page on the album. “Now, these are Lev’s other grandparents, Rose and Jacob. She died two years ago, so he sold his business and moved to Israel. Now for the big surprise.” She puts the album down and gets up. She walks over to her desk.

“She’ll tell you everything about us if you don’t stop her, Sofia.”

"I love it, Dona Larissa. Don't worry."

Lyudmila picks up her violin from the desk and brings it over.

"This is my beauty, Sofia." She holds the instrument as if holding a baby, very carefully. "This violin was found in an apartment amongst fifteen hundred other art objects and instruments stolen by the Nazis. Lev's grandfather was notified in a letter that the Stradivarius belonged to his father, Mesallin Levien, and his great-grandson went to Europe to recover it. I love to play *Rusalka* on it. Music saved me when I myself was in Auschwitz, and I'm happy about that." There is a mix of sadness and hope in her eyes.

My eyes well up. "I'm so sorry, oh; I can't even tell you how sorry I am about what happened to you and Lev's great-grandfather. I feel ashamed for the rest of the world for allowing that to happen." I feel queasy just listening to her impromptu revelation.

"Don't cry, baby. I just told you because I'm hoping you'll sing *Rusalka* to me later. Lev told me that you do it exceptionally well in person. I'll accompany you along with Lev on the piano and Larissa on the clarinet. Will you give me such happiness?"

"Of course, but know that Lev exaggerates and that my Russian isn't kosher. Otherwise, I'll do my best to sing it with as much passion as Dvorjak intended." I try not to think about the nausea but it is building.

She hands me a tissue. "After dinner, then." She puts her violin down on the desk.

"Sofia had a very stressful day in court, Mamochka. Maybe it will be too much for her. Besides, she looks a bit too tired." Dona Larissa says.

"Not at all, Dona Larissa, I'll be happy to sing. It will make me feel happy."

"Agreed, then." Lyudmila sits next to me and shows me a picture of a petite woman with auburn hair coiffed in fabulous finger waves. She has perfectly arched eyebrows, long eyelashes, and ravishing emerald green eyes like mine. "This is Suri, Mesallin's wife. She was a singer at a nightclub where Lev's great-grandfather was a comedian and played his violin in the band. She had your sensibilities, talent, and heart. Wasn't she gorgeous?"

"She's so pretty, so special. No wonder Lev is such a gifted musician, Dona Larissa. He practiced with me at Capella the whole time we were there, and I couldn't have asked for a better accompanist."

"You can call me Larissa, Sofia."

"This is a picture of Mesallin with his toddler, Anais. We found Suri's letters, which had been missing, and in them she says that after they sent Jacob to England to live with his grandmother, Ruth, she got pregnant with the girl, and we think that she might still be alive if it's true that her parents gave her to a French family before they were taken to the camp. Lev hired a detective to find his long-lost grand-aunt."

I focus on the picture of Lev's great-grandfather with his daughter Anais and realize how much Lev looks like him and how much the toddler looks like Lev. I gasp. "Anais looks so much like Lev. She could have been his daughter. Oh, please, tell me you can find her, Larissa. How special Suri was! She was a singer like me. Sorry, Savta, I feel very sick just now. May I please use the restroom? I'm a bit dizzy, too."

"Let's go, honey," Larissa says. "There is a bathroom right here. You look rather pale." She gives me her hands and helps me get up. I sway a bit, but she puts her arm around me and helps me walk to the restroom.

"I'll get Lev," I hear Savta say.

The moment I lift the toilette seat up, I bend over and begin throwing up. Larissa stands next to me and holds my arm.

"It will be just fine, Sofia." She has a reassuring voice. "She likes to tell her story, but I know it's very sad."

I lift up my head as she flushes the toilet.

"How are you doing? Do you still feel sick?" She continues to give me support. "How far along are you, honey?" She speaks in a sweet voice. "You're pregnant, aren't you?"

"Yes, four weeks."

"This is so wonderful, so amazing. I'm having a grandchild. Does Lev know? He didn't tell us anything."

"We were going to tell you at dinner, but I guess you figured it out pretty fast. Oh, gosh, I feel sick again." I bend over and throw up again.

"I've been told that someone is sick." Lev comes in. "I'm going to the pharmacy to get some electrolytes."

"Please don't leave." I lift up my head and wipe my face with the wet towel his mother has given me.

"I've seen this twice this morning. If I don't hydrate you, it would be considered malpractice, darling."

"Oh, yes, you're a medical doctor, but you can't fix this, can you?"

"Actually, I'm reading an article in a scientific journal that might be helpful. I'm on it. But I've got to get you the drink. I'll be right back. Thank you, Mamochka."

"Don't worry. I'll help Sofia. I think it will be over soon." She flushes the toilet.

"See you soon, darling." His voice is mellow. "You're in good hands. My mother will take good care of you, and then I will."

"Thank you. Sorry, I was a bit cranky." I take a deep breath.

"I understand. No worries. It must be very tough feeling sick all the time. Bye." He turns and leaves the restroom.

"Ready to lie down for a bit? You need to rest and hydrate. I'll take your vitals."

"Yes, please. Thank you. I'm so scared."

"I know. I was sick, too, when I was pregnant with Lev. It's just awful. Can you stand on your own? I want to get you a toothbrush. You'll feel much better after you get rid of the aftertaste." She takes the green blanket in her hands. "I'll give it back to you soon."

"I'm okay now. Thank you for everything. I'd like to brush and then lie down for a while if you don't mind."

"Okay. I'll leave you with Savta and go upstairs to get a few things. Please, Mother, take Sofia to the guest room. I'll be right there."

"I have some fresh clothes for you, darling. This nightgown is brand-new. I got it in Russia when I was there last year. It will fit you, and there is a robe, too." She hands me the clothes. "Congratulations, Sofia. How exciting. I love you even more, now. Go on, brush." She reaches out and hugs me.

"Thank you. You're so kind." I put some toothpaste on the brush and begin to clean my mouth. I wish I could stay in Brazil with them, but I know it's impossible. I put the brush down, wash my face, and pat it dry.

"Do you need help changing? Are you still dizzy?"

"No, thank you. I can do it myself."

"Do you have names for the baby, yet?" She whispers.

"Yes. If I have a boy, it's going to be Ariel Dimitri; but if it's a girl, it will be Lyudmila Rose. How do you like it?"

"That's such an honor. Thank you, dear. I'm sure the judge will be happy to know that you're naming your daughter Rose, as well." She leans over and kisses me on the cheek. "No wonder Lev is crazy about you. Please change and come lie down a bit."

"Obrigada, I will."

"I'll wait outside the door." She leaves the bathroom and shuts the door behind her.

I change out of my clothes, thinking that I love Lev and our baby even more. I'm sad to have to part from him, but I must pursue my opera. After the contest in September, I'll return to Rio, and hopefully Brazil will see me differently. I pick up my dress from the floor, put it over my arm, and exit the bathroom.

"You look very pretty." Savta guides me out of her room and into the guest bedroom, which is next to hers.

I lie in a large, solid, Shaker-style, four-poster. I use one of the pillows to prop my upper body against the headboard. Savta hands me the velvet blanket and I drape it around myself.

Larissa returns with Lev.

"My mother told me you got pretty sick, Sofia. You never told me about the results of your blood test yesterday? Do you have them on you?"

"Yes. They're in my purse in Savta's room."

"I'll get them and have a look. I'll be right back. Please take small sips of this liquid. It will help you, darling."

"Thank you." I take the small bottle in my hand and begin to sip through the straw. I feel my hands grow cold and my face flush. I'm getting too exhausted to even stay awake. Being in the courtroom was very upsetting. I almost didn't make it without getting sick.

Larissa puts a tray down on the bedside table. On it are a stethoscope, a thermometer, and blood pressure equipment. She holds an ice pack and a cup of ice chips. She sits down on the bed next to me and faces me. "You look like you're running a fever. Your lips are parched." She takes my pulse. "It's a bit too fast, honey. You don't look well, at all."

Lev steps in and walks up to me. He looks concerned. He shows me the report. "How can you not tell me about these results, Sofia? Your potassium is low. You've lost almost 5 percent of your body weight in about a months' time, and your kidneys are not doing so well. either—and you're anemic. This is serious. You're endangering your own life and the life of our child by not letting me know about this sooner."

"I'm sorry, but I didn't want to add any more stress to your life, Lev. You go to the courtroom every day, early in the morning, and then to the clinic, and then you come home and read through dozens of pages of transcripts, then you talk to the federal prosecutor on the phone. It's just too much for a person who was shot only two months ago. You should be the one taking care of your health. Please, be realistic. I'm just pregnant."

"Still, I asked you to tell me everything about your health so that I could help you. I can't possibly understand why you neglected to show me these results."

He has never spoken to me in this tone.

Larissa puts the stethoscope around her neck. "Lev, I know you're terribly worried about Sofia, and frustrated with her silence about her condition, but it's hardly her fault that the two doctors she trusts have neglected her. Couldn't you see she was ill? She's a pint-size person and has lost 5 percent of her weight. It's noticeable even for me, and I rarely see her. You've engrossed yourself in this trial and neglected the mother of your baby. Haven't I taught you that you never neglect people who depend on you? Please, don't stress her even more."

She puts the thermometer in my mouth.

"I'm sorry, Mamochka, but I asked Sofia to call me as soon as she got the test results, and I even asked her to get her doctor to give me a ring. I'll contact him early tomorrow morning to find out why he didn't take proper care of her."

"She's burning up, and her pulse is fast. I don't like what I see." Larissa puts an ice pack on my head and asks me to take deep breaths.

"I'll call Dr. Aaron and send her records to him, then I'll get a bed for her at the hospital where you work. Do you know who is working tonight?"

"Madalena is. She is a great nurse, and, of course, I'll be there with Sofia. Please hurry, son. She needs medical attention."

I'm entering a kind of dreamy state of mind. I can't keep my thoughts clear. I feel my temperature rising and shiver. My skin is tingling.

Lev leaves the room.

"He had a Dr. Lev moment with you, Sofia. He does that when he is under pressure. Don't be upset, okay? He acts a bit harsh when he deeply cares about someone, and he loves you so much. Just remember that it's not your fault. Your type of nausea isn't common among other pregnant women, and it will take some special care to keep you hydrated and healthy. I'll help you as much as I can. You must have all the support you can get." She smiles. "I'm really happy for you and Lev. It's wonderful news, and I can hardly wait to see my grandchild." She kisses me on the cheek.

I feel my eyes growing heavier. "Thank you so much. I love your son and you and Savta and the judge."

Judge Daniel walks in. "Can I be of some help?"

"She needs to go to the hospital. Please drive us there, Daniel. It's pouring out there, and I want Lev to concentrate on her."

"Yes, of course," his father says. "I'll notify her parents first and then drive you there."

My tears stream down my face. I feel even queasier. "No, please, Judge. My father doesn't know that I'm pregnant, and he might get mad when I tell him that Lev is the father. I can't let him hurt Lev, please. I have to protect him." I motion to get up but Larissa holds me down.

"I know where you're coming from, Sofia, but your father has changed over the course of this trial. He has provided security for Lev and has grown very fond of my son because he knows how much he loves you. You father loves you very much, and my feeling is that he'll be thrilled about having a grandchild."

Larissa gets up and Lev sits down next to me. He has calmed down entirely and is back to his old self. I continue to suck on the ice chips. The more I lick my lips, the drier they feel. I begin to shiver and wrap the blanket even tighter around me. I feel flushed, and my hands and feet are very cold.

"I'm parched, but I don't think I can keep anything down." I give him back the drink.

All of a sudden, I'm fearful of what could happen to me and my baby. I should have asked for help sooner. I feel drained. My breath is labored.

"Can I have this blanket? It's so cozy and smells so good. I want to wrap my baby in it."

"You can have it, sweetie," Larissa says. "It's the color of your eyes and goes well with your brown skin. I hope my grandchild will look like you. Even sick like this, she has the most luminous face, doesn't she, Lev?"

"She's the most beautiful thing in the world." Lev is super-calm, just as he is at clinic emergencies.

Savta comes closer, a smile on her teary face. "Poor baby. She's really sick."

"Don't cry, Grandma. Please take care of my doll while I'm at the hospital. They have a lot of germs there, and I don't want her to catch anything."

Judge Daniel returns. "Your father will meet us at the hospital, Sofia. Ready?" He looks concerned.

"I think we're calling an ambulance," Larissa says. "She needs to get there faster." She holds her cell phone in her hand and taps in the number.

Lev takes off my bracelets, rings, and then my necklace and puts them down on the bedside table.

I watch him and smile. "You match my vibe, Lev. I hope the universe will keep us together forever."

"I'm glad, and I hope so, too. Sorry I was too caught up in the trial to pay attention to you and your needs." He kisses me on the forehead. "I love you so much."

I shiver. "Can I have some butterscotch snaps with candy crunch and covered with powdered sugar, Lev? The ones I gave you at Capella? I'm starving."

"What snaps, darling? You never gave me anything like that. Sorry you're so hungry."

"I guess I have a stash in Los Angeles, but don't tell Didier, okay? Sorry for being so rude, Camarad Lev. If I make it through this and the baby makes it through this and everything is okay in the end, I swear to you that I'll be a good mother to our baby." I lean against his chest.

"And I promise to be a good father to our child, Sofia. Don't worry about anything, meu anjo."

He asks his mother to hand him his iPad and then clicks on the YouTube app. He shows me a clip of me singing in at his apartment.

"Am I going to die, Lev?"

"Not a chance. You'll live another hundred years to continue this gorgeous singing. Isn't her Russian lovely, Mamochka?"

"It's outstanding. She is a great artist and the finest Rusalka."

I hear the sounds of an emergency vehicle. My eyes start to close. "I'm a bit scared of being alone at the hospital."

"I'll be at your side the whole time, and so will my mother."

I remember Anais, Suri's daughter, who was lost due to the war. "Are you going to protect our baby? She'll be so tiny, so tiny. I'm afraid for her."

"I'll protect you and our child, Sofia, that's a promise I intend to keep."

The paramedics come in and as they strap me to the gurney, I promise myself never to neglect asking for help again. I still hear myself singing *Rusalka,* hoping one day to sing it at the Met and at opera houses all over the world.

Chapter 18

I sit on my bed at Didier's house, unpacking my things. It has been a few days since I returned, but I already miss Rio, Capella, and Lev. I hold the Sasha doll Savta gave me that night when I first met her. I miss her, too, and I promised to Skype and talk to her about the baby. She's rooting for a girl so that she'll have a brand-new Lyudmila. I'll also Skype with Larissa. The week at the hospital helped me get my health back. The medication I was put on is helping control the nausea so that I can be ready for the contest in September.

Lev texted while I was in transit to say that the case is in the jury's hands and that he's hoping deliberations won't take long. I long to see Officer Almeida convicted. It will end this painful chapter in my life. I'm opening a new one with Lev and our baby. My love for him only grows, and just thinking that he will change his life to follow me around the world makes me even more willing to do all that I can to support him in his endeavors, as well.

I hear a knock on the door.

"Come in, please."

"Did you take a nice nap?" Didier is wearing his chef outfit and holding his knife case in his hand. He never goes to work without them.

I feel a chill down my spine. "I slept well, thank you. I feel less fatigued, now."

"I missed you and the sound of opera in the house. Did you practice your arias with Dr. Lev even during the times when Madam Prunier couldn't Skype with you?"

"Yes. We spent a great deal of time working on them at Capella. He was extremely patient and followed Madam Prunier's instructions. Sometimes we worked on one phrase alone for a good fifteen minutes. He stayed there with me until we returned to Rio so that I could testify. I stand up. Please have a seat, Didier. I need to speak to you about what happened." I go to the small couch in my room.

His face hardens. "What is it?" He walks to me, sits down, and puts his knife case down next to him. "You got romantically involved with Dr. Lev, didn't you? I can tell just by the way your voice sounded when you said that he stayed with you at Capella."

I look straight at him. "Yes. I found out that I'm in love with him and he with me. It happened, and I'm sorry if that hurts your feelings. I didn't plan it that way. I guess I underestimated my feelings for him."

He looks angry. "I thought you were falling in love with me. You know that I'm in love with you and want to marry you."

"It didn't say in the contract that I couldn't fall in love with someone else. It's a matter of the heart, Didier. I'll never forget how much you've done for me. You're the whole reason I'm singing again, but I can't love you back. I'm five weeks pregnant with Dr. Lev's baby. I'm sorry if I breached our contract, but it happened." My voice cracks.

He slaps me across the face, shocking me. "How could you do that, Sophie?" He raises his voice. "I could throw you out on the street right now, but I'll give you a chance to fix this stupidity by having an abortion. It's the only way you can repair this." His face is flushed.

I touch my face where he hit me and remember my father doing the same thing when he found out I was pregnant with Eli's child.

I get up angrily and turn to face him. "How can you hurt me like that! Keep your hands off me, Didier, or I'll call the police!" I feel tears start but blink them back. "You have no right to hurt me just because you don't like something I did or said. Don't ever touch me again in this manner."

"Sorry I lost my temper." He gets up, walks up to me, and tries to hug me, but I push him away." You've ruined all my plans for you, Sophie. You're supposed to win a tough competition, and there is so much more work ahead. You won't be able to endure the heavy schedule. What is more, this man doesn't love you. He got you pregnant when you have your whole life ahead of you."

"Of course, he loves me. I'm responsible for it, as well. He took responsibility for his action, and so will I. I'll work hard and continue to prepare myself for the contest. There is nothing to fear."

"How about after the competition? We were supposed to get you singing in Brazil, to make you diva number one in your land, but it will never work, now. You'll be tired after spending the night taking care of a screaming infant, and the quality of your work will change, and then your voice will change. It's insane." He softens his tone. "An abortion is the best solution for the problem you created for yourself, for us."

"This is not a problem. It's a baby growing inside me, whom I love already. I'd never have an abortion."

"My mother got pregnant by her manager, Sofia, and she had to have an abortion to keep her career. It's the only way out of this quagmire for you. She had to learn the hard way, and so will you."

"I'm not your mother. I'll make my own choices without your interference. Who do you think you are? Even Lev, who is the father, told me he would not interfere. He wanted me to stay in Brazil, but I decided to return and he accepted my decision. He supports me and loves me."

He stands in front of me. "When I first met you, I thought you were quite naive for a twenty-six-year-old, but as I get to know you, I begin to see how sophisticated you are, so I don't understand why you insist on keeping a pregnancy that will end your career. Please consider getting rid of this baby. You can have ten babies in the future if you want. You haven't even hit your prime, yet. You can also freeze your eggs and choose to have children later when your career has been cemented."

"No. You're not going to decide this for me like my father did years ago when he forced me to have an abortion. It's my body. I get to decide."

He pushes me away. "If you choose to have this baby, Sophie, I'm canceling the contract, and you need to move out right away. You have two weeks to decide. I'll arrange everything for you. I'll get you the best clinic and the most competent doctor. Deep down, you love your opera more than anything else. Please—do what's right." He looks sad. "I have such high hopes for you. You're an amazing talent. Please reconsider."

"I have the right to decide all by myself, regardless of what you're planning to do."

He gets angry again. "You have two weeks to fix this mess you're in. I hope you come to your senses and save your career. You'll shine on the world stage, I promise." He walks to the door and turns. "Dr. Lev was selfish. He took advantage of you. He knew you were dependent on him to help you win that case. He doesn't love you. You shouldn't think of him when you make this decision. I'm the person who was put in your life to take you far. I advise you not to tell him about our conversation or he might influence your decision. From now on, I'm limiting your contact with him."

"Don't speak of Lev in this manner. He's an honorable man, and he loves me."

"I've got tickets for the Met to see Madame Butterfly so that you can get a glimpse of what your life will look like when you become a known diva in America. You will be treated like a queen, stay at five-star hotels, shop on Fifth Avenue, and have everything your heart desires."

"I just want my opera, and now my child. I can have both."

"Nonsense. Nature limits you, and many times a woman can't choose at all. It's just as it is." His voice is harsh. "Get an abortion, Sophie. It's the only way out if you want your career. When we return from New York, you'll have to tell me what you are going to do." He picks up his knife case, turns, and leaves the room.

I focus on the Blue Nestira he gave me, enclosed in plexiglass and hanging on the wall. It makes me sad whenever I think that she never got to live a free existence. I tremble. Just the thought of an abortion makes me shiver. My grandmother once told me that a woman has to figure out her place in the world without killing what she loves. For once in my life, I'm not killing either my baby or my opera. I'll have both. Even though a Brazilian woman is expected to follow the lead of the group and is never empowered to choose anything for herself, I'm shedding old values for new ones. Instead of wanting to belong more, as Brazilians always do, I'm learning to become more self-reliant. I want my voice to be heard, and I won't be forced to do something I don't want. That's it. I'm all grown up, and Didier will have to accept that.

I pick up my laptop and go to sit propped up in my bed. I log on and check to see if there is an email from Lev. He said he would keep me posted. Maybe he has realized that getting involved with me was not the best thing for him. I miss him playing the Bachianas Brasileiras No. 5 to me whenever I felt sick. I click on iTunes and listen to my own voice singing the aria. Lev said that my rendition was flawless. I wonder why he hasn't texted today. He could have, even if he's at his office.

I click on "compose" and begin to write him an email.

Caro Lev,

My love for you is insurmountable. The night has an impressive blue tinge. Only the headlights of a distant vehicle can be seen through the louvered window. Then, I see the moon showing off. Her light obfuscates the stars. I'm all alone and feel lonely without you. I'm quite emotional and still feel sick, even though Larissa gave me many palliatives to help with the nausea. It's just the way my body handles pregnancies. It's tough, but just thinking that this life is growing inside me fills me with a não sei o quê that is difficult to describe. On top of that, this life is 50 percent you and was conceived with love. I can't ask for more than that.

I know that things happened very fast between us. I didn't plan it that way and I have no regrets, although I'm thinking that you might feel overwhelmed by the circumstances. I can already see all the changes that are happening in your life because of this pregnancy. You are leaving the clinic for my sake and the baby's, and I know how much it's costing you. If you do feel pressured, I'll understand, and I'm prepared to raise Lyudmila alone. I just ask that you be honest with me.

Naturally, I want and need you by my side and would nearly die of sorrow if you decided to play it cool. Still, the depth of my love for you is such that, even if you wrong me, I'll never stop loving you. It's just what it is. You're remarkable. You took the time to listen to my father when you know he is an anti-Semite and probably thinks that you are one of the "good ones." Still, you were able to help him when he felt weak after my testimony, and like you said, taking a fall, which you know is very difficult for him. Maybe I'm not being fair. Maybe he is beginning to let go of his prejudices because of you. Thank you so much for being so caring. As much as I want to fight it, I do love my father, at least the father I grew up with. So, you're magnanimous.

Anyway, I got this postcard of a heart from my mother. It's a deep violet against a pale-yellow background. It's asymmetrical, with arias that overlap each other. The unornamented typeface with sans serifs and serifs makes it even more unusual. Isn't that so cool? She also posted a video with different kinds of rain on my wall on Facebook, because she knows I love showers, downpours, torrents, and drizzles. She seems a bit crazy with her Smartphone welded to her hand, posting stuff on Google Plus. WhatsApp, and Instagram. I love her so much. She's happy with the pregnancy and with you in my life. She loves you.

My sister, Madalena, also called me when I was at the airport in Rio. She's super-happy for me. She has lovely, fraternal twin daughters who are very special. They are eight. Melissa is an animal lover like me and wants to be a veterinarian. She has a great voice. Estella is musically inclined and wants to play the cello and the flute, although her mother makes her take piano lessons. I love them so much. Whenever they come to Capella, I spoil them and they spoil me.

Love, I hope you'll respond to this email or call me or Skype soon.

Your favorite opera singer,
Sofia

I send the email.

Suddenly, I feel nauseous and run to the bathroom. I lift the toilet seat up and begin to throw up. I absolutely hate this part of being pregnant. I wonder if I'll be okay in a month's time so that the competition will go on without a hitch. I'll be almost twelve weeks by then, and according to Larissa I should feel perfect by then. I flush the toilet again and wash my mouth with Listerine. I turn the faucet on, fill up the tub, put bubble gel in the water, and watch it run like my racing thoughts. The hydrangeas, tinged with pink, stand bunched in a black container. Nature is perfect.

When I have the baby at Capella, I'll begin to teach him or her about the beauty of the natural world and how to love and respect it. Doralice will be so happy with my baby. She's a second mother to me. Mama was too busy working at the conservatory to spend a great deal of time raising me, but with Lev by my side, I'll be able to raise our children and travel everywhere. I turn the water off and am able to hear the music coming from my iPad.

Butterfly's voice is compelling. She dies for the love of an unworthy foreigner. He didn't deserve a second look from her, and yet she gave him her love, her loyalty, and her own child. She had no other choice, but I do have one. No matter what Didier says.

I put my nightgown on and lay in bed.

The phone rings twice. I pick it up. "This is Sofia."

"Lev speaking. Is it a good time? You sound like you were asleep." His voice is low.

"It's a good time. I thought you'd never call, Lev." I burst into tears. "For a moment I thought you had abandoned me."

"Talk to me. Tell me about your feelings. I'm listening, Sofia."

"When I was a little girl on the farm, I thought I didn't want to grow up, and that being a child forever was a lot more fun, but Papa always told me that I needed to become a more sophisticated girl because, one day, I was going to be an opera singer. He even made me take lessons at the "Socila" spa, a place for women who wanted to become ladies. I had to walk with a book on my head and all, but all I wanted was to ride my horse." I pause. "But it's true that I have grown up. Maybe it's the morning sickness and the idea of having to choose between my child and my opera. It's all so complex being a woman in a world designed for men."

"I get all that, but please tell me what the pain is really about. Why did you think I'd never call?"

I take some tissues from a box on the bedside table and dry my tears. "I thought you had realized that getting involved with me was a big mistake and that the pregnancy was the biggest mistake of all. Didier thinks exactly that, and you were taking a long time to call."

"No, not true. He's mistaken. I love you and love to be involved with you, love this baby you're growing inside you. I just wish you could be here by my side. I miss you so much that I bought a DVD of yours from when you sang at the semi-finals of the competition in London in 2011. God, you look beautiful in that long, black rayon dress and sophisticated hairdo. If it weren't for your childlike face and small frame, people would see that you are a very strong woman who really knows what she wants in life, a woman who makes me feel vulnerable just thinking that she will give up on me any day. I may be many things of importance to you, but I'm kind of reserved while you—you're bubbling with life."

"I'd never give up on you. I love you just the way you are. You calm me down. I'm so emotional, as you know. So, I was dreading the thought that you had realized I was sort of bad news."

"What's behind this, Sofia?"

"Didier said that if you really cared about me you wouldn't have gotten me pregnant, because he thinks this baby will ruin my chances of becoming a great opera singer. He gave me an ultimatum. He wants me to have an abortion within two weeks' time or he'll cancel our agreement and kick me out."

"Now listen carefully, Sofia. You are in charge of your life." He raises his voice. "It's your body, your pregnancy, and it's for you to decide what's best for you. If you want to, you can keep this baby. It's all up to you, darling. Not even I have the right to ask you to keep it or to have an abortion, even though I'm the father. You are the only one who can make this choice. Agreed?"

"Yes. I told him just that."

"It will happen other times, darling. I can't be by your side, now. Carolina, our client, escaped and wasn't found until the next day. The family is very angry and is threatening to sue the clinic. Dr. Fleetly asked me to work a few more days to help him with that. Also, Dr. Cristina is now on vacation, and I have to cover for her. There is no way I can fly to you, but I'll get in touch as often as possible. The reason it took me so long was that I was waiting for the verdict."

"Is there one? Please tell me." I take a deep breath.

"Officer Almeida has been convicted by the jury and sentenced to life in prison without possibility of parole. My father gave him the maximum sentence possible. Justice has been served, and a Brazilian judge delivered it. Even though the Executive tried to favor the party in question, the Judiciary stood its ground, and by evoking the constitution, my father was able to accomplish his goals. It was the first time he spoke for twenty minutes prior to sentencing a felon. He gave a blistering speech, letting him know that the court was astounded by the crimes he committed against Eli and you. He tells me to tell you that he was thinking about you all throughout his speech and wished you were there to hear it. We both think you're an extraordinary woman, because in the end, it was your testimony that sealed his fate. But we both know how much that testimony cost you. You're amazing."

"This is so great, Lev. Thank you for everything you did to bring this case to light, and thank Judge Daniel for doing such a brilliant job. I couldn't love him more."

"He loves you, too, and can hardly wait to see his grandson or granddaughter."

"Well, I'll make it possible in some thirty more weeks."

"That's what I want to hear. Should I send you the money to pay Didier? The sooner you do that, the sooner you'll be free to make choices and take care of yourself."

"Please send it via Western Union to my bank account here in America."

"I'll get on it. I'll help you in any way I can. My mother said she'll Skype with you soon to see how the pregnancy is going. She loves you. She thinks you're so brave."

"I love her back. Thank her for helping me get my health back. She took such good care of me at the hospital. And you—I have no idea how to show you my gratitude."

"No thanking needed. Everything I do is out of my love for you, and that shall never change. Whenever you begin to have doubts, contact me in any way you want. I might not be able to answer right away, but please leave a message marked urgent and I'll be able to get back to you faster."

"How much do you miss me already? Be honest."

"Actually, I taped you singing *Rusalka* for my grandmother and watched it this morning. There is a different sense of gravity about you, and you're very eloquent. There is a poetic depth to you I had not heard before, and I have watched all the tapes you sent me of your singing many times. You're a great singer, Sofia. But I'm afraid this escalation in lucidity and self-expression didn't come trouble-free."

"Do you think ill of me for imagining that you'd abandon me?"

"No, I understand. You're uniquely designed, and that makes you a bit more vulnerable. My grandmother was quite touched by the way in which you were able to feel her pain." He raises his voice. "So, here's a piece of advice— not from your future husband or father of your child—but from Dr. Lev. You must get out of that house and away from Didier. He's controlling, and he's not taking no for an answer. I've seen this in my office many times, and I think you're at risk. Would you please listen to me?"

"Now you're the one who is exaggerating. Didier wants the best for my career, and in a few days, I'm sure he'll accept the fact that I will have this baby and my opera and will help me achieve my goal, which is also his goal. It will be even clearer that it's all business when I pay him in full for all his expenses. I think I can get the money in twenty-four hours after you're able to deposit it. Please don't worry so much. I'm strong. You saw me at the trial."

"Just be careful not to get hurt. I can't take it, so you have to help me." He softens his tone. "I've got to go. Take good care of mother and baby for me, and remember, this important decision is yours alone. And another thing, I love you and I miss having you in my arms."

"You're so cute and hot! I can hardly wait to be back in Rio and make love to you, meu amorzinho, querido."

"Me, too. Take good care, and keep me posted, amor. Bye." I hang up.

There is no way I'll give into Didier's demands. He is in for a big surprise if he thinks I'm Butterfly and will give up the life of my unborn child. Tomorrow, Madame Prunier and Noah will be here, and I will show him that I'm perfectly capable of doing my work. It might take a while, but he will see that I can handle both, my career and my pregnancy.

Chapter 19

It has been three weeks since my return from Rio. I lie in bed in my room at Didier's house. He has given me an extra week to show him that I have what it takes to win the competition at the end of September.

There is a silence that won't go away. It starts in the bedroom. Then it tunnels through the labyrinths of the house. Then it settles in my eyes, and I can't see clearly. I'm unable to fight the dark thoughts fogging my mind. The nausea has increased again, and my energy level is awfully low. As much as I try, it's been difficult to get my work done, and more than twice I had to send Prunier back home.

Didier is obsessed with my preparation and demanding that I practice even longer hours than before to prove myself. I have to show him that I can handle the pregnancy and my career. It's incredibly intense, and whenever I make a mistake, he gets enraged. To keep him from getting angry, I'm in surrender mode. I do whatever he says. Saying no to any of his demands is against the rules. Being so far away from Lev makes everything more difficult, and Didier has exacerbated the situation by taking away my electronics and making me ask when I want to use them. This limits my contact with Lev and makes sure he is present when I talk to him so that I don't complain about the heavy schedule and nausea. Didier tells me he talks to Lev directly and keeps him informed of my situation. I accept his terms also because I don't want Lev to know about what I'm going through, since he'll certainly want to come here and do something about it. I know how angry he gets when he thinks an injustice is being committed against me. It's better to deal with Didier myself.

I turn on the iPad on and listen to *Rusalka*. Lev made a movie of the two of us playing and singing at his house after we made love for the second time, on the day of my deposition. In the video, I wear the diamond necklace he gave me at his apartment in Rio. I'm so taken by The Woman in Gold. After my singing, he did prop me up with love. I dove into the blue oceans that are his eyes and lost myself in their balmy, sensual and healing waters. He has my heart and soul, and yet, he's so far away. But I wanted it this way. I've got to make decisions on my own.

I get up, fetch my jewelry box, and put on the necklace he gave me. He says that I'm his "Woman in Rose," that like the flower, I'm the finest expression of love, the love he craves and says he has found in me. I told him he has my love and gratitude. He gave me the courage to face evil; and together, we've claimed justice for Eli. And yet, being four thousand miles apart and with the upcoming contest, I don't see how this will work. The pregnancy must have been a mistake, after all. I was stupid not to have used protection, and then not to have taken the Plan B pill the next morning. I think I sabotaged my own efforts to have my opera back. There is no way I can move forward with the practice if the nausea doesn't improve.

I touch the marigolds in a vase. I thrive when I dwell in their light, but today it feels impossible to find respite from the conflict between having and not having my baby. Didier is adamant about terminating the contract because he says I can't handle it. Maybe he is right.

The blinds are down. I'm exhausted from throwing up three times today. I look up at the wooden beams across the ceiling. How many trees does it take to make a house, I wonder? I press Pause on the iPad and pick up the clinic report book I brought as a memento and to feel close to Lev. I sit down on the loveseat and continue to read about the work we did together and the clients we shared. Two years ago, I had just started at the clinic, and I was pretty new in that world. He was my Rock of Gibraltar, making sure I didn't feel overwhelmed by the intensity of the world of mental illness. He guided me every step of the way. I turn a page in the book and read my notes about a conversation I had with a client during the last Christmas party I attended at the clinic.

Carolina sat by the piano as Lev played pop songs. Her hazel eyes hid the dimness within, which almost made me forget that hers was a gloomy story. Her dark-brown, curly hair hid thoughts she never revealed. Lithium kept her paranoia under control and her suicide attempts at bay, but it also made her weary. At times, her bipolar disorder caused her to fly off the handle, but that night she was mellow and vulnerable. She looked lovely in her red dress and subtle makeup.

I could hardly believe how festive she looked when, just three weeks before, she had been admitted after slashing her wrists with a barber's razor.

Besides Lev's care and my work with her, her sheer determination to forge ahead while facing overwhelming disability saw her through.

She walked toward me. "Sofia," she said, "you look good in your little black dress, your hair in a high bun like that, and your pearls. How come you don't wear makeup more often? You look stunning."

"Thank you, Carolina," I replied. "Today is a special day, and I decided to look my best."

"I'm sorry I called you a bitch and a witch last week," she said in a low voice. "I was angry at Dr. Lev for keeping me in the suicide watch room so long, and I blamed you for not convincing him to get me out sooner. Sorry."

"Don't worry. You're not the first one—except I've never been called a bitch and a witch at the same time. You get credit for that. I can't imagine being locked up in a room for any amount of time. Sorry I couldn't change his mind, but in hindsight, I think he did the right thing."

"He's a good guy."

"Are you and Rogério together again? I saw him visiting yesterday. Why did you break up with him?"

"He's a good guy, and he is responsible, but in October we had a fight and he turned to me and said: 'I'm boss, I'm in charge and give the orders.' I was mad as hell. I looked at him and said, "In that case, we'd better separate. I'm out of here."' She laughed. "I'm no longer interested in being harassed by a man, stepped on, and squashed by an authoritarian son-of-a-bitch. He got mad and left. Five weeks later, I found out I was pregnant and had an abortion and then we got back together." Her eyes well up with tears.

"What's wrong, Carolina? You look so sad, sweetie."

"I was hemorrhaging as though I was going to die. I couldn't afford to go to an expensive, secret clinic like rich women do, so I didn't get the care I needed. I ended up with incredible bleeding. He took care of me, and we decided to get back together. I guess I was really manic, because you know the rest—I was admitted after slashing my wrists."

"I'm sorry you went through all that. I wish you had told me about the complications of the abortion. Would you like to have a session tomorrow?"

"Yes. I want to tell you everything."

I told her we'd meet there, even though it was my day off.

Remembering my encounter with Caroline brought back my own terrible memories. The fact that abortions are illegal in Brazil has hurt women and claimed many lives. I remember my own abortion and all the bleeding. It felt like dying. The day I went back to Capella after the abortion, I panicked and started packing everything I had bought for the baby. I picked up the yellow blanket, the blue rattle, and baby clothes and put them in a box to be given away. I didn't shed a single tear. Had I started crying, I would never have stopped. But nothing has been forgotten, not a single object, and not the desire to hold my own baby in my arms. I was only seventeen when I had to choose between my baby and my opera, but it is still fresh in my mind. It's wrong for anyone else to make that kind of choice for a woman.

I continue to listen to the music. Even after two years of working at the clinic, I still feel at a loss when trying to comprehend the world of mental illness. Celebrations like Caroline's aside, it is a world impervious to light. It is a world of locked doors, impervious to freedom. It is a world of utter sadness, impervious to joy.

I turn and watch the falling rain, copious and unyielding, thinking that I should have fought back and had my baby back then, but I was so young and so vulnerable, and I wanted my opera, and my father had all the power.

Now, here in Los Angeles, under Didier's roof, I want to be sure about this pregnancy and my music, but everything is confusing. It feels so lonely to be a woman and have to decide what to do about my life.

I get up. How can I possibly have an abortion? Even if Lev says it's my body and I'm the one who must choose, I'm sure he'd be devastated. He wants this baby as much as I do. Oh, have I messed up! I am alarmed at the gravity of my choice one way or another.

A hear the sound of a car on the road. I get up and look out the window. A bird made a nest on the skinny tree in the front yard. I hear the doorbell. It's probably Valéria with the psychic. I head for the door, full of hope. After this guided imagery session, maybe I'll gather the courage I need to make the right decision. I walk down to the living room and open the door.

"Sofia, oi," Valéria says. "Tudo bem?" She hugs me. "This is Ed Miller."

"Nice to see you, my friend." I hug her. "Nice to meet you, Ed."

"Nice to meet you, Sofia," a blond, tall, middle-aged man says. "You have such a bright aura." His navy-blue slacks and long-sleeved shirt make his blue eyes look bluer still. They're the same shade as Lev's, so I like him instantly.

"Please, come in," I say. "Have a seat, please. Can I get you something to drink?"

"Water," he says, sitting down next to Valéria on the couch. "I like to drink water when I work."

"Sure. How about you, Valéria?"

"Water for me, too, querida."

I walk toward the kitchen. Without Didier, it looks too antiseptic. There are no smells of simmering wine. No aroma of chopped tarragon. No boiling tomato soup. It feels as lifeless as I will be if I get an abortion. I fill up a pitcher with water and put three glasses on a tray. I walk back into the living room and put the tray down on the coffee table.

"Is there anything you want me to do before we start, Ed?"

"If you don't mind unplugging the phone, I'd appreciate that." He pours himself a glass of water. "Disruptive noises can break our connection with the spiritual world." He takes a large sip of water. "I like that you have candles lit. Fire is very important."

I reach for the phone on the bookcase and unplug it, hoping Didier won't call until the spiritual treatment is over.

Valéria turns on a small tape recorder. "I'm taping this so you can listen to it whenever you choose to do some guided imagery on your own." She touches my diamond necklace. "This is fabulous."

"My very special friend gave it to me. It brings tons of good vibes."

"I need to get myself a friend like that." She smiles.

"Are you ready to lie on your yoga pad?" Ed hands me a magnetite rock. "Hold it in your left hand to enhance the energy you'll be receiving."

"Thank you." I walk around the coffee table, lie down on the mat, focus on my diamond necklace, and think of the Lady in Gold. I remember that evening in Lev's apartment and how he made me feel so loved and cherished.

Ed sits on a mat in lotus position. "When I get to five, I'd like you to shut your eyes." He takes a deep breath and stays still for a few seconds. "One…two…three…four…and five. Good. Keep your eyes closed and think of a special place you would like to be, now. Think about the meaning of this work and what you want to know. You don't even have to tell me. Just keep that thought in mind, and you'll get the answer you're looking for. Are you comfortable?"

"Yes. I'm at the ocean. The blue water is calm and warm." I think of Lev's place and the sea spreading for miles.

"Good. Blue is good. Listen to the waves. I see white light all around you. Your aura is very clear. A powerful indigenous man is near you. He was a shaman on earth. He says his name is Wide River. He says you shouldn't worry about a person you left behind in Rio because it's just physical distance that separates you two." He speaks softer, yet. "I feel the presence of a female. She says she loves you more than anybody else."

"I'm sure she must be my grandmother!"

"She has a lot of love for you."

He paused, listening, and then said, "She says for you to pray to your guardian angel so that he can help you be strong and not give into anyone's demands. She says she'll always be at your side and will watch over you."

I remember that time I paid a visit to the Amazon forest with her. We visited her Indian nation, and she took me to the spot where the Blue Nestira lived. It was the most amazing thing to see my lovely butterfly take flight and then land on a green leaf. She was the most beautiful thing I had ever seen.

"Can you hear me, Sofia?" His voice grows fainter.

"Yes."

"I want you to breathe deeply. Keep taking big breaths, and then visualize anything that you find relaxing and calming. Slow your breathing down until you've achieved a nice, steady rhythm.

"Good. Good. Now, imagine yourself as calm and relaxed as you can possibly be. Focus on taking action to maintain happiness. Make a decision about what to do about a challenge you face. Once you do, you'll find the support you need to accomplish your goal. Remain hopeful and optimistic. Look after your physical health and get plenty of sleep and rest. Don't lose sight of your purpose, goals, and dreams. Most important, take care of your emotional health. Continue counting your breaths. Breathe. Breathe."

His voice becomes fainter as I enter another level of consciousness. I'm diving in the ocean, just as my baby is diving into the amniotic fluid in my womb. I've loved my indigo sea for as long as I can remember. Before there was history, before there were flowers, before the redwoods.

My ocean is as vast as I make him, as soothing as I make him, as generous as I make him. I dive in unfathomable waters, beneath undertows, across currents, and in whirlpools to find the ghosts of those who died in shipwrecks and buried artifacts from vanished civilizations. I take a dive, swim around orange atolls, and reach the abyss to bring back abalone shells and black pearls in oysters. I think of Lev and how much I miss him, how much I want to speak to him, and how much I want to hear his voice. I will no longer keep secrets from him.

"Sofia, please, open your eyes when I get to five," I hear Ed's voice.

"1…2…3…4…5."

I open my eyes.

"Is that a good place to stop? You look angelic. There is a lot of blue light around you."

"Yes, I've gotten the answer I was looking for. Thank you so much."

We end the meeting with a brief prayer. I pray in Portuguese. Prayer is an activity of the soul, and my soul is still bound to Brazil.

I say goodbye to my friends and walk back into my room. Soon, I hear Didier come in. A shiver goes down my spine. I reach out and grab the Kokeshi doll Isabella gave me when I was in Rio. My doll is made of cherry wood inside. She has a sphere for her head and a cylinder for her body. Her face consists of a few lines, and her expression is pensive. Her hair is as black as mine. She has no limbs. There are a few musical notes imprinted on her yellow kimono, with motifs of white and pink cherry blossoms. She's lovely, although her history is disheartening. How can something so sweet represent murdered infants in Feudal Japan?

My eyes well up. I remember the night Papa took me to have the abortion. I was in a small room. There were modern machines surrounding me. The bright lights were blinding. The sonogram showed a nine-week-old fetus. They told me that he had a heartbeat. I was sinking into a hole, sinking into snow. The doctor turned on the suction machine. I was too numb to punch, kick him, and make him stop. I was too dead to even cry. I wanted my baby, but they erased his breath, his voice, and his fingerprints even before he was made. After the hospital, I bled for weeks. I bled out all my strength, all my desire to live, all my soul. But I had to choose my opera. I knew my father would stop financing my career if I kept the child.

I remember that Ms. Caballé was pregnant with her first child and had a miscarriage shortly after one of her performances. She said to that: "I lost my first child to opera."

I did, too, I realize. I get up, walk down the hallway and into Didier's bedroom. "I want my electronics. I need to speak to Dr. Lev." I reach for my phone, which is on the desk, next to his gun.

"No. I told you can't speak to him until you make a decision." He stops my hand. "I'm sure he's influencing you when he shouldn't have gotten you pregnant in the first place. You're meant to shine on the stage, not walk around the house getting things done before the baby wakes up."

He walks to the stereo and puts on Madame Butterfly. There is a deathlike quality to the libretto that I haven't heard in any other opera. Soon enough, she'll grab her father's dagger and end her life.

"All you do is throw up and skip your practice. You said you could handle the pregnancy and the opera, but you clearly can't." He grabs me by the arm. "I told Dr. Lev that you've decided to get rid of this baby."

"Stop grabbing me! You're a liar. Give me my electronics so that I can tell Lev that I never agreed to an abortion."

He softens his tone. "Sorry, I grabbed you. I just want you to understand that by choosing me, you choose opera, your dream. I swear I'll make you happy." His tone is persuasive. He points to the bed. "Look at this stunning red dress, these shoes, and this magnificent diamond necklace designed exclusively for you." His speech is slightly slurred. He steps closer, and I feel terrified that he might harm me.

"Sorry, I let you down. I appreciate everything you do for me, but I just think we should have this conversation tomorrow. But know that I don't want you to have any illusions about a romantic relationship with me. I never promised you my love, and I love another. I'm sorry."

"Sorry for what, for coming into my life and promising to become a great diva and then getting pregnant and ruining everything?"

"I'm sorry that things didn't turn out the way you wanted, but I didn't mean to hurt you. I wish I could make it all better."

"The only way you can fix this is to tell me that you're having an abortion and never speak to Dr. Lev again."

"No. I love him, and I'll never abandon him. It's my body. I get to decide if I'm going to have a baby or not. No one can do it for me."

"Of course, I can decide for you. I spent thousands of dollars on you and your opera. I own your body, your voice, your soul." He has his eyes locked on mine and steps even closer.

"I have the money to pay you. Please accept it."

"No. You are going to have an abortion. Actually, I made an appointment at a clinic so that you can get rid of this baby, soon."

"No! I'll never agree to that. I've made up my mind, Didier. I'm having my baby. I must. I can't choose between him and opera. But I promise to prepare myself and sing my heart out at the audition. I'll make you proud."

He takes another swig of his drink and puts the glass down on the desk. "This will never happen. I'm canceling our contract right this minute." His face is flushed and his eyes enraged. "You'll pay for your betrayal. You'll have neither Noah nor Madame Prunier to help you at the Met. You're on your own. The only way to fix this is to get ready and go to the clinic with me, right now."

"I'm not going, and that's my final answer."

He grabs my face and holds it between his hands. "You're meant to be my creation. You agreed to that when you signed the contract." His breath smells of whiskey. He leans closer and kisses my lips.

I push him away. "Do not touch me without my permission—ever. Let me go this instant."

He punches me on the cheek near the upper lip.

I fumble over the desk and finally get a hold of his gun and press it against him. "Let me go, or I'll shoot you." I grow cold.

He takes a step back. "No need to shoot me. Put the gun down. I'm sorry I hit you." His gaze is on me.

"Step back or I'll shoot you. I've been trained to do this and hit my target." I remember my grandmother and the black jaguar. "Step back as far as possible." I never felt so sure of anything in my life. I grab my phone and put it in my pocket as I hold the gun steady.

He turns away as I leave his room, still holding the gun. I feel blood dripping from my lips.

As soon as I enter my bedroom and lock the door, I feel as though I'm collapsing. I feel a wave of nausea, run to the bathroom, and throw up. It feels as though I'm on a rollercoaster. I feel that I'm tumbling inside a dark tunnel. Waves and spirals trap me. I'm dizzy. The turns are unpredictable. There are narrow halls, dead ends. It feels as though I've been thrown off the ride. I hang on to the towel holder. I can just barely hear Lev's voice in my head: "Get out of there!" and I stay put so that I can get out alive.

He turns the music louder.

I'm finally able to compose myself. I wet a towel and press it onto my forehead, breathing in and out, trying to calm myself. I'm still dazed as I grab the cell and dial Alondra's.

"Hello."

"It's Sofia. Please pick me up at Didier's. It's an emergency."

"You sound terrified. What happened to you? Should I call the police?"

"No, please, just pick me up. I'm armed." I break down crying.

"I'll be there as soon as possible, honey. Be careful."

I grab a carry-on and begin to pack my meds, my passport, and other important items.

The music is even louder, now.

I think of Lev, and I am able to calm myself down just enough to think straight. He told me to get out, and I will.

My phone rings. "It's me—Alondra. I'm in the driveway."

"I'll be out right away." I hang up, grab my things, and walk to the door. I think of Lev again, and of my baby, and I breathe deeply and go out the door. I grow calmer. I reach the driveway, and Alondra sees me. She gets out of the car. In a few minutes, I'll be gone from this house forever.

"Looks like he hit you." She grabs my suitcase. "I'll drive you to the police station."

"No, please. Take me to the hospital. I want to make sure everything is okay with my baby. I feel some cramping."

"Get in the car." She throws the suitcase in the back of her vehicle.

I break down crying as she gets in and turns the motor on. She switches on the overhead light. "You have blood smeared all over your mouth and nose." She takes off in a hurry. "I'm taking you to the urgent care place close by."

I don't talk. Don't think. Don't feel.

She drives as fast as she can as I collapse on the seat. All I know is that I'm alive tonight. I just hope I don't lose my baby.

Chapter 20

I open my eyes. The lights in the hospital room are excessively bright. The beeping sounds of the machines make me apprehensive, and my hand aches where the I.V. needle is positioned. I no longer feel sick. I'm calmer, but I feel drained. My whole body aches. I feel tears slipping from my eyes. I turn my head to the left. Lev sits in a chair next to the bed, reading from his copy of The Essential Talmud. It's his favorite book, the one he turns to when he's troubled.

He lifts his head and our eyes meet.

"Am I dreaming, or are you really here, Lev?" I reach for his hand and clasp it. "Tell me you're really here."

"I'm right here. I arrived last night and called Alondra. She told me what happened, so I came as soon as they let me in, which was two hours ago." He wipes my tears with his hand. "How do you feel now, Sofia? I was worried about you, but it looks like you made it."

"I feel better now that you're here by my side, but a bit scared." I touch my abdomen, which has been wrapped in a belt connected to a monitor. I don't know how to interpret the data on the screen and panic. "Is the baby okay?" I look at him intensely. "Tell me the truth, Lev?"

He holds my hand. "Yes, darling, the baby is fine. This is just for further observation. You were cramping a little, so they attached the monitor and ran all kinds of blood tests, and they will do a sonogram to make sure. However, the doctor told me that you are depleted of many essential nutrients and that it will take a few days to get you back in shape. Also, your blood pressure is unstable. But I don't want you to be stressed out. You're in good hands."

"Please, explain everything to me."

He reaches for a clipboard on a table by the bed and gives it to me. "If you sign this paper, I'll be able to look at all your records and discuss the prognosis with your doctors and figure out a plan to get you as healthy as possible before we board a plane to New York in a week's time. By the way,

I told them that I'm your husband. You know, it's just easier to get them to open up and share their findings. I want to make sure they get you the best treatment available. I redid all the forms and included all my information so that they'll be in touch with me. I hope you don't mind being called Mrs. Levien."

"I think I can see myself marrying you in the future when I get my act together. You're good looking, a great lover, and a great pianist who'll make a great father." I sign the form and give it back to him. "But you must promise me that you will tell me the whole truth about my condition."

"I promise." He closes his book and puts it on the bedside table. "While you slept, Sofia, I was thinking that I should have come to you earlier, as you came to me when I was shot. It's just that I promised not to interfere, and I wanted to keep my word. Forgive me for letting you down when you needed me." He leans closer and kisses me on the forehead.

"There is nothing to forgive. Please don't apologize. I understand how noble you are and how much you tried to keep your word, and you did well keeping it. I'm the one who needs to apologize for putting myself and the life of our baby in harm's way. You told me that Didier would never accept this pregnancy, but I wasn't prepared to accept it.'" I kiss his hand. "Sorry I hurt you. I needed you all along, but I had to do that for myself, Lev. My father protected me all my life. But now you're here."

His gaze is on me. I feel such love coming from him. I've never loved him more.

"I love you so much, Lev," I whisper in his ear. I'll love you forever."

"And I will love you until death do us part, my beautiful lady." He leans even closer. "By the way, I didn't have a chance to tell a certain diva that when she was on stage for the first time in Didier's restaurant, there was no need for pyrotechnics or anything else. It was just this gorgeous woman delivering through her voice. She knew exactly what she was doing. She had the chops and an amazing instrument. She moved me so much that she gave me goosebumps. Watching the video, I fell utterly in love with her once more. I'm certain she will win the Met competition."

My eyes well up with tears. "My dream of singing at the Met has been shattered. Didier will never allow me to keep Prunier and Noah, and without them, I won't be able to do it. I never want to see him again. It's unreal to lose everything when I was so close to achieving it."

"Your dream is alive and well. I'm offering to accompany you so that you can have your audition. I have all your scores, along with precise instructions from Madame Prunier from the time we practiced like crazy at Capella. I took the liberty of buying two tickets from Los Angeles to New York. I rented an apartment from a friend who's in Europe, and it happens to have a piano. "

"Are you serious?"

"Do you accept my proposal? We can work hard to make up for the time you missed and get you the big prize once we get to New York. I love your determination and passion. It's unbelievable to me what you've accomplished. You never cease to amaze me. It is all going to come to fruition."

"Do you really think I can pull this off? I still get sick a lot, Lev. The nausea has not let up. I hate to think that Didier was right about that. I'm too weak to stand the grueling task of practicing for hours on end. Now, you tell me that I'm depleted and that I need time to get the nourishment I need to make sure I don't lose the baby. I feel so weak."

"As soon as they do the sonogram, I'll talk to the doctor in charge of your treatment plan and will do everything I can to get you out of here well-nourished and completely healthy. My mother schooled me in all I need to know to advocate for you."

"I hope you are right, Lev, but even though I trust you and your expertise, I still think it will be difficult to pull this off. But tell me, how can you be so good to me?"

"I told you I wanted to make changes in my life so that I could be around you as much as possible. It's not a sacrifice. That's what I want, and if you want me in your life, that's all I need to know. I promised you that you'd never face this pregnancy alone, and I'll keep my word. I've applied for a grant to be able to do research on the effects of classical music on the brains of hate-crime victims. If I indeed get it, I'll be able to work on it from anywhere in the world that allows me to connect to the internet. I'll know for sure in two weeks."

"But you love your practice, Lev. I know you do. I was your intern and saw with my own eyes your passion for your work. Please, don't give it up for my sake."

"Someday I might go back to it, but I told you I wanted to do more with my music when you furnished my room at Capella with a piano and I began to play every time I was there. Not only that, your mother started to come over more often, and we played together. See? Now, I can hardly wait to be your accompanist. It gives me much pleasure to know that we'll be traveling the world together."

"I was thinking that if I win the million dollars, I will use some of the money to build an amphitheater at the Amazon Basin, which is next to my grandmother's Indian nation. I want to make classical music more accessible to those who can't afford it. And the proceeds of the first week can be used to save their land—that is, if Didier doesn't demand more money for his efforts."

"That's a terrific idea, Sofia, and I will help you raise a lot more money. My parents have a lot of rich philanthropist friends." He falls quiet, gives me a serious look. "The police want to interview you, later. The doctor in attendance wrote down in your file that you were a victim of aggravated battery."

"No, Lev, I don't want to do this. I pulled a gun on him, and he will certainly file a countersuit. Please don't insist on getting justice for me. I know how important this is to you, but I've got to decide for myself what battles to pick with Didier. I don't ever want to see him again."

Suddenly, I feel my energy drop, and my heart begins to beat very fast. The beeping sounds coming from the monitor grow faster.

"No need to become stressed, Sofia. I want what's best for you and the baby. Let's just focus on your health, darling. I promise not to interfere. Breathe, please. Good. Keep breathing, deeper and deeper." He uses his deepest voice. His energy is still, and he calms me down as he continues to coach me to breathe in deeply.

He begins to massage the back of my neck and whisper words of love.

I shut my eyes. "I'm so blissed out when you touch me like this and when I feel your love for me. Your love is addictive."

"That's the whole point." His voice is mellow.

The sonogram specialist comes in and announces that she's ready. She pushes the curtain out of the way and greets us. She grabs the handle of the machine and brings it close to my bed, right by my foot. "Let's see what's in there, Mom and Dad." She turns on the machine and then the monitor. She comes around, takes the belt off, and lifts the top of my hospital gown. "It will feel a little cold, okay?"

She begins to spread gel from a tube she holds in her hands onto my belly. After she is done, she puts the tube down and then picks up a wand with a handle attached to the machine. She begins to press it lightly on my abdomen, right below my stomach, and as she does, fuzzy images begin to appear on the monitor.

"Are you both able to see it?"

"Yes, I am," I say, feeling very emotional. I tear up just thinking that my baby is in there and is well.

"I can see as well," Lev says.

"Good." she touches a button on the machine and the image becomes clearer. "Can you hear the heartbeat?"

"Yes. It's strong." I see the zigzagged lines making a trail on the monitor.

"Yes, it is. The rate is 157. Very strong, very good, Mrs. Levien. Let me stop here and mark this."

The image on the screen freezes for a moment.

I hold on tight to Lev's hand as tears drip down my cheeks. "It's such a great sound."

"Yes," the technician says. "Your baby is very strong. You're ten and a half weeks' pregnant, a little further than you thought. So, this is really good." She hits another button and the image comes back on the screen. She touches another button and examines what she sees. "Does your family have twins?"

"Yes, one of my aunts has a set, my mother has an identical twin sister, and my sister has a set of fraternal twin girls."

"Makes sense, because I've found another heartbeat. There are two in there."

I attempt to sit up. "What? Did you say I have two babies in there?"

"Please, stay still, I know it's hard, but please try. Let me show you. Do you see this dot here? It's another baby, which I'll call Baby B so that I can differentiate the two."

"Oh, my God! Are you kidding me? Are you sure?" I wipe my tears with the backs of my hands. "There are two in there, Lev. We're having two babies. I'm freaking out."

"Yes, I know. It's exciting." His face shows a range of emotions. "It's the best news I've ever gotten."

"You're having twins, for sure. Do you hear this heartbeat? The rate is 103, not as strong as we want it to be, but you had a rough twenty-four hours, Mrs. Levien. I wouldn't worry so much." She freezes the screen to get a measurement. Then she shows us the image again, and this time makes it much bigger. "Definitely two babies. They are fraternal. There are two placentas growing in there."

"There are not." I laugh. "You're making this up."

"I'm dead serious. One is a little bigger than the other. Again, Baby B has a bit of a smaller house, but it's okay for now. Don't worry. The most important thing is that he has a home."

"What a big deal," Lev says.

"We're having twins, Lev, we're having twins. This is out of this world!" I'm overjoyed, yet also concerned about my second baby. I just feel that things are not well with the embryo. My heartbeat increases again.

"Now, there is another piece to this. The doctor ordered a whole bunch of blood tests to see if everything was okay with the baby, and that's how we found out you were carrying twins. I did my best to keep a poker face so that you could enjoy this moment. Now, one type of blood test reveals your children's sexes. The question is, would you like to know what you're having?"

"Yes!" I nearly shout. "How about you, Lev? Please say yes. I'm freaking out again."

"I'm all for it." He grins.

"Okay. Ready for this? You're having a boy and a girl."

"What? One of each?" I'm just in shock. "Are you kidding me? My mother will be super-happy. She always wanted one of us to have a boy and girl like one of her sisters did."

"I'm dead serious. Grandma will be happy. You're as white as a ghost, Mrs. Levien."

"I can't believe it—we're having Lyudmila Rose and Ariel Dimitri, Lev. Are you super-happy to know that?"

"I'm thrilled. It couldn't have turned out any better, Sofia."

"Do you have any more questions?" she asks as she cleans the gel off my abdomen.

"Will everything be okay with my Baby B and Baby A and me?"

"The doctor will talk to your husband shortly, and then he'll talk to you directly. Try to relax, please. We'll be checking on you a bit later. Dr. Hartford wants me to do second ultrasound after he puts you on another medication that is being made specifically for you in the pharmacy. Everything will be fine if you rest."

"Thank you very much."

"You're welcome. Congratulations, Mom and Dad. I'll leave you two alone, now. You can slide back up, Ms. Levien. I'll give you the pictures, later."

Lev gives her the form I signed. "Would you put this in her file? Thank you so much."

"My pleasure. Make sure Mom relaxes. I'll come and get you soon." She exits the room.

Lev sits down on the bed, facing me. I put my arms around his waist and lean on his chest. "Tell me the truth, Lev. You said you would. I'm not in good shape, and I might lose one of my babies or both." I cry.

"There's no evidence that you'll lose either one of your babies. Everything is under control. In a few minutes, I'll be talking to your doctor, and I promise to share everything I learn with you." He picks up a tissue from the box on the table by the bed and wipes my tears. "Do you trust me?"

"Yes."

"I'm in your corner. Are you happy, Sofia?"

"I'm so happy. It's the best day of my life—well, one of them. Thank you for taking care of me while I was asleep. Thank you for always helping me when things are not going well. Thank you for loving me so much."

"I love you even more, and I promise to be at your side from now on and be the best father for your children and the best husband to you. Are you marrying me soon?"

"When I get my act together, as I said earlier. I've got to win that contest, Lev—that is, if I can get out of this hospital in time."

"You will. When we get to New York, I'd like to take you to the museum to see The Lady in Gold. Then, we are going to see *Rusalka* at the Met. I've bought the tickets already."

"That's glorious."

He kisses me on the cheek. "By the way, when we return to Rio, I'm adding a new layer to your special necklace. How do you like that?"

"You're crazy, as I suspected."

"I may be, but I know that it's important to keep that necklace growing. I love you, Sofia. I'll do anything for you if you let me. I promise to help you accomplish your dream."

"I love you, Lev. I'm so tired, amorzinho. Do you mind if I take a little nap? But please stay at the hospital."

He looks at the monitor. "I'm not going anywhere. Please, go ahead and sleep some more. I'll be here the whole time, watching over you three."

"Thank you." I begin to close my eyes. "Do you think I'll be able to handle twins, meu bem?"

"Yes. You'll be an exceptional mother, and I'll be at your side every step of the way. Don't worry about a thing, amor."

"If you say so."

I take a deep breath and begin to fall asleep. I must get well soon. I hope there won't be anything too bad in store for me. If I were to lose even one of my babies, it would be too devastating. And if I were to lose my chance at winning the competition, it would be as shattering. I've got to put up a fight. As my grandmother used to say, "I'm a daughter of the Aruaques and a warrior by nature."

Chapter 21

I finish putting my makeup on in my dressing room at the Met. There is a print of Maria Callas on the wall above the mirror. She is dressed as Cio-Cio San. I'm also dressed to sing the aria from Madam Butterfly. I wear a gorgeous royal-blue crested kimono with scarlet-tinged maple leaves, plum flowers, and cherry blossoms. The sash is a delicate piece of work made of pink pearl camellias. The tabi socks help with the clogs. It's going to be tricky singing in them, but I've practiced walking in them for months. My hair falls down to my waist.

After a full week at the hospital, I've finally gotten my health back. I'm well-nourished and so are my babies. Baby B's heart rate is now 147, which is pretty strong. The severe nausea combined with the grueling schedule Didier required nearly made me lose my fetuses and my chance at winning the competition.

Lev's presence and expertise helped me heal much faster than the doctors had expected. He proved to me that love and trust are as important as technology and medicine. He helped me turn this whole thing around, and here I am, ready to go onstage for the final round of the contest. There are three of us left out of twenty contestants, and if I win tonight, I'll get the big prize and will put it to good use right way.

Lev and I are planning to raise a whole bunch of money to build the amphitheater. It's truly exciting to think that I'll be able to help the Aruaques Indian nation fight its new oppressor. I might be able to achieve something I never thought possible seven months ago when I first came to America—to find my true voice, not only as a singer, but as a woman who can give a voice to others.

This last round is the decisive one. I'm singing with the Met opera orchestra. Lev will be in the audience taking photos and cheering me on. As long as I can make eye contact with him, all will be well. The dazzling stage can freak a young singer out. Even before I walk out of the dressing room, I'm already thinking about who stood here before me—Callas, Renée Fleming, Anna Netrebko, Lucia Popp, and many others.

I listen to the Tibetan bowls' meditation chakra healing. They are music-scale singing bowls. The varying sounds of the water in the bowls yield a positive energy. It's deeply relaxing. I feel calm and peaceful. Still, I feel something stir inside. Puccini makes me cry every time. His music touches my brain, my heart, and my body, as well.

I refresh my red lipstick, blot my lips, and I'm ready to go on stage. I leave the dressing room and walk down the hall. I hear the applause coming from the audience. The singer who went before me has just finished her audition. I'm glad I got to practice with the conductor. I was able to lay my vocal cards on the table with him and tell him exactly what I needed from him during my performance. It's wonderful when a conductor treats a singer as a respected equal. I hate bullies who scream at singers and the orchestra all the time.

I stand at the entrance of the stage and hear my name called. I take a deep breath and walk into the illuminated room. The Met is as sumptuous as I imagined. I am amazed that I finally am privileged enough to step into a world of great divas and maestros who are destined to change me forever. I walk to the edge of the stage. I hear the applause and take a deep breath so that I can find my center. But it's true that, although I'm nervous, whenever they call me from the pit, I light up. I know that I'm 100 percent prepared. Then, I just hope that the stars align.

The set is perfect. Multicolor parasols cover the ceiling of the whole stage. There are two sakura trees in large vats, one on each side. They are filled with pink and white blooms. There are colorful geisha fans all around. A tall vase next to large yellow fan holds a chrysanthemum arrangement. Earlier in time, the opera was called Madame Chrysanthemums.

"Ladies and gentlemen—and now, on the stage, Sofia de Menezes singing an aria from *Madam Butterfly* by Puccini." The Master of Ceremonies continues with the introduction. "The aria describes Cio-Cio San with her maid Susuki on one beautiful day when Lieutenant Pinkerton's ship will arrive at the port, and she'll be reunited with her American husband. She has turned away from her ancestors to have him in her life. Her love for him is greater than her need to belong in her culture. Yet, soon enough, she realizes he isn't coming back for her, but to claim their son and take him back to America to live with his new American wife."

The orchestra begins to play.

I look for Lev in the front row. As soon as our eyes meet, I feel ready to start. We've practiced this aria countless times. I begin to sing. My voice is rich and full and amplified by the wonderful acoustics. I become Cio-Cio San, remembering that I, too, had to give up a child. Eli's baby never got a chance to come into being. Even though Cio-Cio San and I made similar choices for different reasons, the pain was the same and cleaved as deep. I finish the aria and immediately afterward, I recite Butterfly's haunting verses:

> I felt ready to die...but see, it passes, swift as shadows that flit across the ocean. Ah, I had forgotten...flowers, flowers, yes, everywhere. As close as stars are in the heavens. Pick the flowers as if the wind had blown them. And quickly set thousands of lanterns flaming. We surely have a thousand...No? We're not so rich? A hundred...fifty...whatever the number, the flame shall glow like the flame in my soul.

The audience erupts immediately into shouts and screams, calls of "Brava, Brava, Bravissima!" I look at Lev's face and then I bow my head very slowly. I raise my eyes up and out to the audience, bow again, smile, and leave the stage.

I walk down the narrow hallway until I reach my dressing room. I enter and close the door behind me. I sit down on the loveseat, still feeling the impact of the performance. I look at the orange roses Lev gave me when I first got here. He has been my saving grace, and without him, I'd never have been able to pull this off. I get up to change into my red silky dress he bought me on Fifth Avenue for the occasion. In thirty minutes or so, I'll know the results. I put on my red sandals and brush my hair. I hear at knock on the door. "Come in, Lev."

Even before I turn to look, I can see Didier's face in the mirror. My heart sinks. He offers me a bouquet of red roses. "For my amazing diva!"

I refuse to take the flowers, so he puts them down on the table.

I recoil. My heart beats fast. "Get out." Rage is welling up inside me. Images of that night at his house flash in my mind.

"Hear me out, please. I came to apologize to you." He steps even closer. His breath smells of whiskey." I know I've hurt you, but I was just afraid to lose you. You're the best thing that has happened to me." His face changes and he fixes me with a glare. "I came to tell you that you're shortchanging your goals. It's a tragedy when a person underestimates her talents. You're making a big mistake by giving up on my offer to make you into a world-renowned diva." He puts a manila envelope down on the table. "My lawyer will be contacting you."

"Leave now, or I'll scream for help." I feel nausea and take a deep breath.

"You can rule the world with me. I'm the one who changed the course of your life. I know you love me. Don't hold back. Dr. Lev is manipulating you. He's insidious and harmful to you. He knew that the only way he could win was to create a wedge between us by getting you pregnant." His tone is feverish. "You'll always be my Blue Nestira butterfly, and I'll never give up on you. I was supposed to make you into Brazil's greatest diva!"

He steps even closer and touches my chin.

I raise my voice. "Keep your hands off me." I hit him on the chest.

He steps back, turns, and walks out while I sit back on the chair, trembling. I take deep breaths to calm myself. It's very scary to know that he's not giving up. I pick up the red roses he brought me and throw them in the wastebasket. I'm trembling, and my palms are sweating. I feel another wave of nausea and put my head down between my knees. I breathe deeply. I think of my babies and try to remain calm.

I hear a knock. "Is it you, Lev?"

"May I come in?"

"Yes, please."

He comes in, and our eyes meet in the mirror. I turn to face him.

"You're pale."

"Didier was here."

"Why didn't you call Security, Sofia? There's an emergency phone on the wall." He looks livid. "You can't let him bully you."

"He's drunk, and he'd have made a scene. It's my career we're talking about."

He sighs. "Still, you can't allow anyone to barge into your life and harass you. Remember the night he hit you?" He looks incensed.

"Never mention that night again, Lev. You can't be raging at everything that happens to me. I'm my own woman and can handle stuff like this. The only thing you'll have to swear is that you'll protect our children with all you've got. Promise?"

He takes a deep breath. "Of course, I promise, but I can't stand him getting near you. It's impossible. Don't ask me to just accept it. He's a danger to your life. I can't let people harm you."

"Now you know how I feel when you keep tabs on shady characters who would certainly harm you if they got a chance. You say you'll stop catching neo-Nazis, but you never give up on the idea. I guess we both have to come to terms with those things. Please, let's put this behind us, okay? In a few minutes, I'll know what will happen with my life, and I want to be happy even if I lose. I learned to care for the other singers and would be happy if any of them were the winner. Please, would you mind bringing my duffle bag with you? I want to leave right after the results."

"I'm sorry. I'll do my best not to bring this up again—since you'll be out of his reach." He puts his arms around me. "It's just that your life matters more to me than my own."

"I feel the same way and would give my life for you, so let's just be happy tonight, Lev, and eat that lobster dinner you promised me."

"A promise I intend to keep. We'll just stop at the apartment so that you can rest a bit and then go have a good time in this mad city. And then, I'll knead your head and make love to you. Then I'll braid your hair."

"I can hardly wait." I smile and then grow serious again. "He left this package. Please take it with you and see what it's about. I don't really want to know, but it's probably a lawsuit or something of that sort. Would you do that for me?"

"Yes." He picks up the manila envelope and the bag. "Ready?"

"Yes, as ready as I can be."

I walk out of the dressing room. Lev follows right behind. Didier is nowhere to be seen.

"I'll see you right after the results are announced."

"I'll wait for you." He kisses me on the cheek. "Good luck."

"Thank you." I walk inside the room next to the stage. The other two singers are there. I greet them and sit on the couch next to them. The pressure is on.

I hear a loud voice coming out of the speakers. It's the announcer greeting the audience. He speaks clearly, but I'm too nervous to even understand exactly what's he's saying. Besides, my English is still faulty. I gather he's speaking about the end of the competition and how hard it was for all the contestants and how the level tonight was off the charts.

"And now, without further delay, we're calling onto the stage the winner of the final audition for the role of Cio-Cio San in *Madam Butterfly* by Puccini.

Please, come onto the stage, soprano Sofia de Menezes from Brazil!

I get up and turn to shake hands with the two other women. They congratulate me, and I walk away and onto the stage to a standing ovation. I feel no gravity in my bones. I have my whole life ahead of me and my opera back. The master of ceremonies hands me a bouquet of red roses.

"And here is your winner!" he says to the crowd and kisses me on the cheek. "Congratulations." He bows and walks away.

I bow from my waist and feel tears start. It seems to me that I'm in a dream, that this is happening to another person, a woman I don't know. But as the audience continues to applaud and shout, "Brava!" I begin to believe that it really is happening to me. I've kept my promise to Eli that, one day, I'd sing on this very stage where Gruberova, Callas, Netrebko, and countless other divas have stood. I don't know how long I've been standing here, just bowing. As the applause begins to die down, I bow one last time before exiting the stage and going back into the waiting room.

I hear the orchestra playing and walk to Lev. He holds me tight. "Well done, my diva. You have always looked the part. This aria belongs to you. Your voice is such a stunning instrument, really beautiful, just perfect. Brava, brava, gorgeous! I guess I'm running out of adjectives in English. Maybe I should begin all over again in Portuguese. But first, tell me how you feel?"

"So hungry I could eat a tree. Can we please leave? I'm a bit tired now that it's over. I want to be alone with you and actually order the food rather than go to a restaurant. I want intimacy in a quiet and private atmosphere. Would you go for that rather than eating out? You deserve everything tonight. It's because of you that this night was possible."

"It's your night, Sofia. I merely accompanied you on the piano. You're in charge. Let's go out through a side door I discovered yesterday so that we can escape the crowd." He takes the flowers in his hand and guides me out of the room and through the silent hallway.

We finally exit the building. He hails a cab. I'm in sort of a daze. I can't believe it. I think of the babies I'm carrying and realize that keeping them was the right decision. It makes me extra-emotional. He opens the door for me, and I get in. From the cab, I can see the fog shrouding the streetlamps, looking almost like a solid wall. The mad traffic makes everything look surreal, but what's true is that, in another week, I'll be back in Brazil and will begin raising the funds to build the amphitheater for the community my grandmother was raised in. After only a couple of blocks, we get out and enter the building. As we go up the elevator, I start to feel the weight of what has just happened to me. I panic a little when I remember that this night is just the beginning, and that there will be nearly insurmountable work ahead to prepare many more roles of a lifetime. After winning this, the world will take notice and know that I'm ready to shine on any stage.

Lev lets me in and follows behind me after locking the door behind him. The night air coming through the slit of the open window makes the room chilly. I turn the light on, walk to the fireplace, and turn on the gas. I sit on the bed and take my shoes off. I focus on the painting on the wall; the deep green that washes over the canvas brings back memories of my forest. Lev has promised to take me to Capella after I sing at the amphitheater. I can't wait to see a Blue Nestira flying free.

Lev approaches and kneels down in front of me. He hands me a green satin gift bag.

I take a box out, open it, and hold a music box showing a nymph dressed in a forest-green outfit, sitting by the lake. She has long, black hair. The trees and the moon are behind her. I wind the key and "Song to the Moon" starts to play. The moon on the music box begins to glow, lighting up the whole scene. In the center, *Rusalka* begins to turn.

"This is outstanding, Lev. Thank you."

"There is more. Please open the other box."

I do as he tells me and find a jewelry box.

He picks it up and opens it. "This is a provisory ring so that you get used to the idea of marrying me. I know how much you like owls, and this one is for good luck in your future endeavors."

I focus on the stunning ring by Elina Gleizer at Mystic Owl Designs. It's a unique piece of art, carved with distinct mastery. It's an emerald ring, as green as my forest. "This is so beautiful, so enthralling—thank you. Are you sure you want to marry a woman who will be travelling around the world pursuing her career?"

"Yes, Sofia. You're the only one for me. I'll help you get you where you deserve. I'll play along and support you in any way I can. You'll always be my Rusalka."

"And you're the only one for me. You'll always be my accompanist. We'll be unstoppable. I lean over and kiss him on the lips. "I love you."

I pick up the music box and wind it. *Rusalka* begins to spin and sing "Song to the Moon." On this night in New York, life seems flawless.

Chapter 22

My family and Lev's sit at the dining room table at Capella.

The walls are bright yellow. A painting by a local artist hangs on the wall above the fireplace. Dabs of orange paint scattered evenly across the canvas create a bucolic autumn scene that is free of pretention, and yet sophisticated in a way that only nature can deliver. The painting next to it captures the movement of green foliage against a dark-blue background. The silvery-gray clouds meandering across the canvas add a mysterious touch.

Doralice likes to strew herbs around to make the house smell like a country garden: sage, violet, roses, mints, tansy, winter savory, balm, basil, and daisies of all sorts hang from a line made of rope. After the herbs dry, she bags them and tucks them under sofa and chair cushions, and between the mattress and mattress cover on our beds. She makes Capella attractive and cozy.

There is a new cabinet with Amberina art, amber glass mixed with small amounts of solid gold. The top row holds three tall pitchers in ruby-red, fuchsia-red, and amber. The middle row has flashed-gold punch cups which, according to my mother, are extremely rare. The bottom row holds an acid-etched and engraved amber pitcher and ruby-red goblets. Mama has always been obsessed with antiques and attends auctions whenever she gets a chance. She just gave us the art glass pieces as a wedding present, even though she knows she and I don't share the same taste in house decorations and works of art.

We're having brunch together. Our parents talk about our wedding. They had hoped we would have a big one, but Lev and I have decided to have a small ceremony and put the extra money toward the amphitheater. In lieu of gifts, we will ask the guests to make donations to Greenpeace to help the Indian nation.

Mama wears a white-and-red polka dot dress of pure silk. She always dresses to impress, like many Brazilian women, especially the ones from the upper class. Her facelifts and cosmetic surgeries keep her looking young. For Brazilians, having cosmetic work done is a status symbol. Her dark-blond hair has golden highlights, which make her large green eyes stand out. My father is proud of her beauty and encourages her to do all she can to stop the hands of time.

My sister is a clone of my mother; they look like sisters. Madalena has had her share of aesthetic procedures to keep looking younger than thirty-one. Her CEO husband cares a lot about her appearance.

I'm glad Lev loves me the way I am. I don't want to live a photo-shopped life. The most important thing is that Lev loves me au naturel as well as in my stage makeup. Unlike many Brazilian men, he doesn't micromanage my appearance or tell me what lipstick color to wear. He isn't controlling like most Brazilian men, although he feels a bit jealous when I get mail from male fans who, besides my singing, talk about my appearance. He sits next to me, dressed in a white linen shirt and black slacks. He's so handsome that I too feel a little jealous when we go out together and I see women flirting with him.

My father is back in my life. After the trial, he had a change of heart and wrote me a dozen letters explaining his position. He wrote me about his regrets and has asked for my forgiveness. I still love him, and Lev has helped me deal with the hurt. Someday, I must come to terms with the fact that I have a man for a father whom Amnesty International accuses of using unnecessary and even deadly force against people from the favelas he is supposed to protect by finishing off the warlords in extra-judicial executions. On the other hand, this same man used to braid my hair every morning to keep my mother from cutting it into a buzz. He is the same man who loves Lev like a son and protects him from harm.

The brunch consists of many elements of the northeastern Brazilian cuisine. There are cassava roots doused in butter, tapioca crepes, boiled corn, and Doralice's famous chicken fricassee. She has presented us with jars of jams and jellies made with fruit from the orchard. The aroma of the comfort food is intoxicating. I'm glad the nausea is nearly gone as I enter my fourth month of pregnancy. I'm beginning to gain weight and feel desire for all kinds of foods. There is also orange juice with Piper Reidseick champagne, but I'm not drinking any alcohol.

"Sofia," Mama asks, "how do you like your new, glass art pieces? "

"I love them, but I wish you had told me before you made the purchase. As soon as the baby is born I'll have to put the glasses in storage. It's too unsafe for the baby."

She takes a sip of her mimosa. "I raised you and your sister not to touch art objects in the house. Just train them from the start, and they'll comply."

I put down my glass of milk. "Children need to move freely, Mom. I can't deprive them of movement just so I can have beautiful, fragile things. Sorry, that's the way I think children should be treated."

"Well, darling, in that case, you won't have much of a house. It will look like a nursery." She looks unhappy. She drove herself crazy when we were growing up trying to keep her expensive things from getting damaged, but I will put my children's freedom above material things.

"Sofia," Larissa touches my hand. "Your mother and I are working on your new house in Gávea. I mean, we're supervising the crew who are doing the painting and remodeling of the kitchen. The contemporary red cabinets you picked are gorgeous, bright and elegant. You have very good taste."

My mother puts her glass down. "I went ahead and picked a stove with a wok burner. I know how much you love Chinese food. Larissa loves it, too. What do you think? And by the way, it boils water in a flash."

"Thank you. I know I'll love it, but please, don't worry so much. I'm going to be traveling a lot, and my house should be more like a retreat than a showcase for me and my family, okay?"

Madalena puts her glass down. "She'll meddle in your life, Sofia. Just get used to it, little sister. Like every Brazilian mother, she'll be giving her opinion on everything and calling you and Lev at nine a.m. on a Saturday to invite you guys for lunch. Or she'll just show up to have breakfast with you."

My mother laughs. "That's what my mother did. She would come to my house with a cleaning crew early in the morning to wash all that tapestry she bought me in Portugal. That's just the way Brazilian mothers are, but it's all for the benefit of their children. And by the way, I hired a professional octet for the wedding, the best in town." Mama winks. "But, of course, you and Lev will choose the music."

Judge Daniel speaks up. "Don't worry, Sofia, I'm making sure these two don't touch the nursery, because Lev says that you two want to do it yourselves. My mother was the same way, even though she wasn't Brazilian. She was just Jewish."

I smile. "Thank you, Judge. I think my child should have a peaceful place to live, since we'll be traveling a lot. The nursery should be a place to relax. I'll have a piano in there, too. Lev wants to play the classics for the baby, just like you used to play for me, Mom."

"Are you taking Doralice with you to Rio when you settle there?" Mom asks.

"Of course not. She has her life here, and I need her running Capella when I'm away. Maybe I'll have someone in to help me during the morning hours, but that's it. Lev will help me, too. He'll be doing research from his office at home. We have a plan."

Larissa smiles. "Don't worry about it, Consuelo. We're two doors down and will help Sofia as much as she needs and wants. My mother can hardly wait for the baby to arrive so that she can watch over her great-grandchild."

"Thank you, Larissa." Consuelo rises. "How about if we continue our conversation in the living room? I think Dr. Lev and Sofia have some news for us, and we'll be more comfortable there."

"Great idea," my father says and gets up. "I can hardly wait to hear about it."

Lev gets up. "We have some pictures to go with it so that no one will doubt the news we're about to deliver."

I get up, pick up my handbag, and bring it with me to the living room. I have the sonograms they did at the hospital in Los Angeles, showing our twin babies. I still can't believe we're having a boy and a girl. We couldn't be happier, although I'm a bit concerned about having to give up delivering my babies at Capella if more problems arise during the pregnancy.

I step inside the ample, leaf-green living room. Nesting tables against the wall display exquisite clay works by Brazilian ceramic artists. I sit on the loveseat next to Lev, facing my parents and his. My sister sits in a chair next to us.

My niece Melissa comes in the living room and approaches me. She looks very much like me, unlike her sister Rebecca, who is a clone of her mother. Melissa and Rebecca had their children's breakfast in the parlor.

"Mom said you're having a baby, Auntie Sofia. Is it a boy or a girl?"

"Well, you'll know pretty soon. You've definitely grown taller and prettier." I kiss her on the cheek. "I missed you so much, and your sister," I say, smiling at Rebecca, who has just come in.

"I've missed you, too, Auntie Sofia," Melissa says. "The last time we were here, you sang for us. I like your voice."

"And I love yours. You have perfect pitch, and if you want, I can help you train your voice." She reminds me so much of me when I was her age, so much so that she could pass as my own daughter.

"I want it, but Mom says that opera is too hard."

"I still remember the maddening times before your auditions at the conservatory. Dad always had to comfort you and help you calm down. It was painful to watch him go through that meltdown every week. Besides, she has a weird fingerprint—just like you, Sofia. She will turn our lives upside down."

My father puts his phone on the coffee table. "Don't assume it was a bad experience, Madalena. I was happy to help your sister. It gave me great happiness to help her withstand the pressures of being an opera performer."

"I guess now it's up to Dr. Lev to help her before her singing engagements," Madalena says.

Lev looks at my sister. "Actually, now Sofia is pretty stoic before and during her time on the stage. I'm the one who needs reassurance when I accompany her. It might have been tough to shape her voice as she has done so brilliantly, but she is a master at her craft. "

"Let me help her, Madalena." I plead. "She really wants it, and she's so gifted."

"I'll talk to her father before I give you an answer."

I turn to Rebecca. "I've heard you're learning to play the cello. Is it true?"

"Yes, Auntie Sofia. I love the cello." She speaks in a soft voice. Her manners and dress are always impeccable. Like her grandmother, she hates to be uncombed or untidy.

"Your Uncle Lev plays the instrument. You should hang out with him so he can teach you what he knows."

"Are you going to teach me, Uncle Lev? I'll be good." She walks to Lev and sits next to him. "I love classical music."

"While I play the piano very well, I play the cello only well enough. Still, I'll teach you what I know if it's okay with your mother. I'm glad you like classical music, because I do, too."

"Of course, you can teach her, Dr. Lev. I want my children to play instruments. I never became a professional player, but I find much joy in playing the piano for my own pleasure."

Madalena shows regret. She abandoned her piano training after she married Ronaldo so that she could tend to all his needs. He's the typical Brazilian husband who puts his dreams ahead of his wife's. He expects her to care for the home and the children and, yes, do what she wants—as long as she doesn't let him down.

"It's a deal, Rebecca," Lev says. "We can figure out some times that work for both of us when we return to Rio."

She leans closer and gives him a kiss on the cheek. "Do you love it when Auntie Sofia sings to you?"

"Yes, I do. She is the best soprano on the market, and it's an honor to hear your aunt sing to me."

"She looks so pretty on stage. Grandpa showed us a clip of her auditioning at the Met," Melissa says. "Right, Grandpa?"

"Yes. Your aunt is divine and has been since she was your age."

Melissa edges closer. "This morning, we went to the stable with Eduardo to feed the horses their breakfast. He takes very good care of the animals, just like you, Auntie Sofia." She laughs. "I know you are nice to people, but you are super-nice to the horses, the turtles, the rabbits, the cat—and let's not forget the three huskies."

"When your auntie was your age, she was always finding stray animals and bringing them into the house," my father says. "The animals know where to come looking for shelter."

"Melissa is animal-crazy like you, Sofia. She has a white-and-black cat called Mona, the only living thing who can console her when she is gloomy for some reason," Madalena says.

"I want to have a farm just like you. I love all the animals and the trees like you do, cute little Auntie Sofia." Melissa puts her hand on my belly. "What do you have in there, a boy or a girl? I'm dying to know."

I turn to look at everyone else in the room. "Well, when I was at the hospital in Los Angeles, they did a sonogram, and they found out that Lev and I are having two babies." I smile. "We're having fraternal twins, a boy and a girl." I open my handbag and take the sonogram pictures out. "Here's the proof." I give the photograph to Melissa. "Please pass it around."

"That's so great, Auntie Sofia. You have two babies like my mother, but it's even better because you have one of each. Oh, I want one."

"You can come visit if you wish, but I can't give up either of my babies, little darling."

As she passes the sonogram pictures around, everyone congratulates us with much enthusiasm. Larissa even has tears in her eyes, but my mother looks like she is in shock.

"Their names are Lyudmila Rose and Ariel Dimitri," Lev says. "They will arrive in late February.

"Luckily, Sofia has a birth team of midwives and an obstetrician lined up for her so that she can have her unmedicated water-birth at home." Larissa smiles. "And I've decided to get a certificate in obstetric nursing so that I can help Sofia confidently. If she chooses to have her babies in the birthing center at the private hospital where I work, I'll be her nurse there, too. At least, that's the plan, although having twins is a bit more complex."

"I want my babies to have the gentlest entrance into the world. I don't want medication or an episiotomy. My doulas will help me achieve my goals, and with Larissa at the hospital if I need to be there, I'll feel even more confident."

"You are going to risk the lives of your twins just so you can have them the "natural" way?" Madalena raises her voice. "You have this romanticized idea of nature, Sofia, but nature can be cruel. My water broke during the thirty-sixth week of my pregnancy, and I had to have an emergency C-Section. Doctors don't care about your wishes when they think you or your babies might be in danger. They have all the power. So, I'd be prepared to change plans in a heartbeat."

"I know, but with Larissa's help, I'm sure I'll be able to deliver my babies at Capella, in a special swimming tub, surrounded by family and my husband. I'm healthy, and now that the nausea is gone, I'm sure I'll have a trouble-free pregnancy. "

"Still, Lev, you must know that having twins is very different from having just one baby. Are you going along with Sofia's plan?" Madalena says.

"So far. We are taking it one step at a time."

"You've got to tell her, Mom, about what happened to you." Madalena seems quite upset.

My mother looks like she is still in shock. "May I speak with you privately, Sofia? We can go into your old room where Melissa is staying." Her voice is low, and she blinks back tears.

"What is it, Mom? Please, Lev, come with me." I feel my hands turning cold.

"Let's go upstairs, darling. Of course Lev should come along. Please excuse us. We won't take too long." She gets up and walks toward the stairs. I follow her, and Lev comes right behind me.

I've never seen her look so vulnerable. She is usually in charge. She is far more rational than my father, even though she's an artist. I follow her inside my old room. It still looks like the room of my childhood. My dolls are lined up in the glass cabinet. There are photographs of me lining the walls, a few of them taken during recitals at the conservatory.

She sits down on the bed, and I sit next to her. Lev sits on a chair across from us.

Mama looks pale and fragile as if she had aged a hundred years since the moment she learned I was having twins. This is something new to me. She is usually poised and stoic.

"What happened to you, Mom?"

"You were not alone in my womb. My water broke in my thirty-third week, and the contractions came fast. There was no way to stop them. I had an emergency C-Section. The diagnosis was "failure to thrive." Your twin, Leonardo, wasn't gaining the weight he needed to control his body temperature. He also developed pneumonia. He lived for twenty-nine days. I was by his side every single hour I could stay awake. I held him as much as I could, but I guess it wasn't enough." Her eyes narrow in thought, making her look preoccupied or bereft of all happiness.

My tears drop from my eyes. "I can't believe I never knew I had a twin brother. That's the saddest thing I've ever heard, Mom. I'm so sorry you lost your baby boy. Do you think I could lose mine, too?" I edge closer to her.

"You don't have to. Technology has advanced exponentially, and we have highly trained doctors. Still, you have to be careful, because, like me, you also had to deal with the debilitating nausea in the first trimester. Besides, you're so small. Reconsider your birth choice."

"Was my life in danger, also? Was I tiny, too?"

"Yes, but you were born a little bigger and gained weight a lot faster than Leonardo. Your lungs were well developed, and although you stayed in the NICU for two weeks, you were able to go home afterwards. You were such a miracle baby."

"Oh, poor little me. I'll bet I was an ugly little thing." I pick up a tissue from the box on the bedside table and wipe my tears. "How come you never told me about it? I wish I had known."

"You were so peculiar that I didn't know how to handle you very well. I mean, I had to be careful because you were so sensitive."

"How was I so peculiar, Mama?"

"You were hard to please. When you turned three, you spent long periods just screaming your heart out—and on pitch, I must add. Nothing would soothe you. Dr. Cosme figured you were highly sensitive and couldn't deal with too much stimulation. He recommended a soothing environment and classical music, so I played for you, but it still took a while for you to calm down. He told us to wear earplugs and wait until that phase passed."

"For how long did I scream on pitch?"

"After six months of that evening ritual, you were a happy child again. You loved to lie under the piano while I played for you. When you turned five, though, you stopped talking to the adults. You spoke just above a whisper with your sister and let me know what you needed and wanted. At school, you relied on a few children to let the teacher know what you needed. She was frustrated with you, so we pulled you out of school. Actually, the only adult you talked to was my father, but you only wanted to talk about butterflies with him, and since he was an entomologist, he was able to grab your attention for long stretches. The child psychiatrist who saw you said that we just had to accept it that you chose when and to whom to speak, but not to worry because your needs were being met. So, we just let it take its course."

"When did it end, Mom?"

"Nine months later. Your grandfather recommended we move to a rural setting, but it was impossible due to my work with Rio's symphony and your father's teaching at the naval academy, so we decided to get the ranch so that you could be in that environment more often. Being in nature and caring for animals was the best thing that ever happened to you. You became easier to handle. Now, we know that you are a very artistic woman and a child prodigy. I love you so much, so deeply."

I put my arms around her and lean on her shoulder. "Sorry, beautiful Mommy, that I was so sensitive."

She holds my face with her hands. "You were such a darling. I bought you a tiara with three strands of genuine pearls for you to wear on your wedding day. You're such an authentic Brazilian beauty and such a great artist."

"Thank you, Mom, for the tiara, but I wish you'd return it. I want to have my hair down and wear a crown of roses, like Suzanna in The Marriage of Figaro. I love that aria, and so does Lev. Remember, we're having a small wedding."

"Nonsense, darling. This is an opera singer getting married, not the character of a maid. Tiara of pearls, it is." She gets up. "I've got to go. We've been rude enough leaving the Leviens alone. Thank you for listening to all this old stuff, Dr. Lev. I'm really glad you're marrying my daughter. I know you're the right man for her." She walks toward the door and then turns. "She loves you to pieces."

He gets up. "Thank you, but, really, she is marrying me. I had to ask several times, and I still don't have a date."

"Please convince her to have your babies at the hospital. I'll see you later." She exits the room.

He steps closer and puts his arms around me. "It's your wedding, Sofia. You wear whatever you want on your head."

"She'll make a big fuss. I'll just wear my crown of roses for you after the reception."

"That sounds great. I'm sure you'll look more striking than you already are, if that's even possible."

I let go of him. "I need to ride my horse. I didn't know this conversation would weigh so heavily on me. I need Vento."

"I'm sorry, but you're three months' pregnant, Sofia. It's not safe."

"I won't canter. I'll just let Vento walk around with me."

"Still, if you're thrown off the horse at this point, you've got nothing to protect the babies, and you yourself will get hurt."

"I just ride on the flat. Please, Vento and I sync really well. He'd never throw me off."

"Sorry, Sofia, but I can't agree with that. But I do have a surprise for you! I was going to wait until the wedding, but I think this is the right moment. I've been nursing a rose garden for you behind the pond, and I'd love to show it to you if you want to take a walk there with me."

"Really? Yes, I'd love to see it. You know how much I love flowers. How about your parents? I think we should be with them."

"They'll understand. Besides, they're enjoying the farm so much since they arrived here yesterday. They will be fine."

"Thank you." I kiss him on the cheek. "Do you want to change?"

"Let's go. It's a bit hot out there. Let's bring plenty of water." He holds my hand, opens the door.

We leave the room and go down the stairs. I walk by his side toward the guesthouse. I am determined not to fear the obstacles along the way. I will rise above them and deliver my babies at the right time and in the right manner as long I keep my head on straight and my heart in the right place.

We stop and look at the rose garden. He turns to face me.

"I've named it 'Sofia's Butterfly Garden' because the roses attract all kinds," Lev says.

"It feels just right."

"I'm glad you like it."

"Do you still want to hook up with me even though I have a weird fingerprint?"

"More than ever. It would be crazy not to marry the woman who has my heart, my thoughts, and my soul."

"How about November seventh for the wedding at Capella?" I suggest. "We have three weeks to prepare."

"November seventh is a great date to tie the knot."

"A small wedding first, but after I have the babies, I promise to marry you at the synagogue. In December, I'll be done with my studies and will have converted."

"Are you sure you want to do that?"

"Yes. I told you I want to raise our children Jewish."

"Sounds good, darling. You won't regret marrying me, Sofia, I promise. I fell hard for you for so many reasons, and yet, the more time we spend together, the more reasons I find to fall for you even harder."

"I can't imagine my life without you, Lev. You have my heart, my thoughts, and my soul, too. You are so generous, and I hope I can show you my appreciation."

"You already have."

We enter the cottage. I can hardly believe that our babies will arrive in late February. And then, we'll concentrate on the amphitheater and bring more classical music to those who can't afford it. I can hardly wait to sing to a Brazilian audience and raise even more money to save the Aruaques' land.

Chapter 23

It is February, 2016. Lev and I have settled in Gávea. We are in our bedroom. I had a Feng Shui expert come in to decorate our quarters according to the natural and harmonious flow of energy for sleep and sensuality.

The walls are a rich chocolate brown with gold borders. The furniture is made from Brazilwood. The red of live coals adds warmth to the room. The flowing curtains are also gold . Our bed has ample access on both sides. We put all the electronics in the home office, except for the iPod with hundreds of songs for every mood. There is also Lev's piano. He often plays for me, especially when I have trouble falling asleep. I feel as though I'm back in time, and I'm reminded of my mother playing for me so that I could fall asleep.

The room has multiple levels of lighting that they can be dimmed or brightened as desired. On the small altar next to the fireplace are artfully placed soy candles to clear the air of toxins. There is a gong attached to the wall below the altar.

Lev sits at his desk preparing some documents for fighting Didier in court. He is suing me for breach of contract, even though I've paid back every cent of what he spent on me. He claims psychological damages, but Lev and I are adamant about not letting him get away with it. Even though I didn't talk to the police that night at the hospital in Los Angeles, Alondra did, and she had pictures of my bloody lips to show the cops.

I hear myself singing *Rusalka*, Lev's favorite aria. He does worship me, and there is nothing he won't do for me. He's an attentive husband and a great lover. Little by little, I'm getting to know him even better. He can be as intimate as he is respectful of boundaries. He never spews advice, even when he thinks I need it. His compassion is his most precious gift to me. Even when I make mistakes, he never judges me. Instead, he gives me the space to unburden myself of shame, guilt, and despair. I do my best to reciprocate, but I am far more emotional and bring more fire and verve into our lives.

He is the man who has untapped my sexuality and made sex far more than a physical act. He will father my children, and I'm sure he will be their best friend and a great mentor.

We had a simple wedding at Capella, officially observed by his father. We're planning a wedding at a synagogue for June now that I've converted to Judaism and studied a few months with a rabbi from Lev's congregation in Rio. Our children will be born Jewish and raised in Lev's faith. He never asked me to do it, but I knew it was important to him.

Both sets of grandparents and Savta shower me with gifts for the babies, which are coming next week. I guess I don't have to buy anything. My mother is the worst, and every so often travels to Miami where affluent Brazilians shop. She takes empty suitcases and hops from outlet to outlet, then fills them up with things for me and her grandbabies. Last time she was there, she brought me a special cream to spread on my belly and a therapeutic maternity compression pair of pants to help me avoid stretch marks. She brought me bags of pistachios at Costco because I was craving nuts. She filled a suitcase with clothes for Lyudmila and Ariel. She brought baby bottles that are supposed to minimize colic. I guess this is her way of showing that she cares. Little by little, we are mending our relationship. Now I understand her better. It must have been horrifying to lose one of her babies.

Lev comes over to me. He wears a black suit and tie. He sits down on the bed and faces me. "Are you crying?"

"No, Lev. I'm praying for our babies to be healthy."

He smiles. "So, not only praying, but also doing everything you can to make it happen. Look at you: three days in bed to stop the contractions and delay the birth of our son and daughter. You don't eat sushi or sashimi, even though you crave them. You do your breathing exercises and much more. I'm so proud of you, Sofia. I wish I could do something to take some of the burden off you. You look a bit tired, my love." He combs my hair off my face with his fingers. "It's a bit of a bird's nest today."

"I look horrible, right? Please don't hold it against me. I'm exhausted; drying my hair is out of the question."

He gazes at me. His eyes sparkle as he looks at me in a way that reminds me of that first night we made love, and I fall in love with him all over again. I remember neon lights burning up that night and the depth of his love for me.

"I've never desired you so much, Sofia. It's very sexy to see the woman you love on bed rest to give our babies a better chance to be healthy and strong." He leans closer. "You look so hot, I can barely keep my hands off you." He whispers. "You turn me on."

He kisses me on the mouth. I feel his passion and desire for me. I kiss him back, showing him how much I want him. He is like oxygen itself, and I forget that there were other times in my life when I had no air or very little of it.

"Your sacrifice will not be taken for granted, amor."

My eyes well up. "I want our babies to get a head start, Lev. I'll do anything to keep them in my womb for another week. It's no sacrifice. It's just love, the strong love I feel for them."

"That's exactly why you've never looked so beautiful to me. I love you, te amo, meu bem. You are my whole life." He caresses my belly. "And I love these two little ones in there. I hope they'll look like their mother. How are you feeling?"

"I felt a couple of mild contractions this morning, but nothing else. Dr. Aaron said to call if I have six or more in one hour and if each lasts more than ten seconds. Don't worry. I'll be fine while you're gone."

"My mother is home today. She said to call at any time if you need help, and she'll come by to cook you some lunch, okay? He picks up the huge box and puts it on the bed. "This is from me to you and your babies. Open it, please."

"You didn't have to, Lev. You have already given me so much of everything, especially your love and time and attention."

"I like to please you. So, go on, open it."

I undo the gold bow and open the rectangular off-white box with gilded edges. I take out the first item and nearly cry to see the baby-size scrap quilt. It looks like the one he gave me when we first made love at his apartment the night our babies were conceived.

"This is so gorgeous and delicate. It has been made with great care. Thank you."

"Please take out the next item."

I pick up another present wrapped in pink tissue paper and open it. "It's another quilt just like the one I have. That's just too much."

"We're having two babies, darling. Everything has to come in pairs."

I hold both blankets to my face and smell them. I recognize their scent, a faint aroma of alfazema, lavender, the perfume of my childhood. It seems he has interviewed everyone in my family to find out how I was when I was a baby, a toddler, and a child. He gets me stuff that takes me back to my early days, and I love them.

"Open this, please." He hands me an envelope he picks up from the bottom of the box.

The gold linen envelope contains a stack of gift certificates for Reiki massages. I feel tears start, remembering the time when I used to give him a Reiki massage every day so that he could heal faster from his bullet wound. Just the thought of losing him makes me panic.

"I would have done them myself, but I'm not qualified," he says. "You can just call the practitioner and she'll come to you. Let me know when she'll be here so I can care for the babies. I want you to be pampered and cherished."

My tears drip down my cheeks. "I love you so much. I wouldn't know what to do without you. You are the love of my life, Lev. I'm crazy about you."

"I told you I'd help as much as I can." He reaches out, picks up a tissue from the box on the bedside table, and hands it to me. "Cry no more, darling. Everything will be just fine."

"I hope so, Lev. I'm a bit weary."

"I don't anticipate any problems. I have to leave, sweetheart, but I'll be back as fast as I can."

"Are you going to the clinic?"

"Yes. There is an emergency I have to tend to. Carolina returned this morning, and I have to stabilize her so that I can concentrate solely on you. You know how to reach me during emergencies. Also, I asked my mother to mail your contract to the Met. Are you excited about singing there as a full-fledged opera singer?"

"Ecstatic. Singing Carmen has been a dream of mine, but first, I'll sing in my own land, at the very amphitheater we are building. Thank you for helping me raise a ton of money. I'm glad my father invested mine, and it was helpful, too." I put my arms around him. "I love you, Lev, more than I love myself. "

He caresses my belly. "They seem to be very active in there."

"Do you think I'll lose our boy like my mother lost my twin brother?"

He peers at me. "No. Dr. Aaron is on top of things. The babies seem to be healthy. They'll be small for sure, but they'll gain weight very fast. My mother says that the birthing center is one of the best in Brazil and well-equipped. Besides, she'll be with them most of the time. I promise to help you through this. Pretty soon, we'll have our babies with us, and this house will be filled with even more joy." He kisses me on the cheek.

I smile. "They're going to be so adorable. I think I'm going to cry just looking at the little angels. They'll be so darling."

"Like their mother."

"I'm dreading being away from you today."

"My mother is one phone call away. She is ready to assist you at any point in time, and so are my father and grandmother. I'll return as soon as I can."

"My mother is also coming here after she leaves the conservatory."

"Good. Bye now, darling." He gets up. "If needed, you can also call me at the office and leave a message marked as 'urgent,' and I'll be beeped." He stares at me for a while. "You're safe." He walks away.

There is a pile of mail from fans on top of my bedside table. My fans have been faithful ever since I won contests all over the world. In fact, that's how I met Didier. It's a good idea to go over them before the babies decide to come out. It's impossible to answer all of them, but I always pick a few and respond with a brief, handwritten note. I open a letter.

I feel tired and a little bit nauseated. I feel a small contraction, and time it. It lasted twelve seconds. Maybe I'm just nervous. I breathe in and out, trying to relax. I feel another contraction and time it. I hold the little blanket and try to think of my babies and how important it is to keep them in my womb at least for another week.

I click on the iPod and hear Suri singing Piaf. Lev digitalized all the recordings he could find of his great-grandmother from her appearances at the nightclub. The home movies were found amongst letters to his grandfather Jacob, which did not reach him until a year ago. It's so touching to hear her smooth, warm voice, so filled with depth. She was a great artist. It pains me that my husband lost so many ancestors in the war and in such a tragic and painful manner. But I'm going to use my own artistic gifts to help preserve Suri's memory.

Another contraction comes. It's very painful and lasts twelve seconds. I begin to worry, pick up the phone, and dial my doctor's private number.

He picks up right away.

"This is Sofia Levien. I'm sorry to disturb you, but I feel something is wrong."

"I've just arrived at a meeting with my team, Sofia. What's going on?"

"I'm having contractions that last for about twelve seconds. They are painful. I'm scared."

"Not possible. I medicated you well. The injection is meant to stop labor. Have you been in bed 24/7 as I requested?"

"Yes. I haven't gotten up except to use the bathroom and take a quick shower." I feel another contraction and more pain, and the intensity is increasing.

"Is Dr. Lev there?"

"No. He left for the clinic on an emergency."

"I want you to continue timing your contractions. If there are more than six in one hour, I want you to call me back and also call Larissa. She'll know what to do until you arrive at the hospital. I'll send an ambulance, if necessary. Don't be afraid, okay. I'm in your corner, and I already have my team ready to go."

I feel tears start. "Okay. I'll wait. Thank you so much."

"You bet. Okay, sweetheart. Hang in there."

"Can I ask Larissa to give me another injection?"

"No. I'd rather you wait, okay? I'll call Dr. Lev to give him more instructions if needed. Call me if they continue. I'm very close to the hospital. Bye."

"Bye." I put the phone down and begin to do the breathing exercises I was taught in Lamaze class. It softens my pain and relaxes me. I cry softly, not so much because of the pain, but because my dream of giving birth by supportive midwives backed by sophisticated medical technology is over. I was hoping that, at least, I'd have that at the hospital birthing center, but I know it won't be possible. Dr. Aaron thinks it's too risky.

A sturdy envelope contains photos of the amphitheater's acoustic shell, which is in construction. The design is gorgeous and the location at the Amazon basin is out of this world. Hopefully it will be done by August 2016 when the Olympics will take place, which will help bring attention to the project and festival in which I intend to sing an exclusive Brazilian repertoire.

I open a manila bubble envelope and draw out a medallion. The logo on the pendant is a white cross on a red background. Lev told me before that this is a symbol of white supremacy. My heart skips a beat. The picture sent along with it freezes my blood. It's a photograph of me in my wedding dress. In the center of the forehead, there is a drawing of a bloody star of David, and below the picture, the caption: "Jew!" It's written in a bold, red font. I set the items down on the bed. I feel sweat drip down my temples.

Another contraction hits and then another, and I know that there is nothing stopping these babies. They want to come out. I focus on my breathing, but the pain is just unbearable.

I pick up my cell and press my doctor's number.

"This is Sofia. I think I'm in labor, Dr. Aaron." My voice is barely audible, even to me.

"I'll call the ambulance. I want you to call Larissa so she can be with you when the ambulance arrives. I'll meet you there. I've already spoken with Dr. Lev. I'm giving him another ring, okay? Just hang in there as help arrives."

"Thank you. Are you sure I won't lose my babies?"

"There is no reason to, but we'll have to see if we can keep them in longer. Don't worry. I'll meet you soon."

"Bye. I'll see you soon. Thank you."

I hang up and breathe hard. The pain is increasing. I wish I could get up and walk to the safe to get my gun to take with us, but I'm afraid to hurt the babies even more. Someone will have to get it out of the safe. I reach for a piece of paper, grab a pen, and write the combination number on it.

The phone rings. "Hello."

"It's Lev. How are you?"

"You're not here, Dr. Lev," I say, reverting to my name for him from the old days. "I'm scared. The pain is intense. And they're after me. Can you come soon?"

"I'm sorry, darling, but I'm in Leblon. I had to stop at my old place to get a few documents. I'd rather go straight to the hospital. It's ten minutes from here. I've called my parents, and they'll be with you soon." Suddenly, something I said got through to him. "What's that about 'They're after me?'"

I cry. "They sent me a medallion and a photo. They want to kill me. I need my gun. I can't get it." I can't stop crying.

"Listen, Sofia, my mother will be there soon. The ambulance is on its way. I'm afraid I can't understand you. I'll also call your father to send help."

"Oh, Lev, I wish you were here to hold me close."

"I'll hold you close at the hospital. I have to call my parents again, okay? They must come to you right way."

Larissa hurries in and drops her bag on the chair. "Is it Dr. Aaron on the phone, Sofia? Lev called me."

"It's Lev." I hand the phone to her. I hand her the medallion and photograph.

"Lev, it's Mamochka. She's in labor, I'm sure, but don't worry; everything will be okay, son. I'll take care of her. Pretty soon the ambulance will be here, and we'll all be heading for the hospital. We'll meet you there. Make sure they have a bed for her in my wing." She jumps, noticing the medallion in her hand for the first time. She frowns. "There is something very upsetting going on, Lev. A photograph and a medallion sent to Sofia. I'll take a photo and text it to you. Make sure to call her father to send protection. I've got to go." She hangs up and sits by me on the bed. She takes my wrist in her hand. "Breathe, sweetheart, keep on breathing."

"They'll get me soon."

"No, they won't. We'll protect you. Try to relax."

She takes a photo of the medallion and photograph and texts it to Lev. Then, she wipes my face with a tissue paper. Her phone rings.

"Lev? Did you get hold of her father? Oh, good. Talk to her."

"Sofia," Lev says. "There is nothing to fear. Your father already sent help, and there will be officers at the hospital, as well. You and our babies will be protected, do you hear me?"

"Yes, but they might hurt you. I have to protect you. I promised."

"I'm already at the hospital talking to the officers who are here. I'm safe. I'll see you very soon. I love you." He hangs up.

Judge Daniel comes in. "We're here. Lev told me to get the suitcase you had ready for this, Sofia."

"It's inside that closet." My lips are parched. I grab the paper with the safe's combination number. "Please, Judge, get my gun from the safe. I need to protect myself, Lev, and the babies."

He approaches me and sits down on the bed. "Listen, Sofia, your father is escorting us to the hospital, and there will be enough protection for you and your family, darling." He leans over and kisses me on the cheek. "I promise you nothing will happen to you, to my son, or to my grandbabies. Do you believe me?"

"Are you sure?"

"Yes. You have my word."

The sounds of emergency vehicles come closer and closer.

He gets up and walks away. Larissa sits next to me. "Just breathe, Sofia. Breathe."

I begin to feel numb with pain as the medics put me on the gurney. My tears spring up and fall off the corners of my eyes. "Larissa, please come with me. I'm so scared."

"I can't darling, but I'll meet you at the hospital in no time. Daniel is driving me there. We'll be right behind you. The BOPE agents are going to escort us so that we get there even faster. Don't worry about a thing. Breathe. Breathe. Just breathe."

The medics finish strapping me on the gurney and carry me away. I close my eyes. I faze in and out. I feel like I'm in a fog. I dread what could happen if the likes of Officer Almeida are able to get to the hospital. I must protect Lev and myself. This time I'll be the one to aim and shoot. They'll never hurt the person I love the most in the world again.

The medics stop the ambulance and begin to take me out of the vehicle. They wheel the gurney through the front doors of the hospital and then through the light-blue hallways that lead to the surgical center. They bring me inside a room where I'm greeted by Dr. Aaron and one of his nurses.

"Sofia, you took me out of my meeting. Do you know that?" He smiles. He's in his deep-blue scrubs, gloves, and cap.

"Sorry. I'm really sorry," I say as the medics transfer me to a hospital gurney.

The nurse helps me out of my dress and helps me put on a green hospital gown. The pain is very intense, much too intense by now. They tie my hair into a bun and put the cap over my hair.

"Is Dr. Lev here?" I ask. "Please let me see him." Beads of sweat run down my temples.

"Yes, he is. He'll be with you as soon as we prepare you for the surgery." He examines me. "That's it; these tiny babies are coming out."

Larissa comes in. She's in her scrubs and ready to work alongside the doctor and his team. I breathe deeply and sit up as the anesthesiologist administers a spinal block injection. The contractions are strong, and it's hard to keep still.

Lev comes in and our eyes meet. He walks up to me and stands by my side.

"Lev, do you have your gun on you?"

"Not at the moment, but there are BOPE agents everywhere, and nothing will happen to me or you or our babies. I promise."

I lie back as the anesthesia begins to work. I'm slowly feeling numb from my waist down. Lev holds my hand as Larissa puts an IV line into my arm. I don't move at all, although the contractions keep coming faster and faster. I don't want my children to get hurt. I squeeze Lev's hand. The numbness increases in my belly and legs.

They roll me across the hall to another room, bigger and brighter. I'm now being positioned under the operating light on a firm, narrow bed, slightly tilted. Larissa fits a tube over my nose delivering oxygen.

"Everything will be okay, Sofia. I'm right here. Your babies will be in your arms, soon," she says.

They raise a curtain between my head and my lower body. Machines are checking my blood pressure and oxygen levels. I can no longer feel the lower part of my body as they count the tools they are using for the surgery. Lev lightly squeezes my hand and wipes the sweat off my face with a towel. I feel a wave of warmth knowing he's by my side.

"Don't go anywhere, please." My voice is soft. "I need you."

"I'm not planning on it. I'm here to stay."

His presence alone makes me less afraid that things won't go as planned. He's my solid Rock of Gibraltar. I feel tears start, just thinking that in less than half an hour, I'll have my babies in my arms.

The doctor and the nurses work diligently. I squeeze Lev's hand harder. I feel nervous and very nauseated.

"Is everything okay, Dr. Aaron?" I ask.

"We're almost there, Sofia," he says. "You took me out of my meeting for a good reason."

"Sorry, I'm really sorry, but is everything okay?"

"Everything looks mighty good, sweetie. In ten more minutes, I'll lower the curtain so that you can see your baby girl being born."

"How about my boy? Is he okay?"

"He's fine, but she wants to be born first. She's a tough cookie."

I laugh.

"Oh, good, you're laughing."

I look at Lev and can see a range of emotions on his face, yet he's centered, helping me through the most difficult hour of my life. He sits in a chair by my side and rubs his thumb on my forehead in gentle circles.

Larissa begins to lower the curtain as the doctor gets Lyudmila out of my womb. My heart nearly stops. It's such an indescribable feeling seeing my daughter come out of me. She's finally out as tears run down my face. She cries loud and sharp.

"Here's our baby girl. She is beautiful, isn't she?" Dr. Aaron hands the baby to Larissa. "Her eyes are open."

My mother-in-law enfolds her granddaughter and begins to dry her with a green cloth. She takes her to the warming table and begins to check her. Lyudmila continues to cry vigorously, and her grandmother tries to comfort her. Larissa says that her breathing, color, and heart rate are just fine. She wraps her in a green sheet and brings her to me.

Larissa has tears in her eyes as she hands me my daughter. The moment she puts Lyudmila against my chest, my baby becomes quiet. She looks at me. Her blue eyes are just like her grandmother's, and so is her blond hair. Her eyes are on me.

"Oh, she's so tiny, so small, so beautiful. She's so perfect, Lev." My tears flow down my face, and although I'm exhausted, I feel strong.

"There are three bracelets on her with your name, see: Sofia de Menezes Levien," Larissa says.

"You're so sleepy, baby. So beautiful, tão linda, Lev. She's face to face with me. She has big eyes." I hand her to my husband.

It's an inexpressible feeling to hold such a precious life in my arms and know that she's completely dependent on me.

Ariel comes out. He has black hair. He isn't crying hard. Larissa takes him in her arms and begins to clean him up. It's such a wonderful thing to know that I will sustain his very life.

She brings my son to me, and he begins to quiet down the moment he is in my arms. He's so fragile. I hold him and whisper words of love in his ears.

"He's so gorgeous, Lev. Here, go with Papa."

Lev takes Ariel in his arms.

I feel a kind of urgency I've never felt before. I remember the swastika medallion and the photograph of me, and I panic. They could harm my family! I burst out crying. "Please, Lev, don't let anyone hurt our babies. I'm sure they're coming for them."

He gives our boy to Larissa. "It's all right, Sofia. Don't worry about such things. There are three BOPE officers outside that door to protect our family."

"The nurse will give you a tranquilizer, Sofia," Dr. Aaron says.

"I don't need any shots. I want to keep an eye on my babies. They might be in danger." I raise my voice. "Please."

Lev wipes the sweat off my face. "Please, let the meds work for you, sweetie. I promise you that the babies are safe, and so are you. You look exhausted. Please, get a little bit of sleep. I'll watch over them for you. Do you trust me?" He looks unwavering.

"Do you promise that you and the babies will be safe? I promised to protect you three."

"I do. Please, get some rest. I'll be at your side."

"I'll take the shot, now." The nurse gives me the injection.

I fight a wash of tears, but it's hopeless. "Can you count Ariel's fingers and toesies and then Lyudmila's?"

"Yes, Sofia, I will. Don't you worry about a thing."

"Tell Larissa to be really careful. They're so fragile."

"I'll tell her."

My eyes begin to close. "She's a great nurse, but make sure they are handled with care."

"It's my honor to care for them—and you, Sofia. I love you very much."

His voice gets fainter and fainter, and everything goes dark.

Chapter 24

It is early morning in Manaus. The hotel in the heart of the Amazon state is a gorgeous place. It is hard to believe that there is a whole forest on the other side of this gentrified city. I wear a bohemian night owl robe Lev gave me for my twenty-eight birthday, two months ago. The bird depicted on it has brown, reddish, and yellow feathers and is set against a starry night background.

We sit at the table in the hotel room. The crimson tablecloth is sprinkled with bits of gold foil confetti around the bases of two tall, red candles in clear, cylindrical containers. The napkins are also crimson. Lev lights the candles, and then he picks up a tray from the credenza filled with strawberries, cherries, concord grapes, and sliced red pears. He puts it down on the table and then picks up a maple wooden board filled with all sorts of cheeses. He ordered a special luncheon to celebrate the closing of the opera festival at the amphitheater we built fifteen minutes from where we're staying.

The first notes of Habanera come out of the hidden speakers. I'm looking forward to singing Carmen by Bizet at the Met this December. Lev has been practicing the score with me for a month, and in October I'll start rehearsals at the opera house.

"I believe Bizet wrote this opera with someone like you in mind." Lev pours me a glass of kvass, the Russian drink that packs a punch. I'm the first on stage tonight, and that sure will give me the energy that I need.

"Why?"

"Your smile and facial expression are unpretentious. You are dramatically gifted. And stunning. And sexy, in a classy way. Ah, let's not forget the crystal clear, lyrical voice, which is a heartbreaker."

"Have you seen Carmen Monarcha? She sings it to perfection."

"I have watched her sing on YouTube and find her sensuality exaggerated, while yours is hypnotic. She is beautiful but doesn't have your charisma, and she rushed through a few notes, leaving the orchestra scrambling to catch up."

"You're so biased, Lev."

"Yes, I am, but I am also accurate."

I get up, walk around the table, and sit on his lap. I put my arms around his neck and smell his cologne, a mix of citrus and musk.

"Thank you for practicing with me for this role for so many, many hours. You've helped get me to where I am, and I feel ready for the opening night in two months' time. I hit the jackpot when I hired such a gifted pianist and manager." I kiss his neck. "I think I'll give you a raise."

"I said I was going to change my whole life to help you with your career and the children. How about the husband part? Was that a good deal, too?"

"Phenomenal. You have no idea how much I love you, and I am happy that you are in my life, Lev. You are a great lover and a most caring father. You help me with my career and business. Our lives would be perfect if only you would abandon this idea of dismantling neo-Nazi groups. You promised me last month that you'd never again be doing this type of work. It's dangerous. My father is on top of things."

His face hardens. "I can't sit on the sidelines, not when Officer Almeida escaped from prison. I promised to be working in the background."

"We must protect our children. I'm concerned about leaving them in the hotel with my mother and your parents."

"Our entire family will be protected. There are two agents guarding them, and three more are accompanying us to the amphitheater. Plus, there will be more police during the event."

"I'll have my gun on me at all times, and I will protect you, as well. This time, I'll shoot anyone who tries to hurt you. I will take care of you, Lev, as I promised that night when we first made love after I tended to you. I can't live without you."

"Thank you, but it isn't really necessary. No one needs to be killed. We'll catch him before they have a chance to hurt you or anyone else." He smiles. "You're a tough lady, but I can take care of myself. And I'm the one who wouldn't survive a day without you, Sofia."

I gaze at my husband. My love for him runs so deep. He does everything for me without expecting anything in return. We have conversations about nothing as well as about big, life decisions. He's my biggest fan.

"Are you ready to sing to our own people in a few hours? The amphitheater turned out great. And it was all possible because of you."

"Thank you for all your help. I love the way things turned out. My grandmother would be doing the same if she were alive. She was an activist and fought for the right of her people to continue existing. She was a true native Brazilian warrior. I'm proud to be a brown woman like her." I put my glass down. "Actually, last time we were there, a woman at the synagogue asked me if Lyudmila was adopted. She couldn't believe a brown woman like me would have such a blond, blue-eyed daughter."

"Don't worry about the ignorance of others. It's all about genetics. She had no right to assume anything."

"I told her that Lyudmila's father was the son of a Russian immigrant, and she finally got it that it was you. She said then that my daughter looked exactly like her grandmother Larissa. She was most happy."

"Did you tell her that Ariel is also my son, even though he looks exactly like you, including his sienna skin?"

"Yes. Then, she said: 'Ah, you're the opera singer, aren't you? Dr. Lev raves about you.'"

"It's true. You're brilliant and fascinating. My mother is looking forward to your singing at the synagogue to raise funds for her foundation. She's excited about it."

"I can hardly wait, Lev, especially because you'll be my accompanist."

He clasps my face with both his hands and kisses me on the mouth. He kisses me on the cheek, then chin, then neck, and then both collarbones. "My I undo your hair?"

"No. I was at the salon for a whole hour to keep it in a tight bun. Do not mess it up."

"Okay." He kisses my lips, chin, and neck.

My heart beats fast, and my temperature rises. I kiss him back with the passion of that first kiss in his apartment in Rio. I hold him tight, as if I were going to lose him.

"Lev, I think my milk leaked a bit and wet your shirt. Sorry."

"I know, but I was going to take it off, anyway. I was just hoping someone would unbutton it for me. Will you, Sofia?" He speaks in his low voice.

"You know what happens when I begin to unbutton your shirt."

"Yes, I do." He begins to untie my robe, but abruptly stops when the cell rings.

"Sorry, darling. It's my father. I have to get it."

I disengage myself and sit on the chair next to his.

"I'll turn the television set on, now, Dad. Are the babies okay? Good. I'll come check on them soon." He hangs up, gets up, and turns on the TV.

There is a picture of Officer Almeida on one side of the screen. My father appears on the other side, giving a statement. He says there is a manhunt in the Rocinha favela to capture or kill the disgraced officer. He says that the Olympics are making things more difficult, but he also says he won't relent on hunting the criminal who was once his second in command. He says Almeida is armed and dangerous.

The news ends, and they show the American gymnast Simone Biles on the uneven bars. It's such a nerve-wracking moment for her, and yet she succeeds with a graceful finish. I hope I'll do the same on stage tonight.

Lev turns the television off and puts his arms around me. "There is nothing to fear. He'll be captured and sent back to jail."

"Please go check on the babies and let the grandmothers know what we've discussed. I pumped more milk an hour ago so that they'll have enough until I return from the amphitheater. Please, Lev, make sure the guards follow your precise instructions." I hold him tight.

"No worries, okay." He buries his face in my hair. "Do I get to hear the Bachianas sung exclusively to me tonight as promised? I'll play the cello along with you."

"Of course. You deserve it."

"Then, I think I deserve to have my shirt unbuttoned, too." His voice is just above a whisper. "Please make love to me."

"You'll get everything you've been promised tonight, but now I have to get ready, Lev. I want to get there early so I can prepare myself emotionally and spiritually."

"Yes, ma'am. I'll get you there early." He kisses me on the cheek. "I'll never let you down. You are the greatest woman I know, and a great wife and warrior-mother. And a mighty opera singer. No wonder I'm so in love with you."

"I'm nervous about the show."

"I'm sure you'll steal the hearts and minds of Brazilians everywhere again this evening, Sofia. See you soon." He leaves as I head to the master suite.

I sit at the vanity. I reach out and pick up a magazine called *A Cena da Opera*. I'm on the cover, dressed in a green, form-fitting Versace dress my mother picked for me for the opening a week ago, when the ribbon-cutting ceremony took place and I unveiled a bronze statue of my grandmother.

Opera Scene has an article about the amphitheater with a map of the beautiful acoustic shell built in many shades of green, like the forest in which it sits. I made sure a room was built for mothers with infants so that they could come back to work sooner. I turn a page in the magazine and see a photo of me in a classic dress, leaning against the piano. Lev sits on the bench. My accompanist knows all about my musical moods and understands the nuances of my lyrical voice and also the depth of my vocal gifts. He knows my passions and brings out the best of me on stage. I put the magazine down, get up, and head for the bath.

The floor is strewn with orange rose petals. On the bathtub ledge are lit pillar candles in three different shades of green. Gardenia oil is burning; its scent makes me feel I'm being enveloped by love, Lev's strong love for me. He must have set this up right before he ordered our lunch.

The water runs as I look at myself in the mirror. Even six months later, I still haven't returned to my pre-pregnancy weight. It's a fuller body I never knew was possible, but the five-thousand calorie intake is necessary so I can nourish my babies. The first weeks were nearly impossible to endure— bleeding, stitches, not being able to stand upright or easily walk around. I got cracked and bleeding nipples and worried about producing enough milk. But I'm lucky to have Lev and our families as support systems I can rely on. Our babies have plenty of people who love and care for them.

The water feels warm and nourishing. I think of my grandmother, and now I understand why she left her Indian Nation. She wanted to get an education and fight for her people. Like her, I left my people to return and do good for them. In a few months, I'll make my Met debut in the company's new staging of Carmen. Since winning the contest last September, I've attracted considerable attention in New York. It will be fun to do Carmen, because she is me, the fiery part of my soul. The text, the rhythm, the tempo are there, but as the singer, I provide the energy that makes everything come to fruition. In the end, it's all about my passion, my conviction that through my music I can help others forget their sorrows and overcome their losses. In finding my voice, I can give voice to those who have been silenced by society. I can also help others achieve their dreams. My children push me harder and make my creativity even stronger. Lev makes me into a fuller person.

Before he came into my life, I never suspected such synchronicity existed. Each day that passes, my love for him grows, and so does my devotion. Now that we are parents, our bond has strengthened even more, and I feel there is nothing we can't achieve together.

I step out of the tub, listening to Bidú Sayão singing the *Bachianas Brasileiras No. 5*. My eyes well up. I remember when she died. I mourned her for weeks. No one can sing this aria anywhere near what she did. It's very hard to breathe right; humming vibrates the whole head and tickles the face. The absolutely perfectly poise; the iridescent, dazzling tone; and the magnificent presence throughout the performance was a God give gift. She had a wholesome voice. No one even compared.

Her singing is so haunting and stunning that I know I could never leave my music, my language, Brazil. Grandma said I'm Brazilian to the core. Even though I'll be traveling all over the world and singing on many different stages, I'll always be Brazil's diva.

I put on makeup, still hoping I can do the song justice, tonight.

My black-velvet bodice with matching skirt will look ravishing under the stage lights with the giant moon as scenery. Artfully placed silver embroidery gives me a glittering silhouette. I nearly cry, thinking about this feeling I have; I feel its tug, and I want to follow it. It's an impulse compelling me to give my all. When I sing, it feels as though I am in love for the first time, no matter how many times I sing the same aria. Such feelings have never passed, never faded, and need no renewal. As soon as I sing the first note, it all comes back to me. No arguing against the fact that music has power over me. Opera is my ultimate love.

Lev walks in. He is dressed in a black tuxedo. "I visited with the babies. They're just fine and nourished. I gave the grandmothers your list of instructions." He shows me a video of Lyudmila and Ariel on his cell phone. "They were watching you singing *Rusalka*. See, she is very interested and seems very pleased. But look at him. Look! He's so touched that you brought tears to his eyes."

"Oh, Lev, how lovely. Our boy is so sensitive. He truly loves to hear me sing. She does, too, but she adores when you play the piano."

"I told him that I, too, fell hard for you, but that the good news was that you loved me right back."

"It's true. I love the three of you with all my heart." I pick up my cell. "Here they are on my wallpaper." I show him my own photograph of our babies. "They're both smiling in this one."

"Shall we go? We can leave through the back. There's a BOPE unmarked car and an officer to drive us. Two are already at the amphitheater, doing a sweep."

"Would you please help me with my duffle bag? My outfit is a bit cumbersome."

"Certainly, my beautiful. You look stunning."

"And so do you."

I grab my handbag and we leave. It is a good thing we are in the presidential suite and that no one is around. We take the elevator, and in no time, we are buckled up in the car.

As the vehicle moves through the city of Manaus, I see people walking on the sidewalks who are wearing masks to avoid breathing the dirty smog that poisons the city. It's heartbreaking to think that a mile away, the forest holds tons of carbon dioxide that could give us oxygen. I think of my grandmother and her people. Her tribe had been decimated long before she was born in Manaus to native Brazilian parents. It still puzzles me that she married a colonizer, but he was a sweet Portuguese man who loved opera, literature, and the forest.

I wish I could make the politicians in Brazil understand that they must stop colonizing our indigenous people, taking their land, and destroying their culture, but Brazil is still a racist society that praises the European element even in their soap operas, which emphasize the supposed superiority of the white man. I love my brownness, the blackness of my hair, and the way I look. I'm glad that the world can see an opera singer who looks like many other brown people from her country, millions of them.

"Shall I read my diva the latest review on her singing?" Lev shows me the article in the newspaper.

"Sure. I hope it's a good one."

"Judge for yourself, my love." He proceeds to read the report.

> Sofia de Menezes is born to perform. The Brazilian lyric coloratura established herself as an artist to watch with her New York performance in September 2015 as the endearing Cio-Cio San in *Madam Butterfly* by Puccini. As the flirtatious Violeta in *La Traviata* at the Teatro Municipal in Rio de Janeiro, Ms. Menezes sparkled with the authority of a veteran Parisian. The opera was delivered with a knockout combination of charm, self-assurance, and sensuality, yet, there was a fragility about

her that brought the audience to tears. Last night's performance at the amphitheater in Manaus marked the penultimate of five shows in which the soprano interpreted Villa-Lobos. It's an exceptional and extremely impressive execution. The Brazilian icon will be performing the role of Carmen at the Metropolitan Opera House in December of 2016. She is only twenty-seven but has the gravitas of a Maria Callas.

"How do you like this phenomenal review?" He folds the paper. "Wow, even I am impressed with myself."

The car stops in front of the amphitheater. We get out. Lev gets his cello from the trunk, and we both walk toward the building, which is surrounded by forest. It's an amazing sight. We walk down the hallway that leads to the second floor and go up the steps to my dressing room. He sets the instrument down by the door.

"Would you like your duffle bag in the walk-in closet?"

"No, please, you can put it behind the partition." I put my handbag on top of the vanity.

He comes back to me and puts his arms around me. "I'll be downstairs, tuning my cello. If you need me, just give me a ring."

"Do you know what happened to the lock? It seems to be loose."

"Let me take a look." He puts the duffle bag down and walks back to the door. "You're right. It's broken. I'll call a local locksmith to change it before you go onstage."

"Not a chance, sir. I like peace and quiet. I'm going to prepare myself and do some chanting and meditation. We'll take care of it, tomorrow."

"I'd like to have it fixed tonight, Sofia."

"After we sing, okay?"

"Okay. I'll call somebody after our performance is over."

"Good boy. You may go now." I reach out and put my arms around him. "You worry too much. I love you, baby. Tonight I'm going to play games with you and then sing to you."

"I can hardly wait. I love you, darling. I'll see you in twenty minutes."

"See ya, Lev." I blow him a kiss. "I love you forever."

"Love you more." He smiles and leaves.

I close the door. I like the silence all around me. The building is away from the amphitheater itself. It's good for concentration. I begin to burn some cherry essential oil. I sit down on the easychair and close my eyes. I feel as though I'm surrounded by the spirits of my ancestors. I visualize a green circle of enlightenment, strength, and elegance—a circle of truth and love that comes to my aid.

Chapter 25

I stand on the stage looking at the audience. The house is packed. The night is dotted by billions of stars. The breeze smells of the plumeria blossoms we planted all around the amphitheater. The scenery describes the lyrics in the *Bachianas Brasileiras No. 5*: the rosy evening slowly descending upon the earth reveals the dreamy moon appearing on the horizon. The moon's splendor silences the birds as she sings her mournful songs, complaining of the cruel saudade that weeps and yet laughs at her despair. She longs to hear from her beloved, but fears she has lost him forever.

The "Cantilena" is a moving aria that conveys the melancholy and joy of saudade. My everlasting reverence for this music dates back to the time I was a small girl, lying under the piano as my mother played the song for me.

Lev sits in a chair next to me on stage and begins to play the cello. He offers beautiful, soaring lines in the upper registers, multifaceted vital inner voices, and deep, haunting lower passages. He provides the lush melody that only a native can offer. He is as in tune with the Brazilian folk idiom as I am. Even though I am a girl from the city, through Grandma's stories, I've been to the Amazon Forest a thousand times. My rain forest and I are one. I'm one with my people and my music.

As I sing, I express the deep sorrow hidden in the native heart. I sing with reverence for the life that surrounds me, the green lung of the planet and the promise of life that the Amazon Forest holds. I sing for those who are still fighting day in and day out to preserve the riches that abound.

In an attempt to give my performance an original take, something apart from the other divas, I make an extra effort to temper the melody and the writings of the great composer, even though it's considered almost a sacrilege, especially when I disregard a rest, as if disobeying the mark put there to indicate silence. I am voice, and the breath I take is mine to decide when and how to take. Still, This is my aria Cantilena and we are one, as Lev and I are cello and voice, melded into one.

The applause and cheers of the crowd, "Brava! Bravissima!" bring me back to the moment. Lev rises and stands next to me. We bow several times, and I throw kisses to the audience before I exit the stage. Lev exits to the other side. I pass one of the BOPE officers who stand at the entrance to the stage and continue on toward the end of the ill-lit hallway. I go up the stairs towards my dressing room at the end of the wing. I can still hear the music, but the sounds have grown a bit fainter.

The oil in the green container still burns, and the scent of black cherry permeates the room. I sit down on the chair and face the mirror. After I refresh my makeup, I'll change into my red gown and join Lev at the reception.

I look up and I freeze, seeing Officer Almeida in the mirror. He slides out of the walk-in closet with his weapon drawn. He stands behind me and puts his gun to the back of my head.

"Hello, Sofia! I'm here to take you with me." He steps even closer. "Hand me your cell and change into this camouflage outfit. The getaway car is waiting for us behind the building. When we get to our destination, you'll call your husband and tell him to come to you."

I take a deep breath, think of Lev and my babies, and give him my cell.

"Nice little babies. Let's see if your husband can negotiate with me and set their mother free."

I clasp my black jaguar bracelet. "Please, Officer, I'll do anything you want me to do, but leave my family alone. I have a lot of money, and I can get you out of the country in no time. You'll be a free man." My heart races.

"Change fast, Sofia. My patience is wearing out." He has the look of the cold killer that he is. "Your husband will come to me if he wants to have you back. Hurry up."

"I'll change quickly." I get up. "Behind the partition."

"Good girl. I knew you'd comply. You're still the same sweet girl."

I grab the camouflage outfit and walk behind the partition. The light shines on the jaguar bracelet's amber eyes, and it looks as though it has been hit by fire. Fire, fire, fire, I think.

I fling away the camouflage outfit and find my duffle bag. My fingers fumble with the zipper, and I drop the bag on the floor.

"What the hell are you doing in there?"

"Just a minute. Almost done." I hear him bump against the dresser, coming toward the partition.

I get it open and grab my gun. I force myself to steady my hand. He bumps against the partition. I emerge from behind it, aim, and shoot—once, twice, three times—hitting his arm, shoulder, and then his chest. He collapses, a stunned look on his face.

I open the door, run down the hallway and down the stairs, and see the two BOPE agents coming towards me.

"I shot Officer Almeida three times."

"Are you hurt?" one of the officers asks.

"No, but he's armed." I run into the amphitheater nursery, pick up the landline, and dial Lev.

The Masters of Ceremonies is closing the event, and there is still a lot of noise out there.

"Sofia, are you okay?" Lev says. "I heard the shots while I was putting the cello in the car. Where are you?"

"In the nursery. I'm okay, and I'm still armed." I break down crying. "Please come here."

"Be right there."

I sit down on the couch and keep holding onto my gun.

My mind goes back to months earlier. The day I heard Lev had been shot, everything changed. When I first knew it had happened, I couldn't fully grasp the reality. Then, it sank in. My heart was shattered. Twenty-four hours later, I was at the hospital by his side, and even though the surgery had been a success, he was still in unstable condition with his blood pressure out of control.

I gave him my undivided attention, held his hand, spoke to him about my childhood growing up at Capella and even sang to him. Most of all, even when he was too sedated to hear it, I promised him I'd protect him from harm. Two days after my arrival, the doctors were able to normalize his vitals, and he was ready to go home. I never left his side. I knew I'd love him forever. I knew he was the man who would become my husband, and today, there was no way I'd let Almeida harm him. I would have pulled the trigger a thousand times.

"Sofia, open the door. It's Lev."

I breathe a sigh of relief, get up, and open door. "I had to shoot him. He was going to kill you, Lev."

He takes my gun in his hands. "You did well. I've called my father, and he's calling yours. Let's go back to the hotel." He hands me my handbag. "You are so brave, darling."

The sound of emergency vehicles shatters the silence.

He puts the gun in his backpack, puts his arms around me and guides me out of the room and through the back of the building. As he drives the bullet-proof car, all I think about is the safety of our children. I tremble, just thinking that they might be facing some sort of danger. I hold the bracelet with a firm grip. I hear my grandmother's voice in my mind telling me that there is nothing to fear. As Lev drives past her statue, I hear her voice in my mind:

> You were born with fire inside you, Sofia, and this fire will burn and blaze for as long as you live and beyond. Don't let anyone stamp on it. You must never let anyone blow out those flames within your soul; you must keep on burning bright, because you are a daughter of the Aruaques, like me, and you belong to this earth, to the sun, and to yourself. Do not fret. Do not fear the forces of darkness.

Lev parks the car in the back of the hotel and guides me in. We go up the elevator. I feel like I am in a fog. We pass the two guards at the entrance of the suite. They seem alert, but calm. Lev knocks on the door. It takes only a second for Judge Daniel to open. I follow them in and throw myself into my father-in-laws' arms.

"Please, Judge, help me get bail. I had to shoot. He said he was going to kill Lev if he didn't get me out of there in time." Tears flow down my face. "It was so horrifying to think that I'd lose Lev."

He puts his arms around me. "Listen, Sofia, there'll be only one arrest in this case, and that's Almeida's, and your father wants to do it himself. He's on a military helicopter, heading to the hospital, where that convicted felon is getting ready for surgery. No need to worry." His tone is calm. "Have a seat, darling. We'll take care of you and your family."

He guides me to the couch and sits down next to me. He takes both my hands. "The moment I laid eyes on you in my courtroom, on that day you testified, I knew I was in the presence of a courageous woman who was willing to stand up to the cold-blooded killer of her late fiancé, even though he had promised to take her life if she did. Today, this same woman, who happens to be the mother of my grandbabies, stood up to that killer again and got out alive. I couldn't be more proud of my daughter. Never, even for a moment, even think that you did anything wrong." He wipes my tears with a tissue. "I'm going to talk to the sheriff in twenty minutes and then meet your father, later. Rest assured that you've committed no crime."

I kiss him on the cheek. "Thank you for being so good to me and for raising such a great man. I love your son with all my heart, and just the thought of him getting hurt made me act."

"I'm sure he's thankful to have you at his side. He couldn't love you more, Sofia—and his children. We'll talk more, later." He kisses me on the cheek and gets up.

Larissa approaches me and sits down next to me. "Take this pill, Sofia. It will make you relax a bit. I'm glad you didn't get hurt." She hands me a blue capsule and a glass of water. "It's safe." She puts her arm around my shoulder.

"I want to see my babies," I say, after taking the pill.

"The babies have just fallen asleep. Your mother and Savta bathed them, played them music, and then fed them. I, too, was summoned to play the clarinet. They're just fine. Let Lev take care of you, okay? You did something very difficult, especially for someone as loving as you. I promise to bring the babies to you in a couple of hours. How does that sound?"

"Okay, but if they cry, would you please call me?"

"Yes, I promise, querida. I love you so much. My son is lucky to have you as his wife and the mother of his children. We'll help you through this."

"Let's go, darling. I want to take care of you." Lev takes me by the hand. I follow him out of the room and down the hallway.

He opens the door to our suite, and I walk into the bedroom and change into a red kimono. I wash my hands and face, still thinking that I could have died in the hands of that cold-blooded killer and that he could have lured Lev to his death. The thought is devastating.

The *Elvira Madigan* soundtrack is playing the piano concerto by Mozart that has become our special song since that first night we spent together in his apartment.

He comes in, lifts me up, and carries me to bed. "Let's take good care of you. And then, we'll have a quiet dinner and care for our babies. I'll massage you so that you can fall asleep for a couple of hours."

Our eyes meet. We slowly synchronize our breath. Love flows back and forth between our hearts. It's like quantum love.

He sits against the headboard, and I sit on top of him, facing away. He kneads my head, massaging, pressing, and squeezing my scalp with his large hands. I'm so lazy that I begin to relax. It gives me chills, but in a good way. It feels great to be nestled perfectly between his broad shoulders. His solid body feels good against mine. The stress starts to dissolve. My back starts to unknot. As he continues to knead my head, neck, and collarbones, I'm so full of love, passion, desire, and longing that I don't want it to stop. I don't ever want to let go of him.

His warm lips brush a kiss on my neck as he braids my hair. It's thrilling the way he runs his fingers over my back. I feel the rise and fall of his chest and his heartbeat, as well as mine. I'm caught in his thrall, trapped by the power of his passion for me. Now, with my hair braided, he begins to put orange rose petals in the weave.

I turn to face him. I'm holding my gaze, and his is all love and desire.

He holds my face with both his hands and kisses me on the mouth. He presses a kiss onto my cheek. "You'll always be the love of my life," he says in his mellow voice.

"Ditto." I begin to unbutton his shirt. "I think I left some gun powder on it."

"As evidence that I married a brave woman who didn't hesitate to pull the trigger to protect her man. I'll retire it after today."

"You must give up chasing neo-Nazis if my actions today mean anything to you, Lev."

"You have my word, Sofia. When I heard the shots, just thinking that you could have been hurt was too much to bear."

"Do you have my gun?"

"It's in the car. You don't need it now." He begins to untie the obi on my kimono and run his fingers over the fabric. "This is excellent and rare, like your skin."

"You're so biased, Lev."

"Yes, I am."

I focus on my breathing. I drop underneath the stir and sense my deep feelings for him.

He talks to me in whispers while I fall into an emotionally stirring journey, which brings to mind an expanding universe. I give in to the moment. There is no feeling such as this, when he touches me in such a way that awakens in me the woman I'm meant to be. With him, I've stopped searching for and started finding the road to self-love.

I feel the warmth of his body as he holds me tight. I hold him close.

"I love you so much."

He kisses me on the mouth.

His kiss is everything he is and more. He makes me feel connected to the deepest parts of me. His finger runs down my face. He kisses my collarbones, my tattoo, and then traces my slim scar from the C-Section. He is ever so kind.

"I feel as though I'm on the verge of something." I whisper.

"I'll follow you wherever you go." He begins to kiss my scar.

I close my eyes, feeling only his warm touch. I feel too much. I'm entering uncharted waters, unknown seas. Everything feels organic, native, and restorative.

I clutch him in my arms: kiss his chin, his lips. I want him close. I want his touch. I lose myself in the blue of his eyes, a blue that's achingly beautiful.

In a blink of an eye, I jump in and swim to distant shores. In a blink of an eye, I'm floating above corals and feeling the lightness this sea brings upon me. In a blink of an eye, I find myself reaching deeper into the abyss as he makes love to me.

We're palm to palm, skin to skin, face to face. I feel a part of him, as a wave is part of the sea. I'm a wave, guiding him, keeping him on course, so there will be no shipwreck. He sinks in waters of immeasurable depth. We're ship and sea, sea and ship. I make love to him like I'll never see him again, like there won't be another swim, like there won't be another ship to take me away. I hold him like he'll disappear and I'll no longer feel his love for me, like he'll never come back from faraway shores.

We sync. I overflow. We meld together.

No more rustling of sheets. There is pouring rain outside, but I can still hear the ocean, the waves fading away. Hands down, that was the best swim of my life.

"Are the babies going to be okay? I'm falling asleep."

"They're one phone call away."

"You promise to wake me up if they cry?"

"Yes. Hush now and sleep, sweetie. I'll check on them soon."

"I love you." My voice is only a murmur.

"I love you more than you'll ever know, Sofia," I hear him say as I drift into sleep.

Chapter 26

Lev and I are on the way to catch a plane that will take us to the heart of the Amazon Forest.

It has been seven months since the incident that changed my life forever. I never thought I'd commit such an act of violence, but just the thought of Lev being murdered before my eyes, changed everything. My father has transferred Almeida to a maximum-security prison in Mato Grosso, in the middle of the forest, where he has no access to his helpers. With the help of Judge Daniel, he has also brought the neo-Nazi ring to justice, and they all have been locked up in different prisons so that they can't communicate with one another.

Last night, I returned to the amphitheater and sang the Bachianas Brasileiras No. 5 to my own people again. My Grandpa Otto was present at the event. He now lives in this state. My mother's father continues to pursue his career as an entomologist who loves the forest and devotes most of his time to study and to searching for new species of insects. He wrote books advocating for the most extraordinary place on the planet and is a man who puts nature above everything else. I'm like him in a lot of ways. No wonder, we've been great pals.

I'm delighted that my mother, father, Lev's parents, and the children will spend time at my grandfather's house, away from the city; after Lev and I have finished our retreat in the forest, we'll join them and get to see his insect collection. Too bad, but he has a Blue Nestira in plexiglas like the one Didier gave me, but he promised me he'd not have more than one.

My heart beats a little faster when I think that I'll be in a sanctuary for nearly a week. It's both exciting and a little sad because I'll miss my children. I've never been separated from them. Still, I have to keep my promise to my grandmother. I told her that one day I'd see a Blue Nestira in her own home, and I'm very close to fulfilling my promise. Her people have been in the forest for eons, but now only a hundred thousand Indians are left of the original two million. The Portuguese raped the women, enslaved the men, cut down their trees, and drove them to suicide when they couldn't tolerate the slavery. Now, the Brazilian government seems to be ignoring their pleas to protect their land and save their forest.

The van stops in front of the airstrip where the four-passenger propeller plane waits for us. The indigenous man called Itajaí, who will also be one of our guides, greets us. He has a welcoming smile and very polite manners. He and Lev load our things in the plane as I check my iPhone. There is a message from my mother saying that she and Lev's family are just leaving for Grandfather's house. Lev and I get in the plane, and Itajaí turns the engine on. We're going to spend a few hours where the guide says we'll be able to see the Blue Nestira, and then we'll move on to the retreat the following morning.

The plane takes off toward the forest in weather that's surprisingly cool. In minutes, the roads and houses disappear, and the only evidence of human settlement is the vast area of bare land where cattle were supposed to be raised. They've set huge areas on fire to maintain the savannah for cattle, leaving mile-long lines of flames and charred areas behind the devastating fire. The only things left are blackened spikes of trees, the very ones that have kept the earth breathing, us breathing, my children breathing. The burned-out stretches of forest leave a world of ashes behind and threaten hundreds of species, including the tropical screech owl I so love.

Fifteen minutes into the trip, the charred remains also disappear. Lev gets his camera and begins to click away, to my delight. I want to have proof that my forest is still alive, despite the crimes committed against it. My carbon storehouse is so vast, so powerful, so green, a multitude of greens that spread for miles and miles, breathing life.

I can hardly wait to start the shamanic workshop at the center of the jungle; it has been built by locals, using raw material from the forest. It's also an awareness center connected with the not-for-profit foundation that fights to restore what has been looted in the forest. They are replanting the trees that have been stolen; the company is run mainly by women. I truly think that if we women ran the world, this massacre and others would never have taken place. We have our periods, our pregnancies, our babies, and feel far more intimate with nature than men do. Nature is free. It breathes life, it dies, it spreads its power and sacredness everywhere. I feel so much connection with this world. I don't know how much longer we can take nature for granted without killing our planet.

As we begin to descend, a flock of blue-and-yellow macaws flies overhead. Their vibrant colors and patterns stand out in all the green surrounding us. They're exotic, and a target of illegal trade. They are endangered, and my heart goes out to them. I hope they don't get decimated as other species have been. I hope they survive greed and human brutality.

As we fly lower and lower, I see the vitoria régia. The giant lily pads come in pink, red, and white, and some of them are so huge that this small plane would be able to land on them. It teaches me a new way of seeing things.

We finally land. I see and hear the brassy-breasted tanager. He has brilliant colors: blues, greens, yellows, and even the black of his feathers has a shine to it. I think I'd never get anything done if I had such a beautiful bird to look at all day. I hear the deep heartbeat of my forest like metered music. My whole body resonates with it and begins to relax. It begins to lift me away from the bombardment of life's sounds and erratic rhythms.

I get out of the plane and walk to the stream nearby, holding a Tupperware container filled with cut fruit to attract the Blue Nestira. The grandeur, the serenity, the lightness of this place make my thoughts fly high. I remember why I came here, to seek a spiritual communion with Nature in a non-male-dominated environment. I want to make offerings of herbs and honey to the Goddess Yoruba. Oxum is the divinity of sweet waters. When I was a child, I used to sing for the entity so that she could make me into an opera singer. I unfold a gold scarf I've been wearing and lay it on the ground next to the stream. On it, I place the pieces of fruit as an offering to Oxum so that her energy can attract my butterfly.

Lev approaches and stands in front of me. "How about a crown of flowers for my own goddess?" He places a tiara made of magenta, baby laelia orchids on my head.

"Where did you get this?"

"I put it together myself this morning while you slept in the hotel room."

"Thank you, Lev. You sure know how to score some points with me."

"Itajaí has volunteered to care of our luggage. I'm going to stretch my legs and record this wonderful scenery." He kisses me on the cheek and walks away.

I stay very still and focus on my breathing. I think of my grandmother and evoke her energy, her love for her forest, her loyalty to the most breathtaking place in the world. I remember when I was a child and she first took me to see the Amazon basin. I never felt so free. Already, trees were being stolen, but not near what's happening to the home of my ancestors, now.

I hear the brook, see the moss-covered rocks, and in this very moment, a Blue Nestira lands on a rock a few feet from me. She flaps her iridescent blue wings. I grow stiller yet and think of Goddess—Mother Nature herself. I breathe in, filling my lungs with the purest of oxygen. There is a magic moment in which she flies closer, then closer yet, and lands on the flowers on my head. She is all stillness, and I am all stillness. The simplicity, purity, and evocative emotion of this moment is one I've been waiting for all my life, an instant where my Blue Nestira and I are one. Is it that I feel the haunting presence of my forest love? I thank Goddess Demeter for this outstanding moment.

The Blue Nestira flaps her wings and takes flight. I watch her fly free, unchained. I hear my ancestors laugh as never before, as I imagine they had done countless times before the arrival of their oppressors. I think of my grandmother and all the stories she told me on dark nights in Rio, when the storm caused major blackouts. We sat in candlelight and opened up our minds to a enchanted world that took us far from civilization, a world without boundaries, demarcations, fences, or chains. But I also hear their cries and promise I'll never forget. I'll speak on their behalf through my music and through the stories I tell my children. I shall keep their breath alive, their voices and their dreams alive.

Lev approaches me.

"Did you see that? She came to me and let me have her for a few minutes before flying away."

"I told you once that you're a magical being, and that's proof of it. I took a few shots of you and your Blue Nestira."

"Thank you. Shall I sing something for you when we get settled?"

"Yes, please. I brought Great-grandfather's violin along."

"You've got it, Lev. I'll surprise you."

"They are serving quinoa patties, baked eggplant, and tossed salad with mango and mustard-and-honey sauce. Plus an açaí shake for dessert."

"That sounds perfect." I point upwards. "Look, the clouds are rising up like vapor. There is rain in the making."

"Yes, it will start falling soon, so let's go back to shelter."

We walk toward the retreat center. I can almost hear the pororoca, the tidal bore formed by the meeting of the Atlantic Ocean and the Amazon River. The long and great wave pushes the river further up and changes the orders of things. That's what Lev did for me when he came into my life. He changed the order of things, except in a softer way. He taught me how to set myself free, how to flap my wings once more, how not to be a victim of my circumstances.

We arrive at our accommodations as the sky breaks into rain and storm. The rain falls in haunting drumbeats on the hand-woven palm roof of our sheltering place. All this is mysterious, entrancing, and beyond any kind of ordinary understanding.

"I've set the table for the greatest singer in the world." Lev shows me the simple arrangement with plates, silverware, and a vase with magenta orchids. There is a bottle of champagne in a bucket filled with ice.

"You're just too much, Lev. I love it. I'll wash my hands and be right back."

"I'll pop the champagne."

I walk away, thinking that life has been just perfect since Lev gave up on the idea of dismantling the neo-Nazi rings that still exist in Santa Catarina. He has kept his promise since the day of the incident, and I couldn't love him more for always keeping his word. I walk back to him.

"Please, have a seat, my lady." He pulls a chair out for me. "I poured you some champagne."

"Thank you." I sit down, unfold the red cloth napkin, and lay it on my lap.

He hands me a flute of champagne and sits down across from me. "Please help yourself, Sofia."

"Thank you for all this. You're so good to me."

"Look at this review that came out in the paper:"

> The wonderful Brazilian soprano, Sofia de Menezes, was so deep inside Villa-Lobos' piece that there is no point in making comparisons with other performances. It was just a matter of her singing in our native language; it was as if that delicious voice—rich, creamy, and incredibly luminous—had been created just for that music, or the music written in anticipation of it.

He turns a page.

> Sofia de Menezes' voice has grown fuller and more vibrant, yet. Her rendition was pure beauty—luscious, brilliant, velvety, awe-inspiring, but at the same time humbling. Lev Levien's cello was sublime, making us doubt that he has been playing the instrument for only the past two years, but why would he say something untrue? Another explanation he offers is that his wife's singing brings the best cellist out of him. In the end, husband and wife play and sing in unison. We can hardly wait for their upcoming recording. Bravo!

"Wow, I'm so touched! And it's true that you're magnificent, a cellist like no other."

"I learned the cello so I could play for you, Sofia, and with you, because I knew it was your favorite instrument. And I'm just waiting for the next review. How do you feel about singing the role of Abigaile in Nabucco in January of 2018?" He shows me a contract. "All you need is to sign this, and it will be done."

"Oh, Lev, that's extremely demanding. It's known to have wrecked many voices. I don't think I can do it. Besides, the soprano plays a villain, and that adds another layer to the difficult role. But I sure would like to play the antagonist."

"We have fifteen months to make your voice cast iron and your singing effortless. I know that the vocalization exercises are demanding, but we'll have help from my parents. They decided to retire so that they can spend more time with the grandchildren and accompany us on our trips, if you agree to that."

"Of course, I agree to that. They are so helpful. I trust them entirely. Every time I perform knowing that they are with the children at the hotel, I can just do my job without worrying about them. But I do think we should pay for their expenses when they travel along."

"I'll ask, but I'm sure they won't want you to spend money on them. Both my grandparents were business owners and left a lot of investments in my parents' names. Besides, they made their own money. I believe that all they want is to be close to the children and help us help you with your career. I never told you, but my mother wanted more children, but after two miscarriages, she decided not to try again, so I think being with the babies is very healing to her."

"Oh, that's so touching, Lev. I'm glad they adore her."

"Now, I thought that your mother might want to work for you rather than continue to work at the conservatory so that she, too, can spend more time with the children. And since she helped shape your voice, she'd be perfect to help us rehearse for the role of Abigail. We could pay her top dollar. Besides, she loves to be around the babies, as well, especially Ariel. What do you think?"

My eyes well up with tears. "I don't want anything coming between us, Lev. She will meddle; she always does. We get along so well when we practice together."

"Nothing will come between us. You shot a man who wanted to kill me. Do you know what it means—a bond like that?"

"And you took a bullet for me."

"See? How many couples can tell this kind of story?"

"Okay, but she can practice with me at our house in Gávea, but I don't want her to do that at Capella. My ranch is our world—mine, yours and our children's. She will always be a visitor."

"You make the rules and call the shots. We can draw out a contract where you specify all her duties, times and place, and so forth. By the way, I'm thinking of building a studio for you behind the house at the end of the yard so that the children won't be knocking on the door when you're trying to work. What do you think?"

"I don't want to take too much space from the yard."

"I'll make sure of that. So, what do you say? Are you singing Abigail's role in 2018?"

"I know you especially love this opera because the theme is valuable to mankind. I'll do it." I pick up a pen and sign the document.

"I knew you would take the challenge. We'll go over the details later. Please, eat your food." He helps himself to some baked eggplant. "And you've just become a richer woman after your performances at the Met. When we return, we'll set up a meeting with the accountant and lawyer to see what you want to do with the money you made."

"That's so great, so fabulous, Lev! I'll be able to help a few more causes that are dear to me. I want to make it a better world for our children as well as thousands of others. And I want to do something for you that I've been working on for some time." I get up, grab my backpack, and open it. I take out a file folder and then a sheet of paper that I unfold in front of him.

"Look at the blueprint of the sound studio I'm building at Capella for you. Isn't it grand? You'll be able to record your own music and record it with your wife, as well. Actually, I hired a musical director to produce a DVD with songs by Piaf written from 1942-1944, the music that Suri used to sing at the nightclub in Paris. I'm going to be the singer and you the pianist for the series. And the professional film will include raw footage of your great-grandmother and great-grandfather singing and playing the violin."

His eyes fill up with tears. "This is so generous of you, Sofia. You didn't have to do it."

"You gave up your medical profession to be my accompanist and follow me around the world. Now, it's my turn to help you with your musical career. Now, you can start recording and composing the piano concerto in honor of your ancestors who perished in Auschwitz. I want to pay homage to Suri and Mesallin, as well." I hold a photograph in my hand and show it to him.

In it, I'm dressed in a black, vintage dress from the 1940s, something similar to what Suri wore on New Years' Eve of 1940 to sing in the nightclub in Paris. I'm sitting at the piano, my head, turned to face the beholder, rests on my folded arm. The black hat is as elegant as the bracelet I wear. My makeup makes my eyes greener, but never as green as hers were. Still, we look very similar.

"I'm thinking to use this picture for the cover."

"I don't know what to say. When I think you can't show me anymore kindness, you surprise me again. By the way, the private eye I hired thinks that my grand-aunt Anais may still be alive and living somewhere in France. As soon as he gives me more details, I'll go look for her."

"How great! Can I come along?"

"I'd love to have you by my side."

"Deal."

I walk around and sit in his lap. "Look at this letter my father wrote me. It would never have been possible without you in my life. You are the one who taught me about unlimited kindness, and I will never forget everything you've done for me."

I begin to read the letter.

Querida filha,

I'm honored to be your father. After last night, I was so touched by your singing that I just wanted to be alone with you to talk about many things that are special to me. I want to know more about you, the woman you have become. I want to listen to you speak about things of interest to you, such as your music, family, dreams, your farm. Please, sing to me some time. I'm so happy that my love for opera has found a true artist in you, someone so dear to me. My grandmother longed to have an opera singer in the family. She would be happy to find out about your life as a diva. You are my own Callas! You are incomparable!

Your beauty is truly moving, not only your external beauty but your inner strength and forbearance. You cured my blindness. Forgive me for doubting you and hurting you. I'll make up for it. You're very special to me, and so is my son-in-law and my grandbabies. You're a remarkable woman with a most generous heart. Your accomplishments make me very proud of you.

Carinhosamente,

Your father

I wipe my tears with a napkin. "This makes me so happy, Lev. Thank you for standing by me when the whole world seemed to be against me."

"I wouldn't have done it any other way. I knew all of this about you, and I agree with every word in this letter. You're such a refined soul that I wonder how you could marry a boring kind of guy like me."

"You're my kind of guy, Lev, in every way possible. Here is something else from my father." I show him another paper. "This is the title of the farm and the name on it reads: Sofia de Menezes Levien. My land is officially mine. No one can sell it or do anything to it without my permission."

"Congratulations. I know how much Capella means to you, and to the children and me."

"When I was a child, I used to smell the orange blossoms and stain my fingers with the juice of black berries I picked from the trees. Beyond the bamboo forest, there were uncharted territories and lots of roads that led to the woodside. Back then, the rows of pink floss trees appeared magical to me. I saw that same scenery a million times, so colorful, so green, pastoral.

Oh, Lev, I love my land, but I love it even more nowadays because you are there with me, and so are Lyudmila and Ariel. Our children and you are my treasures. My love for you and my babies is boundless."

"Our children adore you, Sofia. Whenever you're in your studio at home warming up your voice, they don't cease to ask for you. They adore your singing. They can't get enough of your videos, and I can't get enough of your live performances, including when I'm not accompanying you. And here's the mini-article that just came out in Opera Scene magazine:

> Sofia de Menezes, a star of the Brazilian National Opera will make her debut in February 2017 at Carnegie Hall, as Rusalka, the nymph who wants to be human. The aria takes grit, depth, pathos as well as grace to sing it. The diva in question has all the elements necessary to shine on the big stage. Her voice is truly a gift and fits this aria perfectly.

"Look at the picture they took of you when you first signed the contract."

In the portrait, I wear a forest-green silk gown with lacy black roses. My black hair is down to my waist, and my green eyes are shadowed and appear darker. Grayish trees fill the background, and the moon shines through the gaps between branches.

"I like it, Lev. It captures Rusalka's fate, as, sadly, her prince betrays her."

"Yes, indeed, you look perfect." He gets up and leads me to the coffee table where his violin is. "This beautiful instrument has been restored by its very makers in Italy. It has no vestiges of being handled by Nazi hands. It has survived an entire holocaust, and it still sounds pristine. My grandmother has been giving me lessons since we retrieved it."

"Should I sing for you, now?"

"If you are in the mood."

"I am. Please play "La Vie en Rose.""

He stands in front of me. He plays the first notes, and I start to sing.

"Hold me close, hold me fast... I see La vie en Rose... when you press me to your heart." I stop singing while he plays solo. The violin sounds just amazing, so filled with elegance, so filled with love. "When you kiss me...I close my eyes and see La vie en Rose."

He stops playing and puts the violin down. "That was beautiful, Sofia, your voice is truly a gift and fits this song perfectly. You're the cream of the crop. Thank you."

"Oh, and you with the violin, it's so astonishing. Hats off to you. Seriously, it's so haunting just like their story. I'm hooked. I love how your music takes me to another world. I can hardly wait for our album to come out. We'll shine on the stage together. "

"We sure will."

He puts his arms around me and holds me. I close my eyes and listen to his heart beating. Whenever he holds me fast, he makes the torn pieces within me coalesce into a whole that heals old wounds.

He releases me, takes my hand, and I follow him toward the window.

"Would you like to watch the rain for a while? I know how much you love to do that." He turns on the lantern that sits on the small table.

"Yes. This is the best trip ever."

We watch the rain fall, and I'm thinking that I wish I could make a better world for my children and leave them pure water, breathable air, plastic-free oceans, and this magnificent forest but less endangered. I know I will do my part and hope that others will do theirs. Hope.

It rains steadily. There is peace and quiet found nowhere else. It feels wonderful to escape the clatter of urban life. I think of my Blue Nestira, fluttering in the breeze, and the subtle motion of her flight, her pure light when the sun heats. She inspires me to keep searching for beautiful things that will become a part of me forever.

About the Author

Aliete Guerrero comes from coffee, coconut water, and mango juice. She comes from soccer, samba, and Carnival. Growing up in a dictatorship in Brazil inspired her to come to the United States in search of freedom. Writing is her calling, and she carries her notebook and pen wherever she goes. She also loves classical music, taking long power walks, and being in nature with her writers group.

Aliete's work appears in *Catamaran Literary Reader* and *Chicago Quarterly Review*, among other publications. Her writings grapple with complex emotions. Her prose is lyrical, dark, and sometimes funny.

She lives in Los Angeles with her husband, Henry, her youngest son, Chris, and her cat, Derrick Rose.